Body and Bone

Also by LS Hawker

The Drowning Game

Body and Bone

A Novel

LS HAWKER

WITNESS
IMPULSE

An Imprint of HarperCollinsPublishers

Excerpt from *The Drowning Game* copyright © 2015 by LS Hawker.

EPub Edition MAY 2016 ISBN: 9780062435224
Print Edition ISBN: 9780062435217

RRD 10 9 8 7 6 5 4 3 2 1

To Chloe

Body and Bone

Chapter One

Tuesday, May 31

NESSA DONATI WAS going to have to sell her brand-spanking-new car. And all because the rearview mirror hung in the perfect position to display an accidental glimpse of her reflection whenever she reached into the backseat. Typically she prepared herself before facing a reflective surface. But when she was caught off guard, without fail, her mother's disappointed, sour Resting Bitch Face stared back at her.

It wasn't that her mother was unattractive. She was, in fact, far more beautiful than Nessa could ever hope to be. It was that her mother had always used Nessa as a mirror in which to see herself without ever truly seeing Nessa.

So the new black Chrysler Pacifica would have to go.

It was nearing sunset when Nessa parked it on Crestview Drive by the Randolph Bridge, which spanned not only the Big Blue River but the northern tip of Tuttle Creek Lake as well. This was the last stop on a four-day camping trip—just Nessa, her three-year-old son, Daltrey, and their Wheaton terrier, Declan MacManus.

She checked on Daltrey, asleep in his car seat, listing to starboard, mouth open. He'd be okay for a moment, and she was glad she wouldn't have to explain what she was about to do. She felt silly enough about it already.

Nessa and Declan MacManus exited the Pacifica, the dog running ahead, while Nessa locked and shut the door.

She walked the eighth of a mile to the river's edge beneath the bridge as sparse traffic droned by overhead, tires making that *phut phut phut* sound as they traversed the seams in the asphalt. Nessa stood and watched the water flow past, appearing deceptively tranquil until a tree branch rushed by at breakneck speed. Declan sniffed happily around, pausing to mark every object he encountered with a lifted leg.

Nessa looked around to make sure she was alone, then reached into her pocket and withdrew the six-inch-long braid of her husband John's hair. He'd cut it before their wedding five years ago. She had kept it in a velvet box all this time, never dreaming this day would come. She looked at the sky and the water, remembering all their good times on the river. This was the right place to let John's braid go.

The water lapped against her tennis shoes as she wound up and let the braid fly. She watched it arc through the air, hit the rushing water with an inconsequential splash, and disappear. She watched for a moment and let herself cry a little. She needed this sort of closure ritual to move on with her life, like spreading his ashes. Except he wasn't dead. Yet.

Nessa trudged back to the car, Declan MacManus meandering behind her. She unlocked and opened her door, and the dog jumped in and settled in the passenger seat. Nessa noted that Daltrey hadn't even changed position while she was gone.

Nessa started the car, put it in gear, and headed toward home.

Forty minutes later, she parked in the converted hay barn garage behind her house and decided she'd wait until morning to unload the camping gear.

Declan MacManus jumped from the car and ran, whining, toward the other outbuildings, hops vines, and woods beyond as Nessa climbed into the back to struggle with Daltrey's car seat restraints. She draped him over her shoulder, and took him inside and upstairs to his big-boy bed. There, she pulled off his sandals and kissed his fat little feet before slipping him between the sheets. Good. He was out for the night. She left his door ajar, and went downstairs and out the back door to get their suitcase from the Pacifica.

Outside it was full dark, and the woods buzzed with late-spring insects. When she hit the bottom step, she saw Declan MacManus curled up in front of the outbuilding they called the boathouse. He sprang to his feet as if he'd just noticed royalty entering the room. This slowed Nessa down—what was he doing?—but she continued on to the garage, where she retrieved their luggage. When she closed the garage door, the dog jumped to his feet again, in the exact spot she'd left him.

Nessa stood staring at him, and he gazed expectantly back at her.

And then she saw it. The wooden carriage-house door's lock was gone. In its place was a jagged hole, as if God himself had punched a massive fist through it in a fit of righteous anger.

Nessa froze, her breath captive in her throat.

She set down the suitcase and, after a moment of indecision, pulled out her phone and dialed.

Marlon Webb didn't say hello, just, "With a student." This was his way of saying he could be interrupted only for a very specific kind of emergency.

"Call me back," she whispered. "I'm rethinking that whole restraining order thing."

Chapter Two

NESSA'S HEART BANGED against her rib cage and blood roared in her ears. She looked over her shoulder at the house, then back at the broken door, and despaired. Was John inside the boathouse right now, peering out through the shattered door at her? Was he planning to wait until the lights went out in the house to break in?

And how high was he?

Always endless questions, never any good answers.

Call the cops? Ugh. Another police report. Another two hours wasted on minutiae that would change nothing. But if her husband was high on crack, in the throes of a manic episode, he might come after her with whatever tool he'd used to destroy the door.

Fuck.

She walked back to the house, went inside, and drew the dead bolt. Dialed 911, her most-used-digit combination. It seemed to her that she'd used them so much she'd almost worn depressions in the glass phone face.

"What's your emergency?" The 911 operator's flat, mechanical, almost-bored tone irritated Nessa.

"We've had another break-in," Nessa said into the phone. The put-upon sigh in her own voice filled her with self-loathing.

"We'll send out an officer. Do you want me to stay on the line until he arrives?"

Oh, I'm dying for you to, Nessa thought. *Your warm, comforting presence will no doubt ease me through another harrowing stand-off.* Of course, that was unfair—the operator was just doing her job. But would it kill her to be a little more compassionate?

Nessa went into the kitchen and gripped the sink, keeping her eyes on the boathouse.

"I'm Stuck in a Condo (with Marlon Brando)" by the Dickies began playing on her phone, her ringtone for Marlon.

"Hello?"

"It's hell being right all the time," he said.

Nessa laughed. She had his full attention now, which was usually a little too intense, a little too penetrating. A civil engineering professor in his late thirties, Marlon's alcoholism had taken hold during his PhD studies. Vodka had been his drug of choice, and a nearly fatal DUI sent him to rehab at twenty-six. He'd been sober over ten years, and Nessa's Alcoholics Anonymous sponsor for three. Although AA generally frowned upon opposite-sex sponsorships, he and Nessa had clicked immediately.

"He broke into the boathouse," Nessa said, hoping the inevitable police siren wouldn't wake Daltrey, ever careful to shield her son from the chaos swirling all around him.

"Is John on the property? Do you want me to come over?"

"No, thanks," Nessa said. "The cops are on their way."

"You didn't answer my first question."

"The answer is I'm afraid he is."

She filled the teakettle at the sink and set it on a burner.

"I don't want to say I told you so," Marlon said. "But I told you so. You should have petitioned for a protective order the minute you gave him the old heave-ho."

"I know. I didn't want to have to give depositions and talk to lawyers and cops and all that crap. I just wanted him off my property and out of our lives—*my* life."

She glanced sadly out the window above the kitchen sink, which looked out over twenty acres of hops vines. The vines were the beginnings of the niche farm her estranged husband had planted before he relapsed for the third and—for her—final time three weeks ago. Until then, the plants had held the promise of a new direction, a new start. John had come up with the idea of growing hops for local craft beer brewers. She'd made it clear this project was his baby—she was plenty busy with her blog and satellite radio show. But now she'd have to hire someone to care for the hops or let them rot. It made her tired just thinking about it.

"Better get the ball rolling tomorrow," Marlon said. "I doubt this will be John's last unannounced visit."

"I will," she said. She hesitated. "Hey, Marlon. Give me a reality check, will you? I did the right thing, didn't I?"

"Of course you did," Marlon said. "Somebody smokes crack in your house—I don't care if it's a bum or your husband or the pope—with your toddler in the next room, you throw him out."

"I gave him three chances," she said.

"Yes. Which was more than generous."

"Then why do I feel so guilty?"

"Because you have a heart."

"Not according to him, I don't."

"Bullshit," he said. "It's an excuse. You can carry the message; you can't carry the addict."

She knew this twelve-step aphorism—and all the others—from her six years in Alcoholics Anonymous the way some people knew *The Rocky Horror Picture Show*, but hearing it from a man who'd stayed sober for a decade made her feel better.

"In other words, it's not your fault," he said. "You did not enable him. You are not responsible for his sobriety. He is. Your priority has to be your own—not to mention that little boy's health and well-being, mental and otherwise."

"I know," she said.

Nessa turned on the burner, pulled a cup from the cabinet, and dropped in a teabag.

"Keep me updated, all right?" Marlon said. "And keep your head. Remember what's important. Nothing is so bad that a drink won't make it worse, right? Go to your meetings."

"I will. Now go back to whatever it is you do when you're not propping me up."

"I don't prop you up. God does. Remember that."

Marlon said goodbye and hung up. She turned from the window and gasped.

Daltrey stood there, silently staring up at her with his enormous taupe eyes, solemn and watchful. He was almost four years old and hadn't started speaking yet.

What had he heard? She definitely couldn't tell by his expression because even if she'd been doing a stand-up routine, he would've looked at her the same way. His disposition was that of a serious, scholarly, middle-aged man deep in contemplation, preoccupied with thoughts of trash swirling in the world's oceans and the hole in the ozone layer. This was the only reason she was glad he couldn't talk, because she had no answers for the questions she knew he'd ask, that he already asked with his eyes.

He tapped his forehead twice with his thumb, palm out. American Sign Language for "Daddy."

She picked him up, his sturdy, compact little body much heavier than it looked. She hugged him and kissed his hair. "No, that wasn't Daddy. What are you doing up?"

He took her face in his little hands and pressed his forehead to hers.

"It's way past your bedtime," she said.

He nodded and rubbed his eyes. Nessa carried him up the stairs and put him back in his bed, kissed him, and closed the door.

He was toilet trained already and neat as a pin. He didn't talk, but he didn't cry or scream either. No tantrums, no fits, no epic messes. He did laugh sometimes, however—the sweetest sound in the world. One that Nessa would do anything to provoke.

As she descended the stairs, she heard the siren and saw the red and blue lights of a police patrol car.

Nessa took a deep breath and went out the back door.

Declan MacManus howled until the patrol car siren went silent. Then he started barking, his hackles raised when two uniformed police officers got out and walked toward them. Nessa grabbed Declan's collar as he whined, trying to check out the intruders.

"Good evening, Mrs. Donati," one of the officers said.

"Hi," Nessa said, trying to read their nametags.

Officer R. Michaels. Officer B. Watt. Right.

They'd been here before, that first week after she'd thrown John out, the night he'd stood in the front yard screaming like Stanley Kowalski in *A Streetcar Named Desire*.

Michaels and Watt approached and held out their hands palms down for the dog to sniff. Declan's tail wagged, recognizing their scents, and Watt gave him an ear rub before straightening. Now Declan was eager to lead everyone back to the boathouse, wagging and smiling at the cops and Nessa.

"So what happened?" Watt said.

"The lock on the boathouse is broken," Nessa said.

"He in there?" Michaels said, pointing.

"I don't know. I didn't look. I just called you guys."

Michaels nodded and pulled out his flashlight, switching it on.

"Why don't you wait inside, Mrs. Donati?" Watt said, unholstering his gun.

She walked toward the back door and whistled for Declan MacManus, but he ignored her. She had to go back and take him by the collar to encourage him into the house. She locked the door and watched through the window as her dog whined beside her, sad to be missing all the action outside.

"Police," Michaels shouted, walking toward the boathouse, light aimed at the broken door. Watt aimed his weapon.

Nessa tensed. There was no telling what John might do, coked up and manic as hell. He might still have whatever implement he'd used to break the door and try to crack the cops' skulls.

"Anyone in there?" Watt called. He held the gun with both hands and nodded at Michaels, who threw open the boathouse door, shining the flashlight beam inside.

Nessa ground her teeth, waiting and watching as they entered.

After what seemed a lifetime, the lights inside the boathouse illuminated. Officer Michaels exited, surrounded in the dark by a full-body halo.

Nessa opened the back door.

"No one's in there," the cop said. "You want to come out and take a look, see if anything's missing?"

She walked on shaky legs out to the boathouse, simultaneously relieved and disappointed. Inside, Declan sniffed in a widening circle where John had no doubt stood recently.

She looked around but found nothing out of place. John's Old Town Otca 16 canoe was still hanging from the ceiling on its rigging. She'd have thought he'd take it to sell, since it was one of the most valuable things they owned. The tool bench was undisturbed.

But something was off, as if the very air itself had been replaced. It smelled wrong. Instead of the usual musty, combination ancient wood/modern flooring odor, she smelled something else. A mixture of acrid and sour. It was the only indication, other than the broken door, that someone who didn't belong had been in here.

She almost said something about it but stopped herself. These guys didn't need any more crap from her. They must feel like they were constantly chasing ghosts out here.

"Everything looks fine," Nessa said.

Watt nodded, sympathetic. "Let me get my clipboard and we'll fill out the report."

"Come on in through the back door," she said. "I'm going to check out a few things in the house, then I'll meet you in the kitchen."

Back inside, Nessa climbed the stairs to the master bathroom where she looked in the medicine cabinet. Percocet and Vicodin still there. Looked in her underwear drawer where she kept a roll of cash, and it was all intact. At least he hadn't come in the house, or these things would most certainly be gone.

After the cops had taken her statement and left, Nessa changed into her pajamas, washed her face, and brushed her teeth, but she knew she wouldn't sleep, so she went back downstairs and got out her vapor pen. It was the only vice she allowed herself these days, since she'd quit smoking cigarettes when she learned she was pregnant with Daltrey.

It was soon after John had left that she'd discovered a store that had probably once been a head shop but now sold vapor pens. A clerk with gauges in his ears and a neck tattoo had explained how the device vaporized liquid nicotine, then showed her the different flavors. "You can get piña colada, raspberry, lemon-lime—"

"Tobacco flavor, please," she'd said.

"But we have so many—"

"I don't want to smoke limes or vanilla ice cream cones. I want to smoke tobacco, and this is as close as I'm going to get to the real thing."

"Old school, huh," he'd said with mild contempt, but sold it to her anyway.

Now she sat pretend-smoking in the dark, looking out at her beautiful property, deep dark green in the moonlight after the heavy spring rains. She and John had bought the house, buildings, and sixty acres after two things: Nessa's music blog, *Unknown Legends*, had attracted its first major sponsor, and Altair Satellite Radio had offered her a twice-weekly overnight deep-cuts show. John was working at the time, at the job he'd held the longest—two years as a maintenance tech at the Manhattan Regional Airport, so they were able to get their first mortgage.

They'd had big plans when they bought the land and house nine months ago. She and John had agreed to quit his job and become a stay-at-home dad and tend the hops vines. He'd renovate the outbuildings and add on to the house. They would have another baby. But John became depressed and irritable. Picked fights with Nessa. Started disappearing, saying he was shopping for farming equipment, but he somehow never came back with anything.

And then she'd caught John in their bathroom with his pipe and his rock. He'd brought that poison into their home where their son slept, the poison he'd sworn he'd never touch again after relapsing almost four years before. So she kicked him out for the last time.

"I'd rather see Daltrey dead than with you," John had screamed, standing by his truck as Nessa loaded garbage bags of his clothes into the bed. This was the drugs talking, using John like a ventriloquist's dummy, because he worshiped his son, adored him, would die for him under sober circumstances.

"You're a shitty mother," John ranted on. "It's your fault he doesn't speak. You let him get vaccinated."

Not this again. The drugs made him buy into every conspiracy theory circulating on the Internet, especially the anti-vaxxer movement.

"It's your fault," he said. "You're dirty inside and you infected him with your filth."

She hadn't come back with what she'd wanted to say—that her filth was far behind her, and John's was teeming now, this very minute, his cells and brain full of toxic evil.

"You're *my* wife," John shouted. "You can't keep me out of *my* own house, away from *my* son." He'd gestured about. "All this is *mine*. Everything you see is *mine*."

Listening to him rant, Nessa was reminded of her mother. She was always talking about *her* stuff, was fiercely protective of what was hers. "You broke my glass. You ruined my blouse. You can't use my car." *Mine, mine, mine.*

And in that moment, she had a revelation. Instead of marrying a man like her father, the way most women did, she'd married one like her mother.

"You will be sorry you did this," John had screamed. "You will pay for this."

Nessa couldn't help herself. "Of course I will," she'd said. "Because I have to pay for *everything*."

She'd gone in the house and locked him out.

Now Nessa sat at her desk and booted up the ancient Windows XP computer she used for her AA personal inventory blog. It wasn't connected to the Internet so no one could get at the password-protected journal except her.

She got out her Alcoholics Anonymous Big Book and turned to page sixty-four, the beginnings of the resentment inventory, and read the text as she always did, although she had it memorized: "In dealing with resentments, we set them on paper." She sighed and started typing.

Chapter Three

5/31

Hi. I'm Nessa, and I'm an alcoholic. I have been sober for six years, four months and twelve days.

Here are just a few of the things I need to hand over to my Higher Power: At the top of my hit parade is imagining my Higher Power as my mother, Joyce Gereben, standing behind me looking over my shoulder, watching everything I do with disapproval. Hilarious, all things considered. My sponsor Marlon W. tells me that modeling God on a critical and/ or absent parent is common to people like us, although for most it's their father. I can't model God on my dad, because I hardly remember him. He left us when I was five or so.

Sorry, HP. I know you're not actually Joyce Gereben.

First, a confession. When Officer Michaels opened the door to the boathouse, I had hoped John was actually inside with a gun, and the cop would have no choice but to shoot him in self-defense. Then all my problems would be solved. What kind of fucked-up human being wishes another one dead?

At the same time, an irrational, ridiculous fantasy erupted: that the real John, not crackhead John, was hiding in the boathouse with balloons and an I'm Sorry and I'm Done with Drugs Forever banner, and that I'd run into his arms and . . . I can't pine away for something that doesn't exist, that does real harm to my psyche, my spirit, my sanity. I have to go forward one day at a time, stay sober, and raise Daltrey.

Which I don't know how to do without John. Parenting comes so naturally to him, where to me, it's a struggle. I love that boy with all my heart, of course, but the only reason I have any idea what to do with him is because of John.

I wouldn't have guessed this of him when we met, which was after I moved to Denver and got a job at Wax Trax, the record store. John didn't seem like father material, not that I was looking for a baby daddy. He used to hang around the store, and he was this huge presence. He had these big beautiful brown eyes—Daltrey's eyes—and longish hair. He was from Russell, Kansas, and had been a crack addict. But he was as addicted to Narcotics Anonymous as he'd been to crack, which should have been a red flag for me. Still I had the biggest crush on him right from the start. I've always ignored my instincts when I'm in love. That's probably pretty common.

We'd been married less than two weeks the first time he relapsed. We'd had an argument, and he hadn't come home from work. By two A.M., I was frantic, driving all over Denver through the night. I searched for him for five days until I got a call from Denver Health saying that John had been found naked in a park, high on crack. He was arrested and wound up in the psych unit. The doctor there explained that John was bipolar, a fact that John had never mentioned to me. The doctor said the stress of getting married might have triggered a manic episode, making him delusional. And then he'd gone looking for crack to take the high even higher.

After his stay in the hospital, John was medicated and contrite, and things settled down. John swore he was done with drugs—the illegal kind—for life. But then I got pregnant with Daltrey and we moved to Manhattan, Kansas, so John could take a job at the airport.

Then just days before my due date, John disappeared again. He was gone for nine days, only reappearing after he got out of jail for a DUI, when Daltrey was two days old. John had gone off his meds, he said, because he felt too flattened out to want to go on living.

After that episode, I felt differently about John, but I had no intention of leaving him because I knew what it was like to grow up without a dad, and it would probably be even tougher on a boy. So no matter what happened, I was determined to stick with it.

"You can't only think about yourself anymore," I told John. "You have a wife and child now. I'm sorry that the meds make you feel tired. But I can't have you disappearing."

He took his meds faithfully for three years, and I confess I was lulled into a false sense of security. Now I know better, and I can't believe I let myself become so complacent. I guess I thought in a little town like this, drugs would be harder to find. But that's stupid—it's a university town, so of course there are drugs.

The truth is, I thought having Daltrey and me would be

enough to make him want to stay sober, but I'm pretty sure Marlon is right—John couldn't handle my success. Not that I actually blame my professional accomplishments for his relapse. If the radio gig and the blog had never happened, he still would have found an excuse to use.

Would I do it all again? Yes, I would, because I got Daltrey. I just wish John could remember what the Big Book says: "Time wasted in getting even can never be used in getting ahead."

Chapter Four

Wednesday, June 1

NESSA WOKE TO the sounds of Tchaikovsky's Sixth Symphony out back. She got dressed, then went downstairs, poured herself a cup of coffee, and looked out the window above the sink. Daltrey stood on a pallet in the backyard conducting an invisible orchestra using a wooden spoon as a baton, all dressed and shiny clean. Nessa walked out the back door and found Isabeau Revie, her freshly hired nanny, playing air violin on the grass in the morning light, heedless of the heavy dew soaking her jean shorts. She wore a *Firefly* tank top, her long blond hair in a careless ponytail.

Daltrey ran to Nessa and hugged her knees before returning to his conducting post, waving the spoon in the air, a look of concentration and seriousness on his face.

"You need to get him a cardigan and a pipe and a subscription to *The Economist*," Isabeau shouted over the music, which came from portable speakers connected to her phone.

A burst of pure laughter overcame Nessa, the first natural one she'd experienced since John's departure. Isabeau sat there grinning, looking pleased and surprised, and Nessa realized Isabeau probably thought she was a grim, humorless harridan.

"Maybe a little paste-on beard until he can grow one himself," Isabeau added. "Which should be any day now."

Nessa laughed more, and Daltrey smiled. She knew he hadn't heard her laugh much lately either. She needed to make more of an effort to lighten up for his sake.

"We already had breakfast," Isabeau said. Always smiling and enthusiastic, Isabeau was an engineering grad student from New Mexico who was four years younger than twenty-five-year-old Nessa and six inches taller.

She hadn't been what Nessa thought she was looking for when she was first compelled to hire a nanny. Marlon had recommended Isabeau, one of his research assistants at Kansas State who needed a summer job. Nessa had wanted an efficient, impersonal warm body who would be in the house while Daltrey slept and Nessa was working.

But Daltrey had foiled this plan. He'd fallen in love with Isabeau at first sight—with her wide-set brown eyes and ever-present smile, coltish energy, and soft musical voice. He wasn't interested in anyone else, so Nessa was stuck with a warm, engaging personal-space invader who obviously believed they were all going to be besties. Luckily, she hadn't yet noticed that Nessa never offered up any personal information. Isabeau shared everything about herself without reservation. Even worse, Isabeau had mad organizational skills that made Nessa's life easier in ways she never could have imagined.

Isabeau's laptop sat open atop its case on the ground in front of her, one of her long legs extended out to the side, against which Declan MacManus had been lying until Nessa appeared. Now he trotted to her and presented himself for a good butt rub.

"Let's go over your schedule for the rest of the week," Isabeau said. She typed on her keyboard. "Okay, so here's what I've got. Daltrey has a doctor's appointment at eleven this morning. Is it for vaccinations, or—"

"I told you you don't need to do this stuff," Nessa said, setting her coffee cup down on the steps and leaning over to pull some weeds from the flower garden. She didn't want to talk about why she was taking Daltrey to the doctor again. She was embarrassed by her frantic worry over Daltrey's muteness.

She suspected it was because of all the turmoil in their lives, the violence he'd witnessed when John was in a manic phase of his bipolar disorder. She also suspected that her past addictions and risky behaviors had something to do with it, although she'd never mentioned these things to the doctor. She knew she should but, to her shame, she'd hoped a more mundane explanation would come to light.

"But it's easier for me if I know exactly what's going on and when."

Isabeau had gone from nanny to personal assistant while Nessa was preoccupied with grief over the end of her marriage. There was no point in fighting it. Isabeau was a force of nature.

She continued reading from her screen. "I fact-checked your blog post on Wanda Jackson. She was amazing! I'd never even heard of her before that—surprise, surprise. I'll send you a text when that's done so you can look it over one last time before it auto-posts at nine tomorrow. Then I'll work some more on cataloging your music library."

Nessa went on pulling stray shoots of grass and weeds from the flower bed.

"I'm a little more than halfway through the *A*'s," Isabeau said, stretching her arms above her head. "Arcade Fire, I think. Seriously. I've never met anyone with such a huge collection. I always thought my sister had a pretty good one, but hers was like a drop of water compared to your ocean. How did you get started collecting like this?"

"Actually, it was my older brother who got me started in high school." Ack. It popped out before she could even think about it. She should never multitask. Why would she mention personal information so casually? This was the effect of Isabeau's constant presence. Nessa needed to be more careful about what she said. She'd been completely tight-lipped about the extent of John's problems, and she needed to keep to that standard for all other areas of her personal life.

"I'm kind of in awe," Isabeau said. "What did you—"

"I want you to take off early today," Nessa said. She needed to cut this off. Enough talking about herself. "You've been working too hard."

"Okay," Isabeau said brightly. "We made some blueberry muffins if you're hungry. Didn't we, Daltrey?" She turned the music up and returned to playing first-chair violin with renewed vigor.

Attitude of gratitude, Nessa reminded herself, watching this paragon of efficiency, who'd seemingly dropped out of the sky when she needed it most, engage her son. Nessa headed for the door, then turned back.

"Isabeau," Nessa said. "Could you call the locksmith? I need to change the locks again."

She looked up from her computer. "Why?"

Nessa checked to see that Daltrey wasn't listening. She lowered her voice.

"John broke into the boathouse while we were gone."

Isabeau's eyebrows bounced up. "Well, that explains it," she said.

Nessa felt a prickle of apprehension. "Explains what?"

Isabeau stood and walked toward Nessa. "All the splintered wood. I saw it when I got here this morning. I didn't want Daltrey to handle it and get splinters, so I was picking it all up when I found this." She reached into the pocket of her shorts and held out a flat, black triangle.

Nessa took it. It was a Fender medium guitar pick. What was this doing out here? She turned it over and saw that it had been signed in silver ink: BIG.

Big and Rich? Big Bad Voodoo Daddy? Was this one of John's mementos? It must be. Maybe it was one of the things he'd intended to try to sell. What a laugh. She shrugged and put it in her own pocket.

Back in the kitchen, Nessa washed her hands and topped off her coffee while checking the clock. She had thirty minutes before she needed to get ready for their doctor's appointment, so she brought her laptop to the kitchen table and logged in to her blog.

She'd started writing the music blog for fun, as an outlet for her when they'd first moved to Manhattan after Daltrey was born, to a tiny, dark one-bedroom apartment on Anderson Avenue they'd called the Cave. It had started with tentative little reviews of shows she and John had gone to see, often small regional bands; memories of shows she'd seen as a teenager; and explanations of obscure vinyl records she'd picked up at yard sales, rare 78s of old blues and marches, acetates and wax cylinders from the early twentieth century. But soon after, she'd started to say what she really thought. And with that had come two things—Internet fame and vitriolic remarks via her comments section. Thank God she'd avoided the whole social networking thing, or there would have been even more of that.

She usually only answered the positive comments, composing retorts to the trolls in her mind. It had taken her a while to understand that engaging trolls was always a mistake. When she'd started the blog, she'd thought if she explained herself clearly, calmly, and rationally, they'd apologize and everyone could be friends. But that wasn't how it worked. They were like schoolyard bullies—probing for weakness, looking to destroy. Lucky for her and unfortunate for them, it would take more than words to destroy her.

Nessa took a look at the most recent comment posted.

a professional jeweler resized my cock ring
and he made it bigger
Posted by Anonymous | June 1 8:17 AM

This made her laugh harder than it should have. Sometimes it seemed a twelve-year-old boy lived inside her brain and took over from time to time. How many closet comedians were out there, just using the comments section to ply their wares? And how many guys were out there just dying to show the world their junk or at least talk about how big it was?

The narrow spectrum of comments always amazed her. Interestingly, before she'd gotten her radio show and people had discovered she was a woman, she'd never received any personal comments. Before that, when readers assumed she was a man, the comments had been restricted to variations of "idiot." Since then, she'd begun to believe she'd been spelling *whore* wrong all these years, for how often it was spelled *hore*. Why music was assumed to be a masculine interest and area of expertise, she would never know.

Her brother never believed that, and he would be nothing but proud of her if he only knew people were paying her for knowledge he'd helped her accumulate. She cracked open her personal inventory blog, keeping an eye out for her son and nanny.

6/1

I'm Nessa, and I'm an alcoholic. I've been sober six years, four months, and thirteen days.

It's not so much that I don't want Isabeau to know I have an older brother as it is thinking about him hurts. I miss my brother. He and I went through a lot of harrowing, hilarious shit together. He really is the one responsible for my obsession with music in virtually all its forms. The concerts we saw. He started me on a steady diet of excellent, weird, wonderful music from the time I made it out to LA.

He would be so envious to know I have this show. He's the one who should have it. Everything I know I learned from him. It's only fair.

I've kept up with him and my mom via the Internet, been able to watch them from afar. Brandon's on Facebook, without any privacy settings, so I get to stalk his newsfeed all the time. He looks a lot different, but so do I. He's puffier, more sickly looking. I wonder if the cancer has come back.

I often daydream about reuniting with him after Mom passes away, laughing together over the greatest goof of all time. He's always been a very forgiving person—how else could he still be living with Mom at the age of twenty-eight? I would blame his type 1 diabetes and all the shit the whole family went through because of that, but there are plenty of successful diabetics out there who aren't completely dependent on their moms.

But Joyce convinced him of two things very early on: that he can't live without her, and that he owes his very life to her. In a way, he does. Credit where credit's due. Maybe it would have been different if my dad hadn't traded us all in for newer models, a younger, better family, and moved on. Mom always said that Brandon was half her and half our dad. Brown hair from Mom, height from Dad. One blue eye from Mom, one brown eye from Dad. Good from Mom. Bad from Dad.

She said I was all Dad. No surprise there.

Brandon was all good because his biggest goal in life was always to please Joyce. Make sure she didn't get mad, make sure he was always telling her how pretty she was, talented, etc.

Judging from his Facebook feed, he's still that way. Always posting memes like If you have the greatest mother in the world, hit Like! Share this if your mom is Your Whole World! *Crap like that. It makes my skin crawl.*

Brandon never stopped being desperate for Mom's approval. By the time we were teenagers, I held him in contempt. When we were fighting, I'd call him pussy, mama's boy, tell him he was going to grow breasts if he didn't break up with her.

After Dad left, when Mom was between boyfriends, she'd treat Brandon like he was her surrogate husband. I re-

member one time she wanted him to paint her toenails the way Kevin Costner did Susan Sarandon's in Bull Durham. *Creepy as hell. Of course, I didn't understand this at the time, when I was young. I just knew something wasn't quite right in our house.*

Which is why I've done everything I can to make Daltrey's home as freak-show free as possible, but John fucked all that up. And I hate myself because I still love him, even though I hate him for what he's done, for how he's destroyed our family. Because it's stirred up my abandonment issues like a stick beating a hornet's nest.

Nessa's eyes drifted to the clock on her laptop, and she realized that she only had twenty minutes to get ready before Daltrey's pediatrician appointment. Crap. She drained her coffee cup, put it in the dishwasher, and went upstairs to shower.

Forty-five minutes later, Daltrey sat on the floor of the examining room and played with a wire, string, and bead contraption while Nessa flipped through a magazine without really seeing it.

After a quick knock, Dr. Blatter rushed in and washed her hands.

"Hello, Mrs. Donati," she said as she dried off with paper towels. "And how are you, Daltrey?"

He touched his thumb to his chest, fingers extended. ASL for "fine."

Dr. Blatter looked at the file folder the nurse had left for her and said, "What are we seeing you about today?"

"Well, I thought we could do a lead poisoning test," Nessa said, embarrassed but determined. This was her latest pathetic attempt at turning the blame away from herself for Daltrey's muteness.

"How long have you been in the house?" Dr. Blatter said.

"Nine months."

"We can do that, but I really don't think that's what's—"

"And another hearing test, if you don't mind," Nessa said.

"I doubt his hearing has changed since the last one—when was it? Three months ago?"

"I know, but—"

"There's nothing wrong with his hearing, and I really doubt he has lead poisoning. Didn't you say the inspector tested for lead in the house and it was clean?"

"Yes, but—"

Dr. Blatter sat down on her rolling stool. "Mrs. Donati, Einstein didn't speak until he was five. He was too busy thinking to talk."

"That's a myth," Nessa said. Today the folksy country doctor bit was irritating the shit out of her.

"Are you sure? I've read that a lot of places."

This comment annoyed and alarmed Nessa. Had Dr. Blatter also gotten her medical degree from the Urban Legends page on About.com?

"I'm glad you're continuing to use ASL with him so he can communicate until he has something to say."

Nessa wanted to laugh at this—what was he doing with ASL if he wasn't "saying" things? She'd taken a class over at the university in American Sign Language, and any time she couldn't come up with the proper word, she could always find what she wanted on YouTube, which was stocked with thousands of short videos demonstrating ASL words and phrases.

"Yes," Nessa said. "But I'm concerned it's delaying his speech further."

"No," Dr. Blatter said cheerfully. No explanation, no evidence to back it up.

Even if Einstein didn't talk until he was almost five, neither did countless developmentally delayed, disabled, and low-IQ kids. But could those kids use ASL, facial expressions, and body language with such nuance and eloquence at three years of age?

"Please just do the lead test?" Nessa said, hating the pleading tone of her own voice.

Dr. Blatter sighed. "I'll send the nurse in. Okay? I'll see you in four months for his four-year checkup, and I'll bet he'll be talking then."

Nessa laid her hand on Dr. Blatter's arm as she rose to leave the examining room. "Can I talk to you out in the hall for a second?"

"All right," the doctor said.

"Mama and Dr. B are going out in the hall for a minute, Daltrey," Nessa said to him. "I'll be right back."

He nodded without looking away from the toy.

Nessa followed Dr. Blatter out and closed the door behind them.

"I just thought you ought to know," Nessa said, lowering her voice, afraid Daltrey would hear through the door. "Daltrey's dad and I are getting a divorce."

Dr. Blatter opened up Daltrey's file again, clicked her ballpoint pen, and wrote something. "Thank you for letting me know."

"Daltrey's dad is bipolar, you see, and he—well, he self-medicates."

The doctor nodded, her eyes still on the file folder.

"I just couldn't keep hoping his dad would get his act together—I didn't think it was good for Daltrey. You know what I mean?"

Dr. Blatter nodded again, her silence somehow compelling Nessa to continue talking.

"You don't think . . . maybe Daltrey kind of senses something's out of whack? And that—well, it's another thing delaying his speech?"

Dr. Blatter finally shifted her inscrutable gaze to Nessa, who went on babbling.

"John was diagnosed less than five years ago. I thought once he got on the psych meds, the need for . . . the other would go away. But it kind of had the opposite effect. He said they flattened him out. He missed his mania. You know what I mean?"

Of course the doctor knew what she meant. Nessa despised the fact that the situation had changed her into the kind of woman who asked for affirmation after every spoken sentence.

"I'm so sorry," the doctor said, her breezy, dismissive attitude broken through at last. "Has Daltrey regressed in any way since his dad left home? Has he started to wet the bed? Have his sleep patterns changed? Has he lost interest in the things he loves, books and that sort of thing?"

Nessa shook her head.

"If his development slows down or even goes backward, or any of those other things start to happen, then you bring him back in. We'll give you a counseling referral. But kids are pretty resilient. He's a strong little boy."

Nessa wanted to hug her but restrained herself.

"The nurse will be right in to take some blood." The doctor turned away but Nessa touched her arm again.

"Bipolar is genetic," Nessa said. "Isn't it."

Dr. Blatter tucked the file folder under her arm and took both of Nessa's hands in her own. "Listen. Yes. There's a ten to fifteen percent chance Daltrey will develop the condition. But here's the thing. We know what to look for. The fact that John wasn't diagnosed until he was in his thirties means it had altered his brain already. We will keep an eye on Daltrey. If we notice the symptoms, we will manage it. All right?"

Nessa wiped her eyes. "Thank you," she said.

"Take care of yourself, Mrs. Donati."

"You too."

The doctor walked away and Nessa went back into the examining room, where she gathered her son into her lap to wait for another unnecessary needle that would simultaneously assuage her guilt and amplify it.

Chapter Five

When they returned home, a panel truck stood out front, decorated with a golden key, emblazoned with LOCK IT UP! and a phone number.

How had Nessa ever gotten by without Isabeau?

Daltrey held her hand as they walked toward the house, hanging back a little when he saw a kid in a work shirt with long dirty-blond hair kneeling next to the front door, removing the doorknob.

"Hi," Nessa said.

"Hi," the kid said. His name tag read "Brady." "I'll be done in a jiff," he said. "Already got the back door done."

"I'll get you a check," Nessa said, and led Daltrey into the house. He ran for the kitchen, presumably to find Isabeau.

"This is a great house," Brady the locksmith said.

"Thanks," Nessa said.

The kid stood. "Hey, your babysitter or whatever told me you're the Nessa of *Unknown Legends*."

"That's me," she said. She really didn't want to have a conversation with this guy, but she didn't want to be impolite either.

"You're not how I pictured you at all," he said, looking her up and down.

"We never are," she said. She tried to convey with body language that she had many important tasks to attend to, but he ignored this.

"Hearing you on the radio. I never would have pictured you as a soccer mom."

But somehow I could have imagined you as a locksmith's part-time employee.

"I figured you were like a riot grrrl type, you know—covered in tattoos, piercings, that kind of thing."

She almost said, *Oh, I've got piercings, all right. I just don't put anything in them anymore, other than tasteful rings in my lobes.*

And tattoos? Oh, she'd had her some tattoos, all right. An entire sleeve on her left arm, which had taken two years, thousands of dollars, and a lot of pain to remove. Of course, the yellows and greens were nearly impossible to laser off because of those ink colors' reflective properties, so you could still see some parts, which was why Nessa wore long sleeves in every season, even the sweltering, humid, miserable Kansas summers. Too much identifying information.

The only one she couldn't bear to have removed was *The Glimmer Twins* on the soft underside of that arm, which in appearance and location had perfectly matched her high school best friend's.

Candy, her twin, her last real friend. Her soul sister.

Oh, no. Nessa was going to cry in front of this kid. She turned away.

"And you have that blog too, right?" Brady said. "It's pretty good."

"I need to fix lunch for my kid," she said, her sinuses backing up, her eyes filling. "I'll go get your check."

"Okay," he said. "Good talking to you."

Nessa went into the kitchen and leaned over the sink, afraid she was going to vomit.

Every day. Every day it was a struggle not to think about Candy.

Shit. Now Nessa would have to write about Candy in her AA personal inventory blog tonight.

Under "Regrets."

Under "Harms or Hurts."

6/1 part 2

Confession: I judged the locksmith kid. Who the hell do I think I am anyway? Oh, yes, I'm a star, baby. The star my mom always wanted to be, but the irony is no one I ever knew in my old life knows I'm a star.

But that's not what I need to inventory today.

For the first time in a while, I'm going to talk about Candy. It's hard to cry and type at the same time, so I need to cry for a while first.

Okay. When I first saw Candy freshman year of high school, it was like walking toward a full-length mirror. Candy had my exact haircut—short and dark with blond spikes (it was the early '00s, remember), brown eyes like me, same face shape, same general body type. We hated each other immediately.

We went to one of the worst-performing high schools in

the US, which I'm not going to name, because who cares? Metal detectors at the doors, security guards everywhere, lots of gang stuff. I'd already been in trouble for shoplifting at this point, had a solid D average, had been smoking pot and drinking since I was twelve, lost my virginity at thirteen. (Sounds like every cliché bad-kid ever. Pathetic.) Because Mom was rarely home—she was out hustling. I have to give her props. She was always looking for an "opportunity," a way to make lemonade with the lemons life was always handing us. She schemed harder than anyone I've ever met— constantly coming up with crazy get-rich-quick ideas, some of which actually worked out. Getting a job, though, was for ordinary people. Why she thought she wasn't ordinary is a mystery.

She also went on auditions and got a few bit parts here and there. Whenever the movie Death Book *plays on late-night cable, I watch it until the scene where Mom's behind the counter at the DMV and gets a pair of scissors in the ear.*

But every once in a while, she'd get a job—receptionist, or cocktail waitress, or temp worker, until she inevitably got fired.

So anyway, when I found out that Candy was a harlee, what used to be called a goody-two-shoes, I made it my mission to corrupt her. Mostly because I couldn't have her wrecking my street cred with the Latina girls, with her good grades and her . . . okay, I'm going to cry some more now.

So, what made us real friends? Brandon, during a rare extended period of good health, took me to a Queens of the

Stone Age show at the Troubadour in West Hollywood, since none of my girls were interested in "white-boy rock." After the opening band, Brandon went to the bathroom and when he came back he told me he'd seen me out in the hall. It was Candy, of course. What was this spaz bunny doing at a QOTSA show?

I ran out there to find her all by herself, looking completely comfortable alone. That struck me—I needed a gallon of beer and some chronic to get my balls up, but here was this girl, who I thought was a total suck-up, just into the music.

"Hey," she said when she saw me, delight in her eyes, even though we were sworn enemies. Maybe it was because we weren't surrounded by our posses—she hung out with the good black girls. I found out she partied too, but she said something I'll never forget: "You know, you can have a good time without ruining your life. You can party without making it your whole identity. You can do well in school at the same time. You can do both."

"Maybe you can," I said.

"You have to decide what you are. Are you a stoner slut? Or are you a Queens of the Stone Age fan and a writer and—"

"A writer?" I said, incredulous.

"You read some of your poetry in comp class, remember?" She smiled at me. "You never miss comp class. You've got some talent. And I'll bet you read a lot too. You can't be a good writer without reading."

She was right, about the reading part anyway. I know I don't have any great talent at writing. I'm serviceable—that's about it.

After that, we became inseparable, as the saying goes. We called ourselves the Glimmer Twins.

I can't do any more tonight, but I will force myself to write my second-biggest regret regarding Candy.

That we ever met.

Chapter Six

Thursday, June 2

NESSA HAD ANOTHER nightmare about John. They were on the Big Blue River in the canoe, fishing.

"You know I hate to fish," Nessa said in the dream, but even as she said it, she looked around at the early-morning light, the spring-green banks, and felt happy.

"But we're going to catch something really special this time," he said, and cranked on his reel. He pulled up what she thought was a supermarket frozen turkey at first, but then Nessa realized it was a baby.

A dead baby.

He turned to her with a ghoulish smile.

She woke up with her heart battering her chest wall, sweating, out of breath as if she'd climbed five flights of stairs.

Damn you, John.

Nessa's dreams were often so obvious they could be used in a psych textbook. Her relationship with John was like a tiny, helpless baby. And like a baby, if you didn't feed the relationship, if you gave it drugs, it would die.

What we have on our hands is a dead baby.

It took her a few moments to realize she'd been awakened from her dream by the front doorbell. Nessa rolled over and saw it was only eight-thirty A.M. She heard the dead bolt slide, the door open, and a male voice. She listened.

"No," Isabeau said. "He's not here."

A muffled voice saying words she couldn't make out.

"She's asleep," Isabeau said.

More words.

"Well, okay. Would you mind waiting out there?"

Nessa groaned. She suspected siding sales, The Watchtower Bible and Tract Society, or some other equally irritating intrusion. A large No Soliciting sign hung by the doorbell, but the folks who were able to actually find this property eight miles south of Manhattan, Kansas, surrounded by dense woods always suddenly lost their ability to read when they finally made it.

She heard Isabeau take the steps two at a time and then knock on Nessa's bedroom door.

"Nessa?"

"Yeah," she called. She rolled out of bed and pulled on some shorts and a long-sleeved T-shirt.

"There's someone here to see you."

Nessa opened the door and whispered, "Is it a salesman?"

"It's a cop."

This made Nessa's heart pound. She stepped into her sandals and followed Isabeau down the stairs. As she descended, more of the stranger was revealed. Cowboy boots and jeans. Plaid shirt, sport coat. No tie. Dark, cropped hair, full eyebrows, large forehead.

"Mrs. Donati?" the man said through the screen door.

"Yes," she said.

The man pulled a shiny gold badge from his pocket and held it up Iron Man–style, as if ready to blast a hole through her chest.

"I'm Detective Rob Treloar with the Riley County Police Department."

Oh, shit. John must be in jail.

It was times like these when Nessa was grateful that nowadays she reminded people of a Mormon missionary. It typically made law enforcement relax, speak courteously, and look for a reason to apologize for one thing or another. Her childlike, high-register voice only added to the effect, causing people to pause and make a mental adjustment before continuing. But currently, she was speechless.

Nessa closed her mouth, staring at the badge, which confirmed his name and title, and added another piece of information: he was with the general investigations unit. Not vice. Which confused her. She turned to Isabeau, who stood right behind her looking concerned, and said, "Could you take Daltrey upstairs?"

Isabeau nodded and walked away.

Nessa unlocked and pushed open the screen door, then held out her hand so the detective could clasp the tips of her fingers. "I'm Nessa Donati," she said, smiling brightly, trying to relax her jaw.

"Sorry to bother you at home so early," the detective said. "May I come in?"

Again, missionary: gracious, hospitable, warm. That was Nessa Donati. "Of course." She flung her arm wide as if welcoming him onto a cruise ship.

The detective stepped inside, then let his eyes wander to the crown molding and hammered tin ceiling tiles. "Wow. This place is great. How long you lived here?"

"Thank you, Mr.—Detective, uh—why did you say you were here?"

He finally smiled. "Oh, right, sorry. This is just a really nice— I've always wanted one of these old farm properties. You've done a great job on it."

"Thanks," she said cautiously.

"What year was it built?"

"Eighteen ninety-five," she said, trying not to sound impatient.

"And no problems with plumbing or anything?"

"Not yet," she said.

Nessa's *paranoia du police* was probably more acute than most people's, but she couldn't think about that now, couldn't let it show on her face. Somehow, the detective would know.

So she put on her shiniest hostess face as camouflage, ushered him in like a treasured guest, and pointed him to the couch in the living room. Isabeau scooped up Daltrey, who had been playing with Legos on the floor. He buried his face in her neck, shy of the stranger.

Isabeau raised her eyebrows at Nessa before mounting the stairs, carrying Daltrey.

"Can I offer you some coffee, lemonade, water?" Nessa said to Detective Treloar.

"No, thank you," the detective said, unbuttoning his sport coat and seating himself.

Nessa sat at the other end of the couch.

"Is Mr. Donati at home?"

"No," she said.

Detective Treloar had a nice face, but she could tell he didn't brook any nonsense.

"Do you expect him soon?"

"No," she said. "He doesn't live here anymore. We're divorcing."

He cleared his throat into his fist. "Ah. Well." He pulled a miniature notebook from his coat pocket, looked at a page, and said, "Does Mr. Donati drive a 1997 Chevy half-ton pickup, license plate IFL 157?"

"Yes," she said, wary. *DUI? Hit-and-run?* With crackhead John, life was like felony bingo. "But it's in both our names." Then she added, "I think," as if any misinformation, intentional or otherwise, would get *her* thrown in jail.

"The truck was reported to the Park Service," he said. "Abandoned."

"When?" Nessa said, annoyed. What was John up to? Was he living in his truck? But that didn't make any sense, if he'd parked it on some street and left it there. Maybe in his stupor he'd forgotten where he left it.

"It was reported yesterday," Detective Treloar said, looking at his notepad, then at her. "Do you have a phone number for Mr. Donati? Maybe an address where he's living or staying, a post office box?"

You could try all the crack houses in Manhattan or Junction City. Chances are good he's spending a lot of time in one or all of those. Keeping the economy going on three hundred dollars a day.

Under normal circumstances, Nessa would think he'd want to notify the owner of the truck's impoundment. But because it was John, she suspected there was an outstanding warrant. "Is John in trouble, Detective?"

"When was the last time you saw him?"

His question and failure to answer hers irked Nessa. But she guessed it was really none of her business now whether John was in trouble. He wasn't her problem anymore.

"A couple of weeks ago," she said.

"And you haven't heard from him at all during that time? Phone call? Text?"

"No," she said. "We didn't exactly part on friendly terms."

"Oh?" the detective said, his pen poised above the paper, at the ready to take down the lurid details.

She considered. Why not tell him? "John's a crack addict. I threw him out after I caught him using in the house."

Treloar shook his head. "Ah," he said.

Nessa couldn't stop the humiliation from rising like heat through her body, which reacted as if the detective's benign acknowledgment were actually an indictment of her and her failure to keep John clean. As if she wasn't woman enough to keep his interest at home and away from drugs. Nessa shuddered at this pathetic impulse.

The detective fished a business card out of his inner jacket pocket, stood, and handed it to her. "If you hear from Mr. Donati," he said, "please give me a call."

"Wait," Nessa said as she took the card. She didn't want to let him go without getting a few answers of her own. "Where exactly was the truck abandoned?"

The detective straightened. "A half mile north of Tuttle Creek Lake in the parking area by the river slip off Yeti Drive."

She frowned. The river slip? An image from her fishing dream floated before her mind's eye, and another attached itself to it: drug-crazed John parking his truck, walking down to the rain-swollen river, and wading into the water with no intention of coming out again.

Nessa gasped and her heart convulsed, her hands rising to her chest as if to catch it. "You said it was reported yesterday," she said, breathless. "How long has the truck been there?"

"The caller said it had been there for over a week."

"Over a week?" Nessa echoed stupidly. "But John was just here over the weekend."

Now Treloar reseated himself and fixed her with a mock-confused gaze. "But you said you hadn't seen him in a couple of weeks."

Impatient, Nessa said, "I called the police the other night because John broke into the boathouse out back while my son and I were camping. He would have needed his truck to drive out here." She plucked at her chin. How *did* John get here without his truck? Maybe the person who called in his abandoned truck was mistaken about the timeframe.

Or maybe whoever had broken into the boathouse wasn't John.

Treloar's eyes never left her face, and she couldn't discern what he was thinking, but she was pretty sure he thought she was lying.

"You can look it up," she said, her voice quavering. "The cops who came out here were—" What were their names again? "Watt and . . . I don't remember the other's name. But you can look it up."

He nodded slowly. "All right," he said. He stood again and pointed at his business card, which Nessa had placed on the coffee table. "Please call if he gets in touch."

Nessa rose to walk him out. "I will," she said.

Detective Treloar paused at the door. "When I mentioned the river slip," he said, "it looked like you knew what I was talking about. Do you fish?"

"I don't," Nessa said. "But John does. Did. Whatever. He used to put his canoe in the water in that spot."

"So he's a fisherman," Treloar said, nodding. He turned away from the door. "Is he a hunter too?"

"No," she said.

He nodded again and opened the door. "I'll be in touch," he said.

6/2

I have to do this before I go to the radio station tonight, or I won't be able to concentrate. It's obviously more important than ever that I have a steady income.

Hi, my name is Nessa, and I'm an alcoholic. I've been sober for six years, four months and fourteen days.

Today I will concentrate on my Fear ("Wrong Believing" according to the AA Big Book), which are "feelings of anxiety, agitation, uneasiness, apprehension, etc." Here are Fears that have been realized: Fear of abandonment, being alone, change, failure . . . the list is too long. I feel like Charlie Brown in the Christmas special when Lucy asks him if he has pantophobia, which is the fear of everything. That's it!

My fear that I'll never be loved (Daltrey doesn't count because he doesn't know enough not to love me) has come true because John didn't love me enough to stay away from drugs. No one could love me enough. Only God can love me the way I want to be loved, unconditionally, no matter what I do.

I hate even writing this next part, because it shames me. Because it was my mother who taught me that love is always conditional. She knew something that not everyone does— the most effective punishment, the most effective way to keep kids in line, is to let them know you will stop loving them if they step out of line. Joyce knew that better than anyone I've ever met. Each time I did something she didn't like, she let me know she loved me a little bit less. Just a little. But the message was clear: someday the sand in the top of the hourglass would run out, and there would be nothing left.

I learned Joyce's lesson all too well. Each time John relapsed, a little more of my love for him drained away. Please forgive me for being such a good student. But not a perfect student, because my love for John will never completely disappear. Never. Even if he is dead.

At the same time, I know there isn't enough love in the world to stop someone else from being an addict.

Before John, Brandon was the only one who always loved me. Sure, he got mad at me, but we'd fight, and then he'd get over it. He was so easygoing that way. Knew that nothing was so serious between us it was worth severing our relationship. The only thing that could come in between us was—surprise, surprise—Mom. If it was a choice between standing up for me and losing Mom's love, Brandon would jump ship in a heartbeat. I didn't blame him. I was the same way. It was every man for himself where Mom was concerned.

Because of his diabetes, Mom wouldn't let him go out for sports, so he became a role-playing game freak, mostly Dungeons and Dragons. *I made so much fun of him, but he loved it. I actually got kind of worried because he was so completely immersed in these fantasy scenarios that he'd talk about them as if they were more real than the real world.*

One time he tried to explain the convoluted plots and intricate strategies he devised, but I gave up trying to under-

stand, because the truth was it bored the shit out of me. At least he had excellent taste in music.

I hope he's not still in that same head space. I really do.

God, I'm afraid. All my fears funnel into my biggest one: that I won't stay sober. Because if I don't, I might as well be at the bottom of Tuttle Creek Lake.

God grant me the serenity to accept the things I cannot change, the courage to change the things I can, and the wisdom to know the difference. Amen.

Chapter Seven

NESSA ARRIVED AT the station at eleven P.M. every Monday and Thursday night, armed with electronic music she'd chosen from her and John's vast collection of more than 150,000 songs. Her oldest file was a tune from 1895, the same year her house was built, by a group called the Unique Quartette.

She made it a point to never play the same song twice, unlike the other "deep cut" shows on syndicated and satellite radio. She assumed the overplay elsewhere was intended to sell music, but luckily that wasn't the focus of her show. At least, not yet.

KCMA operated out of a lonely building overlooking a field with a tall sign declaring WELCOME TO 98.6 KCMA COUNTRY! It was mostly computer-run with only two live jocks on the job, one for the morning drive (such as it was in a town of fifty-six thousand) and one for afternoon drive (ditto). The rest were syndicated shows from a satellite feed.

Now as she pulled into the dirt parking lot, she saw a Vespa scooter parked next to the car her producer, Kevin, drove.

She hoped she could hold it together tonight. She'd selected a slate of music that was aggressive, drum-heavy—nothing that reminded her of John. She could do this. It was just another Thursday.

The front of the building was glass with a foyer to trap the heat or chill, depending on the season. She went inside and saw Kevin sitting atop the reception desk stretching a rubber band compulsively.

"Oh, hey," he said. "Didn't expect you in so early."

Sitting behind the desk with his feet propped up on it was a young guy in a narrow-brim fedora and skinny jeans with a knapsack on his chest. Ah. The Vespa rider.

"You Nessa?" the new guy asked, making no move to stand or even sit up.

"Yeah," she said.

"I'm your new producer," he said.

Nessa looked at Kevin in confusion. "I wasn't aware I was getting a new producer."

Kevin kept his eyes on the rubber band and said, "I can't keep doing the overnights. My kids are . . . and my wife . . . well, anyway. So this is Otto Goss. He's the guy who makes sure the satellite feed doesn't cut out when no one else is here."

"In other words," Otto said, "I babysit the computer five nights a week. Might as well produce a show since I'm already here."

"Oh," she said.

"I'm gonna take off," Kevin said.

"Good working with you, Kevin," Nessa said, feeling knocked off her game. She wished he'd have given her a little more notice, although what difference it would have made she couldn't quite articulate. Too much crazy stuff going on this week.

"You too," he said. "I'm sure I'll see you around." And he walked out the door.

Nessa turned to Otto, who was texting someone. She waited, but the thumbing went on and on.

"So, Otto," she said.

He held up a finger without looking up and went on thumbing.

She started to feel superfluous and stupid standing there watching him, so she walked toward the break room. As soon as she was almost out of earshot, he said, "So, Nessa."

She stopped and turned.

He didn't look up from his phone as he said, "We need to go over some ground rules before we go live."

"What do you—"

"Hold on," he said, still not looking up.

It took every ounce of her self-control not to walk away. Instead, she waited politely.

"The end," he said. "Just finished my novel."

Nessa didn't say anything to the anticipatory look on his face. The silence stretched until Otto's expression dimmed and turned into a frown.

"Ground rules. One. I'm not your lackey. I'm not going to fetch water and snacks for you like Kevin did. Two. I will not be answering mail for you or anything like that. I'm not your secretary. And three. I need to have some input on the playlists."

Wow. He was talking like he was the "talent." Was he trying to be funny? "I don't think you—"

"Let's go in the studio," he said, and led the way. Once inside, Otto tossed his leather flapped-and-goggled helmet and knapsack into the corner, then switched on the lights and board, hit some buttons and dials. He put his own headphones on upside down, like a beard—in order to not disturb that ridiculous hat.

Nessa felt rushed and jumbled by this guy's dismissive attitude. His disregard for her was stunning.

"You don't look like a malcontent," he said. "You look like a suburban housewife. Which I guess is subversive-lite in its own sad little way."

Her hackles began to rise. "What's that supposed to—"

"All that to say I didn't realize who you were," he said.

"What do you mean?"

"You're the anti-Beatles girl."

This one-line biography irritated her almost as much as his appearance. He had a Van Dyke beard and wore a cardigan and scarf, even though the temperature was in the high eighties. Seeing him, Nessa knew she'd been born too late. She longed for the old days when people meant what they said and weren't ironic, intoning everything with quirked eyebrows and figurative air quotes. But she was grateful because his douchebaggery was just what she needed.

She pointed at his get-up. "You warm enough?"

This threw him off, but only for a beat.

"How old are you?" he said, ignoring her question.

"Excuse me?" She hated the old-fashioned "how dare you ask a lady her age?" tone in her own voice.

"You're in your thirties, right?"

"I'm twenty-five. And how old are you? Gonna go to prom next year?"

He tilted his head. "Do you want my honest opinion of your show?"

"Meh," she said in her most bored voice, looking at her phone and scrolling through emails she'd already read.

"It feels like you're trying too hard."

She pocketed her phone, crossed her arms, and smiled. "Is that right," she said.

"Your desperation to seem relevant is embarrassing."

She shrugged. "Here's the funny thing, junior. I didn't *try* to get this show. They came knocking on *my* door. So the fact is I ain't tryin' *at all* . . . all the way to the bank."

Otto's face turned a gratifying shade of puce.

"You don't deserve to have this show," he hissed.

"Oh? And who does, princess? You?"

Otto punched up his glasses and sat straight. "I graduated from the journalism school at K-State in May after toiling away for four years. I spent hundreds of hours at the campus radio station. I interned every summer for free at shitty little radio stations like this one. I busted my ass. I'm up to my neck in debt, but I can't find a job now." He stabbed the air in front of him with each point he made. "All I can get are hour-long freelance production jobs for minimum wage. And then I find out that before your appearance on WBEZ you'd never been on radio at *all*. You didn't even major in broadcast. You tossed off some little *blog post* about hating the Beatles and now you get to be on *Sound Opinions*? Who the fuck do you think you are? You haven't earned this."

Nessa's temperature rose to a high, rolling boil. Otto had no concept of what she'd gone through to get here, how she'd put herself through college at Metropolitan State University of Denver working in a record store and waitressing, living on ramen noodles and American cheese. She'd earned a bachelor's degree in communications. She had just as much right to be here as this pasty-faced tool. Probably more. She'd clawed her way out of LA with nothing. With less than nothing, doing things he'd only ever read about.

"You don't know anything about me," Nessa said, her animosity sharpening her senses. "And what I do has nothing to do with you. So if you're going to whine like a spoiled little bitch, you can get the hell out of my studio."

"It's not your studio," he said.

"It is from midnight to four every Monday and Thursday."

"This should be my show."

She allowed a slow, sincerely cruel smile to spread over her face and gave him a lazy shrug. "Life's not fair," she said. "Is it?"

According to the countdown clock, she had less than thirty seconds to air, and she didn't have a water bottle or her tissue box set up, and now she wouldn't have time.

"Your blog isn't that interesting," Otto said. "It's hacky and precious."

"So don't read it," she said.

"You're a *poseur*," he said, using the French pronunciation.

Incredulous, she said, "*I'm* a poser."

He nodded at her.

"Let's see." She ticked items off on her fingers. "Pretentious facial hair. Check. Doc Martens. Check. Horn-rimmed glasses. Check. Hipster helmet. Double-fucking check."

"On in five . . . four . . . three . . ."

He pointed at her. She felt razor-sharp and alert like she hadn't in ages.

Her theme music played in her headphones along with the intro voiced by some guy on the coast with balls the size of boulders, his voice deep and rich and rumbling.

"*It's midnight on Thursday, which means it's time for* Unknown Legends *with Nessa, the only radio show that plays the really, really deep cuts.*"

Nessa opened her mic. "Happy Thursday, gang, and welcome to *Unknown Legends*. This is Nessa, and this first song's official video is not exactly my cup of tea—it's lead singer Josh Homme having a night out with a bunch of Asian businessmen. Guess it's indicative of the difficult time the band had putting the album together. I recommend listening on full volume so you can decide for yourself what it all means. Here's 'Smooth Sailing' from Queens of the Stone Age off their album . . . *Like Clockwork.*"

The opening synthesized beats blew into the jangling guitar of Troy Van Leeuwen, and Nessa clicked off her mic, shoved back her chair, and danced like she was at a rave in 2004. She sang loud, while staring straight at Otto. She could feel the hate waves rolling off him like San Francisco fog, and they strengthened her.

They didn't speak for the rest of the shift, but she did her best show ever. She hadn't gotten so many phone calls since the Beatles post, and it kept Otto hopping all night. When the bumper outro for her show played, she stood and stretched. Otto was sprawled on his chair.

"See you Monday," she said, and walked out the door.

Friday, June 3

A NOISE ON the front porch woke Nessa, and she walked downstairs in the dark. She opened the front door, and there stood John, soaking wet.

"I just couldn't get to a phone. It's taken me weeks to walk home, but here I am."

Nessa collapsed in relief, because he was real John, not crackhead John. He hadn't relapsed after all. It had all been a horrible misunderstanding. She got him a towel and tried to dry him off, but she kept finding leaks, and water continued to run from his head, from his nose and ears and eyes.

"What's happening?" she said.

"I'm so sorry," he said as water poured from his mouth in a stream.

Nessa opened her eyes and looked at John's side of the bed, undisturbed, smooth, unslept-in for weeks. She didn't have even a moment's reprieve, no periods of forgetting John was gone, no times of not wondering whether he was alive or dead. It was as if this new fact of her life sat on a shelf suspended above her and clocked her in the head every time her thoughts shifted away from it.

Probably somewhere in the back of her mind, she'd believed if John were to die, it would actually be a relief. Because he wasn't the man she married anymore. He was a burden. But she wasn't like her mother—she couldn't stop loving John even if he was deeply flawed, even if he had destroyed his own life and hers in the process.

She looked at the bedside clock and saw it was six-thirty A.M., four hours earlier than she normally awoke the morning after her radio shift. She tried to go back to sleep, but she couldn't stop picturing John soaking wet on the front porch.

If he was gone for good this time, dead, she wondered how she would raise their boy alone.

Daltrey, who looked so much like his father they'd called him Mini-me, was a constant reminder. The ache that accompanied it was a sharp ice pick in her consciousness. Her love for the little boy was both visceral and transcendent, but at the same time she wished him vanished too—a thought she'd never actually voice.

How was she supposed to go on? How was she supposed to do this alone?

She got up and went to Daltrey's room. He was still asleep, lying on his stomach, his little lips pursed. He looked like an infant when he was asleep, his long straight eyelashes lying across his cheek like angel feathers. He breathed like he was in a hurry. Fast in. Pause. Fast out. His fat little fingers curled in a sweet fist. She lowered her face to his hair and inhaled, the muzzy, sweet toddler scent making her heart ache. She went downstairs and looked out the back window where Isabeau was doing yoga in the morning sunshine.

What was it like to be so young and carefree? Isabeau was only four years younger than she, but Nessa felt like an old crone weighted down with the life experience of someone in her fifties.

Nessa poured a cup of coffee and stepped outside, where Isabeau held the warrior pose, her arms held out parallel to the ground, her legs in a deep lunge.

"What are you doing up so early?" Isabeau said.

"Nightmare," Nessa said, and sat down on the steps.

"Daltrey's not up, is he?"

"No. I just checked on him."

"Good, because I want to talk to you about something." Isabeau rolled up her yoga mat, dropped it next to the steps, and sat next to Nessa.

Oh, no. This was it. Isabeau couldn't handle the crap parade that was life on the Donati homestead.

"Okay," Nessa said, dejected. "I understand completely."

"What?"

"You're quitting."

Isabeau smiled wide, made a *pfft* noise, and a get-out-of-here motion with her hand. "No! You're stuck with me, boss. Actually, it's kind of the opposite. Here's what I'm thinking. It's really kind of a hassle to have to sleep two different places, you know what I mean? Since you're all alone, I wonder if I should just move in with you for the summer until fall semester starts. That way I'm already here for your radio overnights and I don't have to drive back and forth. You have a lot on your mind, and you could use the help with Daltrey. As a bonus, my roommate and her creepy boyfriend could bone all they want without me cramping their style."

Nessa laughed. "I see what you're doing here. But I really value my privacy. Having a roommate is . . . difficult for me."

"I know it. But we'd be helping each other out. What do you say?"

The relief she felt overrode her trepidation. Isabeau was right. With Nessa here alone on sixty acres, departing and arriving at odd hours, it didn't hurt to have an extra set of eyes on Daltrey.

She needed to put the needs of her son above her own selfish needs of privacy.

She took a sip of coffee. "All right," she said. "But that means I'll have to pay you more."

"Oh, you don't have to—"

"You're not a very good negotiator. The proper response is 'Yes, you will.' "

"Yes, ma'am," Isabeau said, and smiled.

THAT AFTERNOON, WHILE Isabeau sat on the floor with her laptop cataloging Nessa's music collection, Nessa sat at her desk and browsed her blog's comments section. The latest one represented the kind of lazy trivia questions she hated.

*What do these diverse artists have in common: Norah Jones,
Tom Waits, Jackson Browne, AC/DC, and Neil Diamond?*
Posted by Anonymous | June 3 8:37 AM

Anyone with a quarter of a brain could get online and look that
sort of thing up. But she always indulged her readers by answering anyway. Usually, this sort of question meant the musicians in
question each had a song with a common word in it, almost without fail. She searched for, copied, and pasted each artist's song list
into wordcounter.com, which found repeated words. She'd then
look through the part of the resulting list where one word was
found five times.

The list came up with fourteen words that had been used five
times. As she started to scroll down, a pounding on the back door
sounded, and Nessa's heart shot up into her throat.

John?

Isabeau started to rise but Nessa said, "I've got it."

She ran to the door and peered out the window.

It was her nearest neighbor, Lauren, and her two boys.

Nessa unlocked the dead bolt, her heart still fluttering in her
chest like a trapped bat, and opened the door to the sound of children's voices and the jingle of Declan MacManus's dog collar. He
crowded inside with them, dancing and happy for the visitors.
Isabeau waved as she threaded her way through the crowd and
walked out the door past the horses Lauren had tied up outside.
Lauren and the boys always rode over inside of driving, sometimes giving Daltrey a ride around the property, one of his favorite things.

"I brought you something from the garden," Lauren said,
blowing in through the door with her long muslin skirt sweeping

in behind. She pulled the hemp pack off her back and emptied it on the kitchen table—two large mason jars full of berries and a basket of fresh ones—while her sons patted the dog before turning their attention to Nessa.

They had no concept of personal space, and the oldest, Ziggy, leaned into Nessa's shoulder, his hot, sweaty skin pressed against her back, while Tosh hung on her shoulder. She'd stopped trying to keep them out of her bubble.

"You okay?" Ziggy said.

It was a weird thing about kids—how they somehow intuited your mental and emotional state in a way that adults would never be able to do, sort of like that high sound that only people under eighteen can hear. It seemed like Lauren hadn't really noticed any problem with Nessa.

"Sure, honey," Nessa said.

"Where's Daltrey?" Tosh said.

"In his room. Go on up."

They scampered up the stairs.

"Where's a bowl?" Lauren said.

She acted as though she and Nessa were close friends, as if they'd shared secrets and confidences. The arrangement suited Nessa perfectly. The appearance of friendship allowed her to keep her secrets and distance without a fight.

Nessa reached into one of the upper cabinets and pulled out a colander and her largest bowl, a brilliant green one Lauren had made at her pottery studio. Nessa sat at the table.

Lauren stood at the sink, rinsing the fresh-picked strawberries, blueberries, and gooseberries. Daltrey's giggle resonated from upstairs as eight-year-old Ziggy and five-year-old Tosh chattered away. They were both named for reggae musicians, of course, and had the long dreadlocks to match. Although Lauren kept them clean, Nessa couldn't help imagining swarms of flies around their heads.

"Why don't the three of you come over for dinner?" Lauren said. "Mac can throw some veggie burgers on the grill and we'll make a night of it."

Lauren's husband, Mac, was an IT genius putting together the computer systems at the new National Bio and Agro-Defense Facility that was being built outside Manhattan. His giant brain intimidated Nessa a little, but he was a nice enough guy, if a little introverted.

He and John had had a cordial relationship, but Nessa hadn't mentioned yet to her neighbors that John was no longer living here, and she had no intention of doing so now.

"Thanks, but I've got to get a blog post up tonight. I'm way behind."

Lauren turned off the water and dried her hands before sitting at the kitchen table. "You'll want to eat these berries today or tomorrow," she said. "Because they're perfect right now. But the ones in the jars will keep for a year."

"Thank you, Lauren," Nessa said. She didn't want Lauren to do anything for her, but it was impossible to stop her, even though Nessa remained aloof and impersonal. Lauren was the most domestic, industrious, artistic person Nessa had ever known. Lauren did most of the talking when they were together, which worked out well. Still, Nessa missed having real friends.

But having real friends required intimacy, and intimacy required honesty. And real honesty on Nessa's part would dismantle the carefully constructed fortress that was her life.

In addition to gardening, canning, quilting, spinning, and

pottery, Lauren homeschooled the boys. They were constantly going on field trips to museums and exhibits. Ziggy and Tosh went around all summer without shirts and grew brown, unlike Daltrey, who Nessa slathered in sunscreen any time they went outside. This drove Lauren insane.

"It's a racket," she said. "You're putting chemicals all over your child, who then is deprived of vitamin D."

"Oh, he gets that in his fortified Sugar-Coated, Honey-Covered, Chocolate-Infused, Artificially Colored Sweetie Flakes," Nessa said.

"It's not funny," Lauren said.

"It's a little funny," Nessa said.

Lauren finished the berries, then called for her boys, who came stampeding into the kitchen with Daltrey hot on their heels.

"It's half-off day on Tuesday the twenty-first at the splash park," Lauren said. Ziggy and Tosh surrounded Daltrey and asked if he wanted to go swimming. His head nod was so enthusiastic, he nearly fell over. Daltrey faced her and traced a circle over his heart with a flat hand, ASL for "Please," his big eyes begging.

Nessa tried not to grimace in resentment at Lauren. Why couldn't she have asked Nessa before the boys came in? She was always doing this sort of thing, forcing Nessa to say "yes" to things she'd rather not do. But in spite of this irritating habit, Lauren was the only mom Nessa spent any time around. She'd stopped taking Daltrey to the playground because she couldn't stand the inane mom talk; the endless complaining about how hard mommying was, about how little their husbands understood; the endless cannibalizing of their children's lives, served up for the entertainment of the other moms, a justification for their existence, to make up for their own nonexistent lives. It was such an identity thing for these women.

They were the ones who posted the creepy mom memes online—like *A son will hold your heart forever*—all this border-line stalker talk: "My children are my heart and soul, my liver and pancreas. I'm incomplete without them, blah, blah, blah."

Nessa had been horrified when she'd learned she would be having a boy, because apparently something happened to a woman's brain when she had a son. She became a servant, hopelessly tied to the boy's wants and needs. She poured all her energy into this male life, the only one in existence who, for at least a short time, only had eyes for her. These women believed they could mold their sons into the men their husbands could never be.

She'd been relieved to discover she could love her son but not have that weird, desperate longing for him, to serve his every need.

Lauren appeared to be the same way with her sons. That's why Nessa could tolerate her better than most. And Lauren was interesting. She did things, didn't just follow three paces behind her sons as if they were demigods.

"Okay," Nessa said, "we'll go to the splash park."

Daltrey and the boys held hands and danced in a circle. She couldn't help but smile. He'd probably forget before the day came.

"How about we pick you and Daltrey up at nine on the twenty-first for the splash park?" Lauren said.

"Okay," Nessa said. But she already had an excuse ready. She'd call Lauren the night before as soon as Daltrey was in bed and say they had sore throats, and she was so sorry but they wouldn't be able to go after all, darn it to heck.

"All right, we're off," Lauren said, rising from her chair. "Tell DJ goodbye, boys," she said.

Nessa hated the familiar use of his initials, but it seemed petty to say so. They didn't get together with Lauren and her sons all that often, and Daltrey lit up whenever he saw them. Maybe being around them would actually encourage him to talk. Food for thought.

Lauren gave Declan MacManus a jowl rub, strapped her basket back on, and put on her hat. Her sons ran out the back door.

"See you the twenty-first," Lauren said as she and the boys exited through the open door to their waiting horses. Nessa locked the door behind her and watched through the window as the family mounted their rides and rode west through the woods toward their property.

Nessa gathered the berry jars Lauren had left. "Daltrey," she said. "You want to go down to the cellar?"

He signed "Yes" over and over. He loved the spooky dirt-walled hole in the ground where she kept canned goods and holiday decorations, and where they'd be safe if a tornado ever came their way. John had made a practice of leaving small items around in the cellar for Daltrey to find. He didn't want Daltrey to be afraid of dark places, so he would leave a little plastic animal, or a quarter, or a shiny stone, and tell his son the little people had left it there for him to find because they wanted him to be happy.

Daltrey followed her out the back door and down the steps to the side of the house where wooden doors concealed a cement staircase leading down into the earth.

She had been scared to death of her grandmother's storm cellar when she was a kid, thinking of it as a tomb, a dark, dank place where she imagined demon hands would reach out and grab her ankles before she could get to the string that when pulled would illuminate a single bulb. Her cellar was much the same, and she still got a creepy feeling going down there. So she was glad to have even little Daltrey with her, because her protective instinct tended to drown out her fear.

She lifted the heavy wooden doors and then felt her way down the stairs until she found the string and yanked it. Daltrey came down backward, as if descending a ladder, then promptly sat on the damp cement floor while she shelved the berries.

Daltrey rooted around, looking for his prize, but there would be none this time.

"Let's go, honey," Nessa said. "I don't think the little people have—"

But to her utter surprise, he held up a little red die cast car, his face awash in delight.

Nessa felt unexpected tears spring to her eyes as she took it from his outstretched hand and turned it over.

"How about that?" she said, handing it back to him. She led him up the stairs and out into the sunshine. She shut the cellar door and they went back in the house.

Daltrey ran into the living room to show Isabeau his new car.

"What have you got there?" she said. He placed the new toy on Isabeau's palm and she looked it over. "This is way cool." He nodded and ran up to his room, no doubt to put the car with his other "little people" treasures on his bookcase. Nessa wiped her eyes and sat down in front of her computer.

Right. She'd been researching that trivia question. On the screen was the list of words common to all five artists' songs:

part

ground

roll

vine

old

water

rosie

She stared at her screen in disbelief, an electric buzz covering her skin.

A quick search confirmed it.

Norah Jones's "Rosie's Lullaby"; Tom Waits's "Rosie (Closing Time)"; Jackson Browne's "Rosie"; AC/DC's "Whole Lotta Rosie"; and Neil Diamond's "Cracklin' Rosie."

Rosie.

Nessa's real name.

Chapter Eight

THERE WAS SIMPLY no chance someone out there had figured out who she was. Or, more precisely, who she used to be.

Nessa had taken every precaution to make sure her photo was nowhere on the Internet, no link between her current identity and her birth name. She had it written into her Altair contract that they were prohibited from using her photo in promotions, using the excuse that it helped retain an air of mystery. If she wrote about John or Daltrey, she referred to them as J and D. She used Hushmail for email, Tor software that allowed her to browse and post anonymously, and the Tails OS, an operating system that prevented anything being written onto her computer's main drives. Everything was designed to mask her IP and leave her untraceable by anyone except security experts.

She had a flash of John's abandoned truck. Were these two things connected somehow?

She dismissed this as paranoia of the most insane kind—bipolar, crack-addict paranoia. No. It was a fluke that the commenter had come up with this particular trivia question. It didn't mean he knew Nessa had been Rosie in another lifetime. There was no traceable connection between Rosie and Nessa. They were two different people. She had to believe that. She had to.

She looked at the question again, and the name attached to it was of course Anonymous. Maybe she should make signing comments mandatory, but that would cut way down on interaction if people had to identify themselves, and it was her numbers that kept her sponsors paying her.

It was just a coincidence. A very specific coincidence.

Nessa had to try and work, even though her concentration was shot full of holes. Too many things crowded into her brain. But with or without concentration, Nessa had to finish and put up a post before midnight, and nothing could get in the way of that. Her advertising agreement demanded she put out three posts a week, even if her estranged spouse was missing or dead, even if she was encapsulated in an iron lung, even if she was off-planet. Advertising marched on.

She sat down at her desk in front of the window that looked out on the hops vines and opened her laptop. Best thing to do was start typing. But she was interrupted by a quiet gasp from Isabeau.

"Hey, boss, I need to show you something."

Nessa swiveled in her chair as Isabeau picked up her laptop, walked over to the couch, and sat down. She beckoned to Nessa, who got up and sat next to her.

"What is it?" Nessa said.

Isabeau set her laptop on the coffee table and tapped the trackpad.

"Okay, so I know you don't do social media and all that, but I thought it might be useful to see what's going on in the 'sphere, see if you're being talked about out there. I know your advertisers are always looking for ways to increase your exposure, so anyway, I created a couple of Google alerts—with search terms like *Nessa*, *radio*, *Altair*, *deep cuts*. That sort of thing. So I got a couple of alerts this morning—"

Isabeau typed into the address bar and pulled up her Google alerts page.

"So as it turns out," she said, "you have a Twitter account. Where 'you' tweet all kinds of really idiotic shit. No offense. And from the bad grammar and the weird topics, I don't think Altair is responsible." Isabeau typed on her keyboard. "I'm pulling up Twitter and searching for @RadioNessa."

Nessa's cell phone rang. Her contact at Altair. She let it go to voicemail and pocketed it before looking at Isabeau's screen. A Twitter profile page appeared with the bio: *Obamma was born in Kenya. He has no right to be the presdient. Someone should assinate him.*

Nessa whipped her head toward Isabeau, her mouth so wide she could swallow a dinner plate. "We have to delete this."

"We can't," Isabeau said. "It's not your account. It's not, is it?"

"Of course not! Look at the spelling!"

Was that really what she was so twisted up about? The spelling?

"I voted for Obama," Nessa said, the defensiveness in her voice making her cringe. "Both times."

"Oh," Isabeau said. "I didn't. Not crazy about his foreign policy. But I definitely don't want him dead."

"How do we get this taken down?"

"We can't. Unless we can prove this person meant you harm, meant for people to think this is actually you."

"Of course I can prove it. Look at my voting record. Look at my *spelling*, for God's sake."

Again with the spelling.

"Anyway," Isabeau said, "I don't think that's going to be enough to persuade a judge to issue a take-down order. But I'm going to report it to Twitter."

Who was this girl? Where did all this knowledge come from?

"Keep reading. It gets worse."

Nessa read through some more politically incorrect invective, and then she saw this:

> *The earthquake in Java was retribushon for legalizing gay mariage.*

Nessa groaned. "Enough," she said. "I can't read any more."

"Well, you obviously haven't gotten to the worst one. You need to see it."

Nessa kept scrolling until she got to a highlighted tweet, one that was twice the size of the others, and it was one of "hers."

> *Thanks to vacines, my son can't speak. He'd be better off dead. Don't get your kids vacinated!*

Nessa's skin tingled. She'd never mentioned Daltrey wasn't talking yet on the blog or on the radio. She was certain of it. She normally didn't talk family on the radio and only rarely on the blog, and only as it pertained to whatever music she was discussing.

But . . . John had endlessly speculated on Daltrey's lack of speech, although he'd never said Daltrey would be better off dead. Had he? Of course not. But John had bought into the whole vaccine conspiracy movement, no matter how many articles she'd shown him debunking this ridiculous myth.

"You don't believe that, of course," Isabeau said, as if to reassure herself Nessa wasn't a crackpot.

"Of course not." Nessa regarded her. Did she think Nessa was doing all this to generate publicity or something? What did Isabeau think, and how could she possibly ask Isabeau to be real with her when she had no intention of being real in return?

"I didn't think so," Isabeau said.

"Are you sure you didn't think so?"

"Yes." But she wouldn't meet Nessa's eye.

Nessa's computer dinged from her desk. She brought it back with her to the couch, sat back down, and opened Hushmail. There were several messages from Altair and a couple from sponsors.

She clicked on the one from Rick's Music Shop and Guitar Services:

> *Dear Ms. Donati,*
> *We are sad to say we are pulling our sponsorship from your blog* Unknown Legends *due to the offensive nature of your recent tweets. We wish you the best of luck.*

Nessa typed a reply to Rick's:

> *Dear Rick,*
> *The Twitter handle is a malicious spoof account. I can see how some people might become confused, but this happens all the time. If you're in the public eye, you attract haters, and those haters do what they can to destroy your credibility. If you'll notice, the spelling is horrendous, and mine is not. I of course know how to spell* Obama *and* president. *;) As you*

know, I've never made any of these kinds of comments before, and now there are many, obviously an attempt by someone to discredit me.

I hope you'll reconsider. If not, I understand.

Best, Nessa

Nessa then got on her blog and whipped off a quick note to her subscribers and sponsors explaining what had happened and asking them to hang in there with her while she sorted the insanity out.

"I have one more thing to show you," Isabeau said. "So you read about the Air Capital plane crash over South Dakota over the weekend, right?"

Of course she had. There'd been no survivors, but in a bizarre twist, much of the baggage was intact.

"Well, as it turns out, you also have a Facebook fan page. And here's the most recent thing 'you' posted."

#AirCapital597 Glad the valuble stuff survived!! Who's going with me to the auction??

"Good God," Nessa said. This was the kind of thing that ruined people's reputations forever. She remembered the story of the PR exec who posted a thoughtless tweet and had to change her name and move.

"Trolls, right?" Isabeau said. "Nothing to do but sit in their parents' basements and smoke weed and anonymously heckle people who are actually trying to create something. I'll bet this guy's some jealous asshole who's trying to spook your sponsors.

He probably has a shitty music blog with two subscribers—his mom and a girl named Desiree who keeps asking him if, for just $24.95, he'd like to take a look at some of her nude photos."

Nessa laughed. "You really think that's all it is?"

Isabeau rolled her eyes. "Probably," she said. "If you ignore him, he'll probably get bored and try to find somebody more fun to flame." She stretched. "Hey, I'm going into town here in a little while—meeting some friends for dinner and a movie. I should be home about ten. Cool if I bring my stuff with me and do a little move-in?"

"Oh, sure," Nessa said. "Have fun."

Isabeau closed up her laptop, slung her purse over her shoulder, and went out the back door.

Nessa spent the rest of the afternoon calming nervous and angry sponsors and her Altair bosses, then made a stir-fry for herself and Daltrey for dinner.

After they ate, the two of them went out back to walk their property with Declan MacManus. The dog cavorted happily, running to and fro, barking over his shoulder at them as if they were an irritatingly slow tour group and he was their guide. They walked into the wooded area beyond their outbuildings, and Nessa pointed things out to Daltrey as they passed them. "Look," she said. "A sunflower. Sunflower. Tree. That's a tree. It's an oak. Weeds. Those are weeds."

The sun dipped below the horizon, and Daltrey looked happy to be outside in the warm dusk later than she normally let him stay out.

Finally, what she'd been waiting for happened, and a tiny light ascended from the tall grass.

"Look, Daltrey! A firefly! Can you say firefly?"

His eyes grew bigger and his mouth dropped open, as more and more of the lightning bugs appeared and rose in the air around him.

Daltrey and Declan MacManus chased after the fireflies and leaped at them. Daltrey finally twirled, his arms overhead, never letting go of the toy car, his eyes closed in rapture as the tiny lights floated all around him.

She wished Isabeau were here to see this. She wished John were. And she was crying again.

After Nessa put Daltrey to bed, she sat at her desk and paid bills until Isabeau returned at nine-thirty, suitcases and a few boxes in tow for her move-in.

"You should have let me help you do this," Nessa said.

"I only have a few things," Isabeau said. "No biggie." She dragged everything up to the guest room and Nessa could hear her putting things away in dresser drawers.

Nessa felt relief at having another adult in the house, and she knew she'd made the right decision. She went upstairs and knocked lightly on the guest room door. Isabeau opened it and threw her arm out wide as if she were welcoming a treasured guest.

"Do you have everything you need?" Nessa said.

"I think so. You going to bed?"

"Yeah. I'll see you tomorrow."

Nessa closed Isabeau's door and went to check on Daltrey. He was sound asleep, still clutching the car. She eased it from his hand and looked at it. It was a Hot Wheels replica of a Tesla Model S, which had been John's current dream car.

"Good on the environment," he'd told her, "but still hot."

She placed the Tesla on the top shelf of Daltrey's bookcase next to the Fender guitar pick and the other artifacts John had hidden for him.

She gazed at Daltrey's lovely face, thinking, *My dad went out of his mind and all I got was this lousy toy car.*

Chapter Nine

Sunday, June 5

NESSA SAT AT her desk after dinner while Daltrey and Isabeau played Legos and wrote her Monday blog post.

> The Disintegration Loops *is a four-volume album by William Basinski, and I don't know when I've been so disturbed by a piece of music as I was when my friend Marlon, who knows all the freaky stuff out there, even though he's middle-aged (or maybe it's because he's middle-aged) played it for me. . .*

She gave herself a chuckle, calling Marlon middle-aged even though he was only in his thirties. She knew he'd have plenty to say about that at their next sponsor meeting.

She finished up the post, proofed it, changed a few phrases, and cut a few words, then attached *The Disintegration Loops'* cover art as the featured image, added tags, and posted it a day early. Good for her.

Nessa navigated to the front page of her blog to read the latest comments. Most were nice, some were thoughtful, funny, interesting. But there were also the odd nasty, profane, personal, ugly comments from trolls. And then there were the Beatles Avengers, who could never let go of her apathy toward the all-time greatest band the universe had ever known. When she felt like punishing herself, she read these brilliant, witty ripostes like *You're writting sucx.* This served a three-fold, evil purpose—it stirred up angry feelings, put a sword through her already aching heart, and made her feel superior all at the same time. Today's gem: *Your mind is so small, you probably like Norman Rockwell.*

That made her laugh. She did like Norman Rockwell. Fuck 'em.

After Daltrey went down, Nessa and Isabeau watched a movie in the living room, a romantic comedy, which didn't help distract Nessa because of its utterly predictable storyline. Isabeau went up to her new room about ten minutes after the movie ended, and Nessa followed her upstairs to check on Daltrey, who was sleeping peacefully, then washed her face and put on her pajamas before returning to the living room. She made herself a cup of green tea, got out her vapor pen, and opened her laptop, ready to do her inventory.

But first she refreshed her blog and saw the Basinski post already had several comments below it.

Awesome! Next time I have +7 hours to sit still and think about collapsing buildings I will know what to listen to.
Posted by Anonymous | June 7 7:38 PM

Beatles rule
Posted by Anonymous | June 7 7:46 PM

Profiting off of the worst day in American history FTW
Posted by Studtman | June 7 7:55 PM

7:55 go back to sleep DAWG
Posted by Anonymous | June 7 7:59 PM

Great records! I love this stuff. BUT, if want music for sit-
ting around thinking about "collapsing buildings" as 7:38
suggested, I would obviously be playing Einstürzende Neu-
bauten.
Posted by Anonymous | June 7 8:02 PM

remember the days when people actually wrote songs instead
of hitting three notes on the "strings" setting of a synthesizer
and then repeating it for 11 minutes?
Posted by LIghtning! | June 7 8:02 PM

This was the type of comment she felt duty-bound to respond to.

So it didn't strike you . . . that's fine. But for me, TDL is the
very definition of art. It provokes a response. It disturbs, it
delights, it wears brand-new neural pathways in your brain,
and redistributes the chemicals. It changes you. TDL changed
me, and for that I thank William Basinski.

Some of the comments on her blog were so brainy and
well-reasoned she wondered if Marlon wrote them, like the

Einstürzende Neubauten comment (which, she learned, was a German industrial band—thank you, Interwebz). But she didn't dare ask, because she didn't want to sound like a self-obsessed me-monkey, as if he spent all his time pondering her brilliant words and thinking of pithy comments to add.

One more comment appeared:

What you need is another good raping.
Posted by DeadJohnDonati | June 7 8:37 PM

Nessa choked on her tea, which sent her into a violent coughing fit.

She heard a door click open upstairs.

"You okay down there, boss?" Isabeau called.

Nessa continued coughing, and Isabeau appeared in the doorway, then charged into the room when she caught a glimpse of Nessa's face. "What is it?"

Nessa turned her laptop toward Isabeau and pointed.

"What is—oh, my gosh," Isabeau said, her hand over her mouth. "What kind of sick asshole would do that? I mean, that is just beyond the pale."

The commenter's handle scrolled through Nessa's brain like a Times Square news ticker marquee:

DeadJohnDonatiDeadJohnDonatiDeadJohnDonati

"TOS violation," Isabeau said. "We're banning this guy from the blog. That is unacceptable. But first I'm going to screenshot it." She did so, then sat staring at the screen. "Another. Why does this guy use 'another'?"

Another *good raping*?

Nessa fought down the panic that rose in her chest. She'd been so shocked by the handle that she'd missed it completely.

It didn't mean anything. It was just another anonymous testosterone-fueled hate message.

It didn't mean anything.

"Boss?"

Nessa's breath came quick and shallow, depriving her of the oxygen she desperately needed to stay conscious. She bent forward and willed herself to breathe deeply.

"Go on to bed, Isabeau," Nessa said. "I'm okay. Just go on to bed."

"But—"

"Please, Isabeau!" Her voice was high and sharp, and Isabeau obeyed.

What you need. . .

What she needed was for all this stress to stop. What she needed was for John to come back, alive and drug-free.

What she didn't need was another raping, good or otherwise.

Chapter Ten

Wednesday, June 8

SHE DREAMED SHE was being crushed, a dead weight on top of her, being unable to breathe through her broken nose, smothering. Until last night, she hadn't had this nightmare for years, but it stirred up past terrors, those feelings of despair and futility she'd hoped she'd escaped, back when suicide entered her fevered, grief-stricken mind on a regular basis. She longed to go to sleep and never wake up, but there was Daltrey, her brown-eyed boy, who she couldn't leave. She was selfish, but she wasn't that selfish.

She woke before it was light and went into the kitchen to make coffee and wait. She couldn't read or watch TV. She couldn't concentrate. She should do something productive like Lauren would—maybe make apple dolls with dried corn husk skirts or bake vegetarian lasagna or make artisanal sheep's milk cheese to sell at the local food co-op.

Since Nessa couldn't do any of those things, she caught up on laundry. Finally at a little after six, Daltrey came padding into the kitchen, his beautiful thick taupe hair an apostrophe over his head, rubbing his big round eyes with one hand and dragging his Timmy Chicken behind him. Then he glanced at the door to the garage and back at her, his eyebrows a question mark. He signed "Daddy."

She didn't know what to say. The only thing now that redeemed their doomed union was standing before her clutching a colorful stuffed chicken.

"You want some eggs for breakfast?" she asked him.

He nodded, and she got busy cooking.

Isabeau came into the kitchen tentatively, worry etching her face. "You okay, boss?"

"Yeah," Nessa said. "Sorry about the meltdown last night. I'm all right."

"You want to talk about it?"

Nessa turned her eyes toward Daltrey and shook her head, hoping Isabeau would catch on that she didn't want to talk about any of this in front of her son. What Isabeau wouldn't know was Nessa had no intention of talking to her at all.

After breakfast, Isabeau turned the television on to *The Octonauts* for Daltrey before sitting on the floor next to Nessa's desk to work on her computer.

Nessa opened her own laptop. Isabeau had added a new search term to their Google Alerts—DeadJohnDonati—and this morning, Nessa's inbox was stuffed full of alerts from the comment section on her blog. This was the first one:

Nessa Donati steals cars and kites checks.

Interesting that this particular comment was spelled perfectly.

And something else . . . who used the phrase *kites checks*? That was an archaic term, wasn't it? She called Isabeau over and showed her.

"Before you delete anything," Isabeau said, "we need to screenshot everything so we have a record of what's going on. It's a good thing you use this spam plug-in, because each commenter's IP address appears next to their comments. I've started a spreadsheet."

"Even if we delete these things, stuff on the Internet is forever, right? Daltrey will see this one day, and he'll—"

Isabeau put her hand on Nessa's arm, a first. "Just hold on. He'll know this is a lie. But in the meantime, I need you to remain calm. It doesn't help to get all freaked out."

Nessa went through her email. Another sponsor asking for reassurance that the odd comments on her blog would be stopped.

The clothes dryer buzzed, so Nessa folded the last of the laundry and lugged the full basket upstairs. Her first stop was her own room. After she'd unloaded her things into her closet, she went to Daltrey's room, where she filled his dresser drawers. And then she lingered over Daltrey's treasures atop his bookcase.

She lifted the things one by one: the Tesla Model S, the little green army man with a bazooka, the amethyst geode, the Fender guitar pick. As she grabbed it, she heard Isabeau gasp downstairs and say, "Oh, my gosh."

Nessa ran down the stairs, the pick still in her hand, and when she got to the living room, Isabeau's expression stopped Nessa dead. The now-familiar feeling of alarm filled her stomach.

"Oh, shit," Isabeau said. "Oh, this is so bad."

"What?" Nessa demanded. Isabeau rose from the floor and pulled out Nessa's desk chair in front of her desktop computer.

"Go to NessaDonati.com."

"But—"

"Just do it!"

Nessa sat, put the pick in her pocket, and typed the URL into the address bar, then watched the website materialize. The home page of the site was a fairly generic splash page with the following menu items: Show / Blog / Appearances / Game / Photos. Had Altair put this site up without her knowledge?

She looked at Isabeau, whose expression was tense and worried, her eyebrows knotted.

"You better look," Isabeau said.

On the Show page, it listed the times she was on the air. Under Blog, it said Coming Soon. She was beginning to think it was Altair, until she clicked on Photos.

There she found dozens of nudes: her legs spread-eagle, having sex in every position imaginable and some she couldn't imagine, and even grosser things. *Hustler*-grade stuff. Of course her head had been Photoshopped onto the airbrushed bodies. She didn't look anything like that. But it was more than a little unsettling to see herself in that context.

She glanced again over her shoulder, and Isabeau met her gaze.

"That's not the worst of it," she said, reaching for the mouse and clicking on Game. A headshot of Nessa appeared, filling the screen. Beneath the headshot were instructions: *Use your mouse buttons to punch Nessa's face. If you knock out a tooth, you win!*

Just to see what would happen, she clicked the mouse, and fists shot out, punching the face. Each punch made her eyes swell a little more, bruising develop, blood come out of her nose, eventually knocking out a tooth. Fireworks exploded on the screen, accompanied by the words *You Win!* The effects were spectacularly realistic.

She scrolled further.

New Rape Game Coming Soon!

"This is beyond trolling," Isabeau said in a hushed voice. "This is menacing. It's threatening. It's *personal*."

Yes, it was. Nessa turned the pick over in her hand, and the silver BIG written on the back of it suddenly grew in her brain, filled the room and her consciousness as "Dead Wrong" blared in her mind. That song. It was by Notorious B.I.G.

BIG.

She had to do an Internet search. Alone. Now.

"I'm going to take a bath," Nessa said, snatching up her laptop.

Isabeau's eyes traveled from the computer in Nessa's hands to her face.

"I'll be back down in a little while. I need to calm down. Okay?"

"All right," Isabeau said.

Nessa went upstairs and locked herself in her bathroom and opened her laptop. She navigated to the California state prison website. After almost an hour of searching and being bounced from one worthless, confusing, badly designed website to another, she finally had to plunk down $4.95 for seven-day unlimited access to governmentsearch.com. Then Nessa finally had the information she needed and dreaded.

He'd been paroled fourteen months ago.

Nathan. Her high school classmate who'd served seven years in Chino, effectively blowing his full-ride football scholarship to USC. For raping Nessa.

She sat shaking in her bathroom using her vape pen. It was a poor substitute for what she really needed, what her very cells cried out for, which was a shot. She kept having to swallow to keep up with the constant salivating, to tamp down the germinating nausea that mimicked withdrawal.

It was clear to her that Nathan had posted the Rosie trivia question to let her know he knew who she really was. But did he know *where* she was? That she was in the middle of Kansas?

No, she reassured herself. If he did, he'd have shown up in person.

Right?

He was terrorizing her to try to flush her out, to expose her, or more specifically, to make her expose herself. So the cops would find her and haul her off to prison now that he was out. He would finally have his revenge.

Nathan was a rapist, but was he also a killer? Maybe not before prison, but very possibly yes after doing his time. He'd had seven years to learn. To allow his bitterness and acid-rain hostility to build. To think about his stolen future, his life playing college football and then the NFL, all the money, all the women, the fame he'd been robbed of. By Nessa.

She didn't like to think about what had happened after the rape, because it was nearly as bad. Nessa had just wanted it all to go away. But Joyce had insisted on pressing charges, overriding Nessa's terror at testifying at trial and facing her attacker. Joyce gave Nessa a touching speech about empowerment and justice and saving other girls from this monster, and when Nessa still resisted, Joyce showed her a contract from a television producer. She had actually contacted the man with an idea for a reality show—mothers of rape victims sitting around rapping about how their daughters' lives had been destroyed. The deal would only go through, Joyce said, if Nessa participated, if she outed herself.

"What do we always say?" she'd said to Nessa. "When life hands you lemons, make lemonade, right? We need to turn this sad situation into a blessing."

"What does that mean?" Nessa said.

"This is our one shot," Joyce said. "We'll be set for life. This show will make us famous and rich. Don't you want that?"

"Or," Nessa said, "you could get an actual job."

Joyce had given Nessa the death stare, the one that used to scare Nessa into silence, but after the rape, it had no effect. Then her mother had pulled out her trump card, the one that always worked.

"What happens the next time Brandon gets pneumonia or an infection? Or he goes into anaphylactic shock? Do you want him to have to go to County? He almost died from a staph infection the last time he went there. If we do this show, Brandon will have the best care. *You* can make that possible."

Joyce had had the contract in hand. Nessa could save her brother. She shouldn't be selfish, although she couldn't shake the feeling that if it were Joyce who had to do what she was asking Nessa to do, Brandon could damn well go to County.

The trial was just like Nessa had read and heard about. The questions about her sex life, about her sluttiness and her drug use. It really was like getting raped all over again, but in front of a judge, jury, and lawyers. The two bright spots were Candy's testimony, which was heartfelt and strong, and the testimony of the kid who'd walked into the room and saved her. That was pretty much what put Nathan away. Not Nessa's testimony, not the testimony of a slut.

And then they did the reality show, and they got five grand a month apiece, plus a signing bonus, plus a ratings bonus if they were high enough.

Nessa could imagine Nathan watching this show on the prison

TV, his rage growing, his revenge plot coalescing in his mind, becoming his life's focus and goal.

At the same time, Nessa's focus and goal had gelled, bankrolled by the allowance Joyce gave her out of their show earnings. And that was heroin.

Thursday, June 9

"JEEP'S BLUES" PLAYED on Nessa's phone, waking her from a sound sleep.

"Hello?"

"Mrs. Donati? This is Detective Rob Treloar from the Riley County Sheriff's Department. How are you doing today?"

She tried to sound like she'd been up for hours. "Great," she said. "I'm fine. How are you?" Although why he'd care if the call had awakened her, she didn't know.

"Doing well," he said. "I'm calling because I have a request. I wondered if you might have an item that would possibly have Mr. Donati's DNA on it."

Nessa gasped, and it sounded showy and theatrical to her own ears. "What did you find?"

"I'd rather talk about it in person. Could you come down to the station with a hairbrush of his or a toothbrush? Do you have anything like that?"

"John took all his—"

"Or a close relative."

Nessa's breath caught. "You mean my son?"

"Was—is Mr. Donati your son's biological father?"

For whatever reason this question rattled her propriety. "Of course he is!"

"Well, ma'am," Detective Treloar said, infinitely patient. "Would it be possible for you to bring him to the station for a cheek swab?"

"What did you find?"

"Let's talk when you come in. Tomorrow about ten? Would that work for you?"

Nessa was unable to breathe. "Okay," she said, but no sound came out until she cleared her throat and repeated herself.

"I'll see you then." He clicked off.

Nessa sat up and gazed out the window across from her bed, which looked out on the fields beyond her property. She'd been right. John had jumped into the river, drowned, and the police must have found his body, and it was unrecognizable. The carp and catfish must have stripped most of his flesh off his bones, and now the only way they could make sure it was him was with DNA.

What had she expected? Had she really expected for John to live that long after he started using again? No, she hadn't. But this reality, the idea that he might really be gone, made her realize her little girl's heart had hoped for a storybook ending, where John would clean up, sober up, grow up. Come back to her, never to use again. What an idiot she was. That's not how this worked. She'd read all the literature. Only about twenty percent of crack users were able to stay clean, it was that addictive. It ate holes in the brain, destroyed the pleasure center, made life without it seem colorless and joyless.

Nessa wept, imagining John's torment. Unable to fight off the insatiable predator that had subjugated his life, surrendering to the river's current.

She had to stop picturing it, had to turn her mind away from it. She took three deep, slow breaths and forced herself to get up and drink a glass of water. She didn't know anything for sure yet. It was possible she was imagining it all wrong. Maybe the police wanted DNA in case they found anything. Or because he'd committed some crime. She preferred this line of thinking, because anger was energizing, and she needed energy to keep functioning.

The sun shone into the kitchen windows, and the very presence of light straightened her posture and helped her breathe more deeply. Maybe they'd go to the park today. After a cup of coffee, Nessa went out back to feed the dog.

"Declan MacManus!" she called.

He didn't run for her, didn't bark his "I'm coming, I'm coming, hold on, be right there" bark. He must be way off the property chasing pheasants or something. He'd be home when he was hungry or wanted to play ball.

She turned back toward the door when a large clump of crabgrass caught her eye, annoying her—John wasn't here to maintain this sort of thing, and she wasn't going to do it. But as she got closer, she saw it wasn't a clump of grass, but a mound of fur.

She ran.

Declan MacManus lay on his side, not breathing, flies on his open, milky eyes. Dead.

Nessa fell to her knees and the flies scattered momentarily before going back to business. She looked him over, looking for blood, cuts, wounds, and noticed the remnant of a foamy substance on his mouth and nose. For a moment she wondered if it was rabies. But she'd played with him yesterday, and there'd been no sign of the disease. It wouldn't have killed him this fast.

Maybe it was one of the plants in the woods or he'd eaten something off the ground that was poisonous to dogs.

Nessa raised her head, tears rolling down her face, and looked around. These woods had always seemed friendly and welcoming to her, but now they appeared to be full of dark shadows and predators and poisonous plants. Even in the sultry morning, a chill covered her.

She went in and woke Isabeau, who, when she heard the news, ran outside in her underwear and cried over Declan MacManus's body.

"Oh, poor baby," she said, and then before Nessa could stop her, Isabeau was hugging her into her shoulder. This was the first hug she'd received from someone other than Daltrey in months and it loosened something inside her.

Daltrey would be destroyed by this news. Declan MacManus had watched over the boy since birth, always a gentle presence, cuddling with him on his bed, picking up whatever Daltrey dropped, and returning it to him—even food, like Nana the nursemaid dog in *Peter Pan*. Two huge losses in less than two months for a three-year-old would definitely have consequences.

"Isabeau, I need you to be here when Daltrey gets up, but I'll break the news to him when I get back from the vet, okay?"

"Nessa, he's dead," Isabeau said. "There's no point in—"

"We need to find out what killed him," Nessa said.

"He was such a good dog," Isabeau said, crying and ruffling his fur.

Nessa picked Declan MacManus up and put him in the Pacifica, and drove into town to the vet's office.

She waited for almost an hour before the vet came out, shaking her head. "It was antifreeze," she said.

"No way it could've been rabies or anything like that, then," Nessa said, her hopeful denial ebbing away.

"No. He must have found a spilled puddle in your garage."

"Our garage has a dirt floor," Nessa said.

"Do you have a fence?"

"No," Nessa said. "We live on sixty acres. We just let him roam."

"Do you have neighbors within running distance?"

"Yes."

"He might have wandered into one of their garages. A lethal dose for a dog of Declan's size is only about a third of a cup. That's one of the reasons to keep your animals fenced. I'm so sorry for your loss. We can cremate the remains for you here, if you'd like."

"Please," Nessa said, crying bitter tears. Maybe she should try to find a replacement dog and bring him home before Daltrey got up from his nap, but he'd know. Of course he'd know. He was not a stupid little boy, and she could not try to fool him that way.

When Nessa returned home, she found she couldn't get out of the car. She was going to have to tell Daltrey, and she didn't know how to do it. She sat there for so long that Isabeau came out to the garage and knocked on the driver's side window, startling Nessa. She opened the door and got out of the Pacifica.

"You all right, boss?" Isabeau asked.

"No," Nessa said. "I'm going to cry now." Nessa burst into tears, and Isabeau reached for her, but Nessa wrapped her arms around herself and stepped away. A look of hurt crossed Isabeau's face.

"I need to tell Daltrey," Nessa said, wiping her eyes.

"I'll help you," Isabeau said.

They trudged toward the house and went into the living room, where Daltrey was constructing an elaborate tower out of Legos. He looked up, first at Nessa, then at Isabeau and back again. His eyebrows drew together. He knew something was wrong. He was such a smart kid; if he ever started talking, they were all in serious trouble.

"Daltrey," Nessa said. "Come sit on my lap. I've got something to tell you."

She sat on the couch and made the sign for "Come here." He continued frowning and didn't move. He probably thought if he didn't sit on her lap, whatever bad news was coming could be held at bay.

"Come on, honey," Nessa said. She signed "Come here" again.

He sighed, set down the Legos in his hands, and reluctantly came to sit on her lap.

Isabeau sat in the wingback chair, tense, ready to offer condolences.

"Daltrey, I need to tell you something."

He nodded.

"Declan MacManus—" Nessa couldn't go on. She'd almost said "ran away." But that was unfair and untrue.

Daltrey nodded encouragingly at her.

"Sweetie, our good dog died this morning."

He looked at Isabeau, confused, then at Nessa.

"With Daddy?" Daltrey signed.

Isabeau's mouth dropped open.

Daltrey's question was a spear through Nessa's heart. He knew something horrible had happened to his dad. But she wouldn't confirm that to him, couldn't.

"Well, Declan MacManus is in heaven now," Nessa said. "We won't see him again in this . . . life. In this world."

Large, fat teardrops fell from Daltrey's eyes. "Goodbye?" he signed.

Nessa nodded, and he slid his arms around her neck and cried.

"We'll see him again in heaven, a long time from now. But we will see him again. I promise."

Nessa knew in her bones that this was just a warm-up for another, more difficult conversation she'd be having with him very soon.

Chapter Eleven

Friday, June 10

THE NEXT MORNING, she woke before anyone else and went down to the kitchen for coffee. She sat at the table, staring out the window at the hazy day, unable to work or read. When Daltrey got up, she busied herself making him pancakes.

Isabeau came down to breakfast, rubbing her eyes.

"I overslept," she said.

"It's okay," Nessa said. "It was a rough one yesterday."

Isabeau nodded and reached into the cupboard for a plate.

"I'm sorry that you're having to be here through all this shit," Nessa said. "I'm grateful you're with us though."

Isabeau smiled sadly at her and poured herself a cup of coffee before sitting down to dig into her pancakes.

"I have to take Daltrey down to the cop shop to get a cheek swab," Nessa said. "Do you want to go with us?"

"Cheek swab?" Isabeau looked shocked.

This was good. Having someone else to calm down always helped Nessa stay calm herself.

"No big deal," she said.

"Yeah, I'll go," Isabeau said. "I've never been in a police station on purpose."

Nessa looked at her, alarmed.

"Just kidding," Isabeau said, winking. "Actually, my dad was a cop."

Nessa didn't react. Typically, people would respond with a tidbit from their own past, but this was not that kind of relationship, and Nessa needed to keep it that way.

Nessa showered and put on her makeup. She hoped to ask Detective Treloar if there was any way he could find out Nathan's whereabouts. If he'd checked in with his parole officer recently. If it was possible for him to travel outside of the state at this point in his parole.

After putting on a long-sleeved almost matronly white dress, Nessa peeked into Daltrey's room, where he sat on his toddler bed looking at a board book.

"Let's get you dressed, and then we can get a bacon, egg, and Gouda sandwich at Starbucks, huh? And then, guess what?" She made her voice excited to get him excited. "We get to go to the police station."

His eyes got wide and his mouth made a silent, round O.

He jumped from bed, pulled open his dresser drawer, and selected an outfit consisting of swim trunks and an old bib that said *Bad to the Bone*.

"How about instead . . ." Nessa said, pulling out shorts and a T-shirt.

When he was dressed, she pointed at the book and said, "Do you want to bring that in the car?" He stuck it under his arm and followed her out to the Pacifica, where Isabeau was waiting.

They drove on Highway 177 North to 18 West, ate at Starbucks, then headed toward their final destination.

"There's the police station, Daltrey, isn't that cool?" Isabeau said, pointing at the nondescript tan brick-and-glass building.

Isabeau was so good, so natural, with Daltrey, so unlike Nessa before she'd had a child of her own. She wouldn't have known what to say to someone else's kid.

"You'll get to meet some police officers," Nessa said. "What do you think about that?"

She parked in the west lot and got Daltrey out of his car seat. He smiled and took her hand as they walked into the station. It echoed inside.

There was a female cop at the front desk.

"I can't remember the name of who I need to talk to," Nessa said, her voice tremulous as sweat rolled down her sides, tickling. Unlike Isabeau, she'd been brought to a police station in hand-cuffs more than once. "My name is Nessa Donati, and I'm here to have a cheek swab done on my son. Detective . . ."

Her mind went blank. What was his damned name?

The woman behind the desk smiled encouragingly at her.

"His name starts with T, I think . . ."

"Detective Rob Treloar," the officer said. "Is that who you need to see?"

Nessa nodded, wiping the rest of her makeup off. Daltrey stared silently up at her.

"Detective Treloar got pulled out on a call, but we can have a tech do it. Have a seat."

She, Isabeau, and Daltrey went to the waiting area and sat. Daltrey climbed into the chair next to Nessa and held her hand, staring solemnly ahead, like a priest at a wake. She patted his hand and handed him his book. He crossed his legs at the ankle, his feet straight out in front of him, and looked over his book like a little old man reading the *New York Times Book Review*, licking his index finger to turn the pages like his dad did when reading a magazine. Her breath caught in her throat.

"He is so freaking adorable," Isabeau said.

Twenty minutes later, a female technician in a lab coat came out and said, "Mrs. Donati?"

Nessa stood and Daltrey followed suit.

"Here for a buccal swab?" she said.

"I'm sorry, I don't—"

"Cheek swab. For DNA. Is that right?"

"Yes."

"Follow me."

They followed her down a hall. As they walked, she said over her shoulder, "I'm Amanda. We're in there." She led them into a small room where she told them to have a seat. While Amanda washed her hands in the stainless steel sink, she said, "What's your name?"

Daltrey looked at Nessa, who said, "His name is Daltrey."

"How old are you, Daltrey?"

"He's three," Isabeau chimed in.

The tech looked at Nessa suspiciously. "Can't he talk?"

"No," Nessa said.

"Oh," Amanda said. "Sorry." Then to Daltrey: "Is your mouth empty, honey? You chewing gum, or did you have a snack in the last fifteen minutes?"

He shook his head and opened his mouth to show her.

"Well, he seems to understand what I'm saying."

"He does," Nessa said, hoping she wouldn't have to explain.

"Okay, Daltrey, here's what's going to happen. This isn't going to hurt at all. In fact, it might tickle a little, okay?" She put on gloves. "I need to put these on and a mask to keep everything nice and clean, but it's still me under here, all right?"

Daltrey nodded, watching her closely.

She slipped the mask on over her nose and mouth, then tore open a paper pouch and carefully removed a long swab.

"Now," she said, her voice muffled by the mask, "I need to make sure that this swab doesn't touch anything else besides your mouth, okay? I'm going to need you to open your mouth as big as you possibly can, bigger than you ever did before."

Isabeau demonstrated by opening her mouth wide.

"Just like she's doing right now, okay? Can you do that?"

He nodded and opened wide.

"Now I'm going to touch this cotton end to the inside of your cheek and roll it around. I need you to be a big boy and keep your mouth nice and wide until I'm all done. Got it?"

He nodded, his mouth still open.

Amanda gently touched the swab to the inside of Daltrey's cheek and rotated it for about ten seconds. Nessa could tell that it did indeed tickle, because his nostrils flared and his lips were trying to curve into a smile, but he was brave and held his mouth open. The tech withdrew the swab, taking care not to touch the end to his teeth, lips, or tongue, then placed the swab into a tube, which she then corked with a rubber stopper.

"That's all there is to it, young man," she said, removing her mask. "How was that?"

He kissed the fingers of his right hand and slapped it into his left.

"He says, 'Good,'" Nessa explained.

Amanda smiled.

"Any idea why they need a DNA sample?" Nessa said, trying to sound casual.

"Nope," the tech said, peeling off her gloves and removing her mask.

There was a knock on the door, and Amanda opened it. In walked a man with a round, smooth face topped by heavy eyebrows and dark hair. He carried a half-inch-thick file folder under his arm.

"I'd like to speak with Mrs. Donati," he said to Amanda.

As Amanda regarded him, her expression changed from open friendliness to visible dislike. When she turned again to Nessa, her smile returned.

"Thanks for coming in," Amanda said, and then gave Nessa a look like *Good luck with this jerk*. Nessa prayed she was reading the tech wrong.

"Thank you, Amanda," Nessa said as she exited the room.

The detective didn't acknowledge Isabeau or Daltrey, just kept his eyes fixed on Nessa.

"I'm Detective Greg Dirksen."

She looked at the gold badge on a lanyard around his neck.

G. Dirksen, it said. *Homicide*.

Nessa stared at the badge, a chill constricting her throat.

Homicide?

Out of her peripheral vision, she watched Isabeau's mouth drop open.

"Mrs. Donati, I have a couple of questions." He set his file folder down on the counter and stepped closer to her.

Nessa didn't answer for a moment, just gazed steadily at the detective. She was very familiar with this sort of subtle male physical intimidation. She put her hands on her hips and stood her ground for a count of five. Then she turned to Isabeau and said, "Could you take Daltrey out to the lobby and wait for me there?"

"Sure," Isabeau said, looking concerned. She held out her hand to Daltrey, who took it, and followed her out the door.

"What can I do for you, Detective?" Nessa said, smiling her Mormon missionary homemaker smile.

"Do you own a gun, Mrs. Donati?"

The question came so fast her mouth started to form the answer before her brain caught up and stopped it. She cleared her throat. "Why do you ask?"

"Please answer the question. Do you own a gun?"

Of course she owned a gun. She'd purchased it recently, after John's two nocturnal visits the week she'd tossed him out. She just hadn't had the lady balls to learn to shoot it yet. She kept it in a box at the top of her closet.

Nessa composed her face, her facade starting to crack under the strain, but she maintained her smile. "Do *you*?"

Her motto when it came to cops was *Avoid at all costs*, and when that failed, *Don't make eye contact*. And finally, *Offer no information*. Wait to be asked, and answer as succinctly, plainly, and respectfully as possible. But the number one rule was *Don't be a smartass*. Never a good idea to antagonize a cop, but his brusque, disrespectful manner was bringing out the biker chick in her.

He just looked at her.

She pulled down her sleeves. She knew her rights and she knew she didn't have to answer any questions. If he'd asked nicely, the way Detective Treloar had, he would have gotten his answer.

"I need to get my son home," she said. "It's his nap time."

"Why won't you answer the question?" He leaned toward her, giving her a hard stare.

She still stood her ground, but she began to shake. "Did you— did you find my husband? Is that what this is about?"

"I'm not at liberty to say."

"Then you're not at liberty to interrogate me either," she said. "Unless I'm under arrest. Am I under arrest?"

"It's a simple question, Mrs. Donati."

"So is mine." She spoke slowly, no doubt antagonizing him further. "Am I under arrest?"

There was another knock at the door, and Detective Dirksen cracked it open so Nessa couldn't see or hear who was outside it. That person whispered something and the detective hissed something back, obviously not pleased with the interruption. "Fine." He turned his frown toward Nessa and said, "I'll be right back." He slipped out the door and closed it behind himself.

He'd left his folder on the counter.

Before she could think about it too hard, she opened the folder and saw the police report about the abandoned truck in the front. There were photos beneath more paper. After a split second of indecision, she pulled out her phone and started snapping photos of every page, turning each quickly, glancing at the door between snaps, trying to hear the terse conversation outside the door, but she couldn't do both.

She wasn't even seeing what she was photographing, so concentrated was she on the sounds outside, until the doorknob started to turn. She slammed the folder shut, reached for the faucet and turned on the water to give the appearance of being at the counter to wash her hands. As the door whooshed open, one of the papers slid from the folder and drifted to the floor.

"Guess I bumped it," Nessa said breathlessly. "Sorry about that."

Detective Dirksen watched the paper land at his feet, then looked at Nessa, suspicion etched into every feature of his face.

Nessa turned off the water and saw who the detective was trading tense words with. It was Rob Treloar.

"Well, hello, Detective," she said with her warmest smile.

He smiled back while Dirksen continued to glower.

"Hi," he said. "How are you doing?"

"Holding on," she said. "Can you answer a simple question for me?"

"I can try," Treloar said.

"Why is this homicide detective interrogating me about whether or not I own a gun? Was my husband murdered?"

Treloar's eyes shifted away from her for a microsecond. "We're keeping all possibilities open."

A roaring filled Nessa's ears. Was it possible that John hadn't killed himself? That someone else had?

She cleared her throat. "Is that why you need a sample of DNA?"

Treloar nodded. "For comparison purposes."

"Comparison to what?"

Dirksen said, "Mrs. Donati—"

"Why won't you answer my questions?"

"Because this is an open investigation."

She stared at Dirksen, then addressed Treloar.

"Did you find John?"

"No," he said.

Dirksen shot him a grimace.

"May I leave?" Nessa asked him.

"Of course you can," Treloar said. "Just one thing though. Would you have enough time to give us a fingerprint sample before you go?"

Everything froze. Nessa couldn't seem to move her mouth for a moment. "A what?"

"We're processing your husband's truck, and we need to eliminate your and your husband's fingerprints. His are on file, is that correct?"

"Um, yes," Nessa said, trying to think clearly, but it wasn't working. She looked at her watch. "We'll have to do that another day. I really have to go. Daltrey's got a . . ."

A what?

"A birthday party to go to, so . . ."

"A minute ago, you said it was his nap time," Dirksen said.

Of course she did. She nearly smacked herself in the forehead.

She walked to the door. "I'll give you a call and set up an appointment to come back. All right, Detective?"

The detectives exchanged a glance.

"Sure," Treloar said. "Give me a call."

She opened the door and walked through it, having to restrain herself from holding her middle fingers in the air as she walked away.

A rural housewife didn't act that way, even if she was a person of interest.

But if they took her fingerprints, they'd *really* be interested, but for an entirely different reason. Because her fingerprints belonged to a dead person.

Chapter Twelve

AT DALTREY'S BEDTIME, Nessa read him five books before helping him brush his teeth and put on his pajamas. When she tucked
him in, he stared up into her eyes stoically and signed "Daddy"
with one hand, the red toy car still clutched in the other.

What was she supposed to tell him? *Your father loved cocaine
more than he loved you. He was willing to give up everything to be
with drugs. And one way or another, they're what killed him.*

It would be years before Daltrey would be able to understand
any of this, and the emotional and psychological fallout would last
years beyond that. For now though, he was a nonverbal almost-
four-year-old who needed to go to sleep.

"I love you," Nessa said, then kissed and hugged him, his pudgy
arms around her neck, the puppy smell of him tugging hard on
her bruised heart. She turned on his night-light and rain sound
machine, then closed the door most of the way.

She went downstairs and found Isabeau sprawled on the couch
in the living room watching TV, remote in hand. She muted the
sound with it.

Daltrey had been around them all day, so Nessa hadn't had a chance to tell Isabeau what happened at the police station. She snapped off the television and sat in the wingback chair. Before she could tell the story though, she said, "I'm going to cry now."

She did, for a good ninety seconds, and then dry-sobbed her way through the story, at one point allowing Isabeau to get a glass of water for her.

"Why didn't you tell me about Mr. Donati? About the crack and all that?"

"I'm a very private person," Nessa said.

"I get that, but it kind of seems like crucial information to give an employee who works in your house."

Nessa's head thundered and her eyes stung. Isabeau was right, especially since the information in question might have prevented her from taking the job in the first place. "I'm sorry," she said. "I didn't think it would be an issue."

"I guess I thought you were a single mother or something," Isabeau said. "Marlon didn't tell me any of this."

"It's not his story to tell."

Marlon's recommendation of Isabeau was further AA rule-breaking, but nothing about their relationship was conventional AA. Marlon did what he wanted.

"I'm really sorry," Isabeau said. "About all of this. You must be devastated."

"I don't know what I'm . . . going . . . to tell . . ." And she was sobbing again. How were you supposed to explain this sort of thing to a nonverbal three-year-old? John's best trait by far was that he was one of the most engaged fathers she'd ever seen, and his permanent absence might lead to Daltrey's permanent muteness. Her precious son, fatherless. But what had she thought? That she'd allow visitation with a crack addict? Never.

"Is there anyone I can call for you?" Isabeau said. "Family or friends or something? Somebody who can come and be with you?"

"No," Nessa said.

"What about your parents?"

Nessa shook her head.

"Mr. Donati's family?"

This hadn't occurred to Nessa. She was going to have to tell John's brother and sister, not to mention his parents, who were scheduled to pick Daltrey up later in the month and take him to Kansas City for a few days. Sadly, they would not be that surprised. They'd suffered through his mental illness and addictions even longer than she had.

"You know what," Isabeau said. "I think maybe you ought to wait to tell them anything. If they're anything like my parents, they'll freak and be all in your face, and you probably don't want that right now, am I right?"

Nessa nodded.

"Besides, there really isn't anything to tell them, until after the police drag the river and the lake and maybe . . . find . . . *something*. You know what I'm saying?"

Nessa did know what she was saying.

Isabeau pressed a finger to her lips. "But . . . what if they *don't* find anything?" she said. "What if he's, like, dead, but they never find his body? What happens then?"

She slid to the floor, opened up her laptop, and began typing furiously. Nessa watched as Isabeau's eyes tracked back and forth, reading, her eyebrows drawn together, her lips moving a little.

"Oh, wow," she said. "It takes seven years after a person goes missing to have him declared dead, unless you go through the courts with a petition and apparently it's a big old hassle." She typed some more and read some more. "Did—does Mr. Donati have a life insurance policy?"

"Yes," Nessa said.

"You're not going to see any of that for seven years either."

Daltrey would be ten by then, almost eleven, with very little memory of his father.

"Boy," Isabeau said. "It's a good thing you're the main bread winner, huh?"

It *was* a good thing. This tactless statement actually surprised Nessa so much that an equally inappropriate laugh escaped Nessa. She covered her mouth with her hand to quell it.

"So you never did tell me what the vet said yesterday," Isabeau said.

The vet. That seemed a lifetime ago. It was only yesterday? She felt like she'd aged five years. "The vet said it was antifreeze. That's what killed him."

Isabeau looked confused. "Antifreeze?"

"Yeah. I guess it's lethal to pets. It causes their . . ."

Isabeau's face had gone white.

"What is it?" Nessa said.

"Is antifreeze green?"

"I'm not sure," Nessa said. "Maybe."

Isabeau pulled out her phone, thumb-typed on the tiny keyboard, and waited. She focused on the screen, then her head dropped back on the couch and she closed her eyes.

Nessa took the phone out of her hand and saw an image of antifreeze. Green.

"I found a plant water-catcher next to the boathouse with, like, this acid green liquid in it. I didn't know what it was so I tossed it out—didn't want Daltrey to get into it." She opened her eyes and lifted her head, then covered her mouth with both hands. "I didn't even think about poor old Declan MacManus."

By the boathouse.

"Was that before or after the break-in?" Nessa said.

Isabeau's eyes tracked upward as she thought. "It was after," she said in a flat voice.

Did John deliberately leave antifreeze out to kill the dog and punish Nessa? There was no way. John loved their family pet. But crack had made him do horrible things. It was certainly possible.

It was after ten when Isabeau finally went to bed, and Nessa still needed to work on her personal inventory. But first, she wanted to go through the snaps she took of Detective Dirksen's file folder. While she waited for the photos to download to her laptop, she made a pot of tea and got out her vapor pen. She was so exhausted she thought about waiting until tomorrow, but dread and curiosity got the better of her.

She sat on the couch, poured a cup of jasmine tea, and opened the first image.

Disappointment washed over her as she tried to read the blurry, off-center typewritten report pages. She clicked through the all-but-unreadable text pages until she got to the first photo.

It was a side view of the copper-colored pickup truck. She couldn't immediately discern what the next one was, until she'd looked at it for a moment. It was a close-up of one of the interior sides of the truck bed. She puzzled over this, looked at every inch, but couldn't figure out what she was supposed to see. The next image seemed to be the same thing but must have been the opposite interior side of the bed, along with drawn circles, arrows, and handwriting. The next photo was a close-up of the same area with what looked like two metal rivets in it surrounded by irregular patterns of splintering, again circled.

She clicked over to the next image. An overhead shot of the truck bed with dark streaks running parallel to the contours. She brought the computer close to her face. Was that mud?

She gasped, her sharp intake of breath sending her into a coughing fit, and let go of the laptop as if it were electrified.

That was blood.

Blood that would need to be compared to a DNA sample of a close relative.

Nessa clicked back a few to the photo of the interior truck sides. She now realized what she was looking at.

Two bullets.

Next to the arrow pointing to the slugs someone had hand-written *.38 cal.*

That was why Detective Dirksen asked if she owned a gun.

Monday, June 13

NESSA HARDLY SLEPT the next few nights, trying to come up with a plan to keep the police from fingerprinting her. As she flopped around in bed, she reasoned that the police would have no impetus to run her prints through NCIC. Why would they do that? They were just trying to eliminate any fingerprints they found on the boat as hers and therefore not a problem.

But then she thought . . . what if they lifted one of her fingerprints from the truck and ran that through NCIC accidentally? That. Would be. So. Bad.

She had to hope that there would be no usable prints of hers, and she tried to remember the last time she was in the truck. Her head felt like it would explode, her blood pressure was so high.

It was seven forty-five A.M. when she finally gave up and got out of bed. Since she'd only been asleep a few hours, Nessa tried to go back to sleep, but at eight on the dot, her default ringtone played. The Riley County Sheriff's Department was calling.

She contemplated letting it go to voicemail, but she was only postponing the inevitable.

"Hello?"

"Mrs. Donati? This is Detective Rob Treloar. How are you today?"

"Yes?" Her brains were so scrambled she couldn't seem to answer appropriately.

"Good," he said, as if she'd said, "Fine." "I mean—I wondered if I could come by this morning and talk to you about some things. I just have a few more questions."

She was wary. "What is it?" she said, breathless.

"We'll discuss it when I get there." He cleared his throat. "So would about an hour from now be convenient? Would that work for you?"

"That's fine," she said. "See you then." She was reminded of reality TV, where information couldn't be revealed until after the commercial break. Dread filled her.

She went downstairs and found Isabeau and Daltrey in the kitchen. Her son sat on the floor, playing drums with wooden spoons on some old Tupperware bowls. He set down the spoons and gave her a big smile. He held his arms out, and she picked him up.

"Daltrey," Nessa said. "Would you like to go to the park this morning?"

He signed "Yes" over and over again, squirming with joy in her arms.

"Can you go upstairs and put on your shoes?"

He nodded and ran for the stairs.

"Can you take him and come back by about eleven?" Nessa asked Isabeau.

"Sure," Isabeau said. "You're not coming with us?"

Nessa poured herself a cup of coffee, and tried to make her voice sound unconcerned. "Detective Treloar is coming out here to ask me some questions."

"You sure you don't want me here just in case?"

"Just in case what?"

"You know," Isabeau said. "Police brutality."

This comment made Nessa smile. "I think I'll be all right. I'd prefer that Daltrey wasn't here."

"Got it," Isabeau said.

The two of them drove away ten minutes later, and Nessa took a shower, got dressed, and sat in the living room.

At nine, the doorbell rang and she ran to it like she was anticipating a homecoming date. She opened the door, and there he stood, wearing a royal blue shirt and clashing tie. He must not be married, she figured. And then she saw that Detective Dirksen was with him.

"You've met Detective Dirksen, Mrs. Donati," Detective Treloar said. She couldn't read his expression, but he must have known Dirksen would be coming with him.

She felt betrayed, but put on her gracious hostess face and treated Dirksen with respect. No antagonizing him this time. She would be on her best behavior, cooperative and charming. Even though she was pretty sure she was now a "person of interest" in a possible homicide.

"How have you been?" she asked. "Come on in." She ushered them inside.

"Thanks," Treloar said, stepping over the threshold. Dirksen followed him, his eyes never leaving her. Dirksen was looking for a fight. He was probably always looking for a fight.

She pointed the detectives toward the couch in the living room. "Have a seat," she said.

Treloar did, unbuttoning his jacket, but Dirksen remained standing, his arms crossed over his chest.

"Can I get you some coffee or water?" she said.

"Some water would be great, thanks," Treloar said. Dirksen shook his head.

She immediately regretted offering, because she'd have to leave the room, and she was afraid they'd go through her stuff, the way she herself had gone through Dirksen's folder. But of course they wouldn't. They were cops.

She got two chilled bottles of water from the refrigerator and returned to the living room, where she handed one to Treloar and sat down in the wingback chair. This was so she could keep an eye on Dirksen, who stood in the wide doorway behind her.

"It looks like you're growing hops out there," Treloar said, pointing out the back window.

"Yeah, we are," she said. "Were." She cleared her throat, trying to keep the tears at bay. "We'd planned to sell them to local craft brewers."

"Wow," he said. "Where did you get that idea?"

"Well, John was looking for a small crop that was worth a lot, and marijuana and poppies were out . . . So anyway, we figured all these buildings could be converted to storage and packaging and shipping and all that stuff. John was in charge of all that."

"So I recorded your radio show the other night."

She felt her face redden. "Oh, really?" she said, and tried to keep from glancing at Dirksen. She wondered if he meant the night she met Otto. She hoped so.

"It was really interesting," Treloar said.

Nessa figured this was a little game of good cop/bad cop. Treloar was nice and personable, but before long, Dirksen was going to shine a light in her eyes and start yelling questions. Tension began building in her chest.

"We ran your husband's name through NCIC and KCIC. We got a hit on NCIC. Seems your husband was arrested in Denver, is that correct?"

"Yes," she said, her cheeks burning even hotter.

"Indecent exposure, disturbing the peace, disorderly conduct, drug possession. Does that sound right?"

"Yes," she said.

"Did you know him then?"

"Yes."

"We ran you through the computer database too," Dirksen said, startling her.

Nessa held her breath and spots swam before her eyes.

"Clean as a whistle," Treloar said.

She expelled her breath slowly.

Dirksen jumped in. "The reason we're here—"

"I'm sorry," Nessa said. "First, I wondered if you all could look into something for me. I haven't mentioned this to you, but I have a troll, and I think it might be someone I knew back in California. He was recently paroled." She recounted the incidents online. Dirksen looked bored, but Treloar listened intently.

"What makes you believe he's the troll?" Treloar asked. He pulled out his notebook and jotted down some notes.

She swallowed. "This guy raped a friend of mine back in California about eight years ago, and I testified against him at his trial. I think he may be trying to get back at me."

Dirksen and Treloar glanced at each other.

"His name is Nathan Zimmer." Saying it out loud produced a sour taste in her mouth.

Dirksen said, "I don't think it's—"

"But it's not only online harassment," she said. "My dog was poisoned with antifreeze. I'm afraid maybe he's come out here to harass me in person."

"I'll look into it," Treloar said.

"Thank you. I really appreciate it."

Treloar and Dirksen traded glances again.

"So let's talk about your husband," Treloar said. "Did he have any enemies? Any people he'd pissed off?"

"Well, you know how it is in the drug culture—everybody's always pissed off at everyone. I mean, it's possible he pissed off a dealer, but—"

"So you know quite a bit about the drug culture, do you, Mrs. Donati?" Dirksen asked.

Her right hand went automatically to the inside of her left elbow, and as soon as she realized what she was doing, she dropped her hands to her sides. "When you've got a drug addict for a husband," she said, "it kind of comes with the territory." She held his gaze until her eyes watered. But his face showed that he didn't believe this was the whole truth.

"So, let's continue our conversation from the other day," Detective Dirksen said. "Do you own a gun?"

She was ready this time and answered smoothly. "I do."

"Would you be willing to let us take a look at it? Maybe run a ballistics test?"

Why not? She didn't have anything to hide. She went upstairs, got the gun, and found the registration papers for good measure.

"How long have you had this?" Dirksen asked.

"Just a month or so," she said. "I've never actually fired it. I felt like I needed protection since my husband lost his mind."

"May I?" he said.

She handed it to him, butt first.

He opened it, looked inside, then ejected the clip and emptied it.

"This is an eight-round mag, right?"

"I don't know what it is," she said, but then realized why he'd asked.

She counted five bullets. Her skin felt cold, bloodless. Why hadn't she thought to check on the gun after she looked at the photos from the police file? Damn it.

Dirksen gave a smug, satisfied smile. "You want to explain this to me?"

She opened her mouth but nothing came out.

"Mrs. Donati?" Dirksen said. "Why are there three bullets missing?"

She cleared her throat. "Maybe that's how it was when I bought it."

"Highly, highly unlikely," the detective said. "You still good with us running ballistics? Or should we get a warrant?"

She couldn't answer.

"Mrs. Donati?"

And she knew. The bullets in this gun were going to match the ones in the truck bed exactly.

Chapter Thirteen

THEY BAGGED UP her gun and the clip with the missing bullets while she watched, sweating like Nixon during his resignation speech.

"Thank you, Mrs. Donati," Dirksen said. "As I'm sure you know, we will be in touch soon."

Treloar shook her moist hand. "Sorry for the intrusion. Call me if you have any questions. We'll return the gun after the test."

"Maybe," Dirksen said, giving her a piranha-like smile.

Treloar made an annoyed face but didn't say anything.

"And we still need to fingerprint you," Dirksen said.

They walked around to the front of the house, got in their vehicle, and drove away.

Nessa went back inside and sat on the couch. How could she prevent the police from taking her fingerprints? Should she force them to get a court order? Or should she go ahead and get a lawyer?

She looked at her phone and saw that she still had thirty-five minutes until Isabeau and Daltrey returned.

Boy, did she need . . .

A dangerous, ancient set of emotions bubbled just below the surface. If she didn't acknowledge it, didn't let it spring into form, she could tamp it down. She could keep it at bay.

A shot.

The thought slipped through the cracks.

Just one more time. But there was never just one time. She had to remember that.

What she meant to think was that she needed some loud-ass music to dance to. Her savior. She grabbed her phone and dialed through the alphabet until she came to an appropriate song. "Good Lovin' " by the Grateful Dead from 1977's *Shakedown Street.* (The worst-reviewed album in the Dead's catalog, but fuck 'em.) Plugging her phone into the speakers, she let it rip.

Sweet relief. Nessa danced as if she were at a real live Grateful Dead show back in the day. Listening to Bobby Weir's joyful singing let her twirl like a dervish across her lonely living room. The song ended and she fell back on the couch, listening to the rest of the album at a lower volume.

More tea. Fire up the vape. It will be fine.

She stood and paced in front of her laptop, pretend-smoking, trying to get a grip.

John. What did you do to us?

He'd brought that ugliness into their home, that dirty world they'd both escaped—or thought they'd escaped. His very absence, the vacuum he'd left, was filled with crack dust.

Now she got out her copy of *101 Common Clichés of Alcoholics Anonymous: The Sayings the Newcomers Hate and the Old-timers Love.* Even though she technically was an old-timer, she hated the sayings, but they had helped her keep it together more than once. She didn't want to bother Marlon again, even though he always said she should call him any time she was feeling like this. She opened the book at random, as she usually did, as if consulting the *I Ching*.

We have a disease that tells us we don't have a disease.

We. There was no "we." She was alone. Alone in the universe. No one to protect her, and no one to help her protect Daltrey. She went to meetings sporadically and never spoke. She didn't socialize with the other freaks. She went because Marlon told her to go. When they all held hands at the end of the meetings and recited the serenity prayer in a circle, she never made eye contact with anyone.

She read another one. Damn it.

We are only as sick as our secrets.

MOTHS FLITTED AROUND the light over the front door of the station as Nessa put her key in the lock and turned it. Otto was already there, sitting at the receptionist's desk and using the desktop computer. Without looking up from the monitor, he shoved a stack of envelopes toward her.

"Mail call," he said.

"Thanks," she said, picking them up. The Altair website listed a PO box in LA for fans to send mail to. The Altair people collected her mail, bundled it up, and sent it to her at KCMA once a week. Nessa was amazed that anyone would actually write on paper, put it in an envelope, write an address on it, scrounge up a stamp, and put it in a mailbox. But there was the stack, twenty high. Some people still liked the old ways, and she could sort of respect that.

"Let's turn on some lights," Nessa said, like she always did. Otto liked sitting in the dark, with only the glow of the screen.

She flipped on the overheads, and he flinched like a mole.

"What are you working on?" she asked.

"Screenplay," he said.

This week. Last week it was a chapbook. The week before that, a web comic. She had to give it to him, he was always creating something. Unless it was just a big show. But who would do that? Put on a show just to impress her?

She pulled up a chair, opened her iPad, grabbed a letter opener, and started slicing open the envelopes.

Dear Nessa, the first one read. *Love your show. But would it kill you to play some Beatles?*

She got one of these every week. She shook the paper in Otto's direction. "Why don't people understand that there *are* no Beatles deep cuts? That every song they ever did has been played and overplayed and dissected like the Zapruder film? Do people seriously not understand that?"

The hostilities between them had cooled somewhat, but they were nowhere near friends. Still she needed to talk sometimes.

Otto held up a finger, then continued to type. She tried not to read what he was writing, but she suspected it was *The quick brown fox jumps over the lazy dog.*

"Maybe they're just messing with you," he said. "Everybody knows you hate the Beatles."

"I don't hate the Beatles," she said. "All I said was that they were not a rock band. They were a pop band. That's all I said. And they're the most overplayed band in history, which isn't saying much since every sixties and seventies band has been overplayed to the point of—"

"We know. We know. That's the whole basis of your shtick. That's the whole reason you got this show." He pushed up his glasses and focused on her, deadpan.

"That's not the only reason," she said, stung. "I also happen to have a pretty vast knowledge of—"

"Right. Anyway. I don't want to have this same conversation over and over again. It's boring as hell."

She was only four years older than he, but the chasm was wide. She felt like a fossil, saying things like, "In my day . . ." But she had to remind herself that he was a jealous brat, a kid whose parents had paid for his college. Nessa had had to do everything herself with no support. But she'd already told him that. Telling him more than once would make her sound like she cared what he thought.

She slit open the next envelope and out tumbled a photo of a guy in a Speedo. She promptly threw the letter and photo away without even reading it because she knew what it was going to say. Any time there was a photo, it was a proposal.

The next envelope enclosed a handwritten letter. *Dear Nessa*, it said. *You have the best deep-cuts show I've ever heard. I wondered if you could scrounge up some music from an Australian band that was popular over there in the seventies called the Saturday Night Club.*

She made a note of the band name on her iPad, then did a quick search of her music file database. There it was. She'd play a song called "Burns" and give a shout-out to the letter-writer on air.

The next envelope had a letter gushing compliments, along with a flash drive and a request for her to plug the guy's band during her show. She set a reminder on the iPad so she'd remember to listen to the contents of the flash drive and decide whether she would do as he asked. She didn't mind promoting good music, but if money or gifts were sent, she promptly returned them with a brief bio of Allan Freed from history-of-rock.com for their information and edification: " 'Payola' is a contraction of the words *pay* and *Vic-*

trola (LP record player), and entered the English language via the record business. The first court case involving payola was in 1960. On May 9, Alan Freed was indicted for accepting $2,500 which he claimed was a token of gratitude and did not affect airplay."

Nessa glanced at the large clock on the wall: eleven thirty-eight. She grabbed a water bottle from the break room fridge, scooped up the rest of the envelopes, and went into the studio. The smell hit her as soon as she got into the room—male BO. She groaned. Dale must have worked a shift, because every time he did, the studio chair reeked.

Otto actually laughed. "I'll take it," he said. "I'm not as sensitive as you are."

They switched chairs.

"Why don't they do something about that?" she said.

"The general manager is one of those 'really nice guys' who doesn't want to hurt anyone's feelings," Otto said. "I guess he got everyone together and said, 'Let's not forget to shower before we come in.' But everyone knows it's Dale."

"Why doesn't the program director do it, then?"

"He's a coward too."

"You know what?" Nessa said. "I'm just going to buy my own chair and haul it in here every week."

"Or you could do the show standing up," Otto said.

She shrugged and sat in the uncontaminated chair. Otto busied himself turning on the board, doing a sound check, making sure all the machines were in working order like he always did.

Nessa opened her water bottle and took a drink, then picked up her iPad, ready to pull up the requests. But it made a *ping* sound, indicating a text message. She glanced at Otto—the producer would often text her during broadcasts if he needed to tell her something. But Otto was busy with board stuff, not fiddling with his phone, plus the number was the cell phone equivalent of an 800 number.

An image appeared on the screen. At first, she didn't understand what she was looking at. A super-grainy, zoomed-in photo. She couldn't figure out what it was until she pinched toward the center and the image resolved. Then a sharp intake of breath sent her into a coughing fit, and still she couldn't take her eyes off the image in her hands.

"You all right?" Otto asked. "You're on air in two."

Nessa couldn't breathe. Her eyes burned as she stared at the picture. It was Daltrey's face.

With black X's drawn over his eyes. And the words *He Will Die* scrawled below.

"What the hell, Ness?" Otto asked. "You're on in one. Get it together."

Nessa watched the secondhand sweep mercilessly, faster than normal, it seemed, toward the top of the hour. She took a deep breath and held it, stars swimming before her eyes, trying to focus her mind.

This was not a photo from her collection. Daltrey was wearing his striped overall shorts and a white T-shirt—his outfit from the day before. It was a photo that had been taken yesterday, in the grocery store parking lot with a telephoto lens from some distance away.

Nessa blew out her breath slowly, trying to concentrate. She pulled on her headphones and repositioned the big microphone in front of her.

Otto, eyes full of actual concern and curiosity, counted down. "Five, four," then the rest of the way with his fingers.

Her theme music played over her introduction.

"*It's midnight on Monday, which means it's time for* Unknown Legends *with Nessa, the only radio show that plays the really, really deep cuts.*"

Otto pointed at her and she spoke into the mic. "Hey, everybody—"

She couldn't get the image out of her mind. Only in it, Daltrey was really dead.

"I just got a letter from—" she looked up at the Internet screen above the board "—Chuck, who wanted to hear some Saturday Night Club, an Australian band that played every crap bar in the country during the late seventies. This is 'Burns.'"

Nessa clicked her mic button and shoved off her headphones.

"What the hell, Ness?" Otto said again.

"Sorry," she said.

"What just happened?"

Nessa's voice was shaking. "I must have just gotten my first dose of stagefright, I guess," she said.

She put the cover on her iPad and clutched it to her chest.

"Are you sick or something?"

But she knew he knew that something on the iPad had rattled her.

"I'm fine," she said. "I'll be fine."

"Anything you want to talk about?"

"With you? No." Being mean steadied her a bit. She looked at the music clock and saw she only had two minutes and twelve seconds. She was about to screw up the order by having Otto play a song she'd held in reserve for just such an emergency as this. She was going to make him put on the twelve-minute-sixteen-second "Starless" by King Crimson from 1974's *Red* album.

"Cue up track three sixty-five," she said.

"It's not on the list," he said. "You can't just—"

"Cue it up," she barked. "I need a minute. Are you really going to tell me you can't do this? I thought you were all about breaking the rules and going against the grain and bucking the system. So prove it."

"Aye-aye, Cap'n PMS," he said.

As she walked out of the studio, she depressed her iPhone button and heard the familiar chime. "Set timer for eleven minutes," she said into it.

"Okay," Siri said. "Setting timer for eleven minutes."

Nessa went into the bathroom and locked the door behind her. She opened up her iPad and looked at the photo again. Then with shaking hands, she pulled out her phone and dialed Isabeau. It rang and kept on ringing. By the fifth ring, Nessa was frantic.

"Hello?" Isabeau's sleepy voice answered.

"Why the hell did it take so long to answer?"

"What?" Isabeau said. "What time is it?"

"Where's Daltrey?"

"He's asleep, of course," Isabeau said, yawning.

"Go in his room right now."

"What?"

"Do what I said! *Now!*"

"What's going on?"

"Just do it!" Nessa yelled so loud her voice cracked.

"Okay."

Nessa watched the time count down on her phone, at a glacial yet speed-of-light pace, her breath loud and panicky.

"Yup. He's asleep. Just like I said."

"Is he breathing?"

"Of course he's breathing! What in the world is going on?"

"You need to call the cops." She went on to explain what had happened.

"You better screenshot it, Nessa."

"Why?"

But as the word left her mouth, the photo began to pixelate and dissolve.

"What's happening? It's fading, and—"

"Click the power button and the home button at the same time," Isabeau said.

Nessa let go of her phone and fumbled with the iPad, which slipped from her sweaty hands and dropped to the floor. As she scrambled to pick it up, the photo disappeared altogether, and a logo appeared: TempHoto.

Nessa screamed in frustration.

She heard a knock. "Nessa?"

"Just a minute," she called.

"You okay?" Otto called. "It sounds like you're filming *Saw* in there."

She looked at her phone. Six minutes until she had to be back in the studio.

"Just give me a fucking minute, will you?" She lowered her voice before speaking into the phone again. "Isabeau, I want you to go down and make sure the doors and windows are all locked."

"All right," Isabeau said, wide awake now but not fearful. "But everything's fine here."

"I want you to call 911 right now and get a patrol car out there to search the woods, the whole property. Tell them what happened."

"Okay," Isabeau said, not as enthusiastic as usual at Nessa's request.

"Call me back as soon as you're done."

She clicked off and waited, staring at her phone. Was she overreacting? It was possible, but she didn't care. It was another few minutes before "Jeep's Blues" played.

"They're on their way," Isabeau said, yawning again. "They said if you don't have a copy of the image sent to you, there's just not much they can do. Those temporary photo apps are pretty much untraceable."

Nessa growled in frustration. "All right. Thank you, Isabeau. I've got to go. I'll be home at four-fifteen."

"See you then," Isabeau said, and clicked off.

Nessa made her way back into the studio with two minutes to spare. Otto didn't look up, obviously stung that she'd rejected his concern.

"Sorry, Otto," she said. "Had a bit of a panic attack there."

He looked up then and said, "Fine. Whatever." His body language got even more defensive and injured.

"Oh, now," she said. "Don't be like that, princess."

He shook his head, his eyes still on whatever he was reading tonight.

When King Crimson ended, Nessa got back to the original play order.

"Hey, Otto," she said.

"What," he said, head down, pretending to read.

"What do you know about these temporary photo apps? You know, the apps that you can text a photo to someone's phone, and within a few minutes, the photo deletes itself?"

He looked up, interested. "You want to send someone a pic of your junk, or what?"

"Yeah, no," she said.

"Why do you ask, then?"

She sighed. "Never mind," she said.

"Okay," he said. "Does this have something to do with what just happened?"

She nodded.

"Is someone . . . harassing you?"

She nodded. He regarded her for a moment and said, "Good."

6/14

Hi, I'm Nessa, and I'm an alcoholic. I've been sober six years, four months, and twenty-six days.

I might as well stop even trying to sleep. The Riley County Sheriff's Department is going to think of me as the little girl who cried wolf. Of course, the patrol they sent to the house turned up nothing and nobody. Poor Isabeau.

I talked to the patrol officer, and he confirmed what Isabeau said—that without any record of the photo, there's nothing they can do.

I can't even think about what life would be like without my little guy. I can't even go there, because I'll go insane for real, and he needs me to stay sane.

I've read that losing a child is the worst thing that can happen to a person. My mom knows what it's like, and I'm sorry about that. But it was my death that helped her pay for Brandon's frequent hospital stays.

I read all about it in the LA Times.

I've known people say they wish they could be at their own funeral so they could see who their real friends are. Seeing my obituary in print was nothing like that. The sad, pathetic circumstances surrounding my "death" play out every day in big cities around the world. No one gives a shit.

But my mother, as I knew she would, made big-time lemonade out of my death. I have to admire her for that. If she hadn't hit the talk show circuit again, speaking about what it's like to lose a child, the dangers of drugs, the crappy county Medicaid we qualified for would have killed Brandon for sure. Plus she became a minor celebrity in the bargain, which she parlayed into some parts in TV shows and B movies.

I haven't seen her in anything in a while now, and treatment for Brandon's periodic pneumonia thanks to the radiation therapy ain't cheap. I've actually thought about trying to send him some money on the sly, but he'd give it to her, and she'd use it on quacky facial treatments to keep herself looking good for possible television appearances.

She's got be getting pretty desperate about now.

Chapter Fourteen

Thursday, June 16

THE NEXT TWO and a half days were mercifully uneventful, although the tension in her back and neck made turning her head nearly impossible. There were no new comments from Dead-JohnDonati, no new websites, no sponsorship cancellations. Nessa had even gotten a decent night's sleep the previous night. But on Thursday, the silence had an unsettling effect on her, one of dread and horrible anticipation. The troll was not done with her, she was sure of that, felt it in her bones.

At eleven P.M., Otto called. "Hey," he said. "I'm going to be late tonight. I've been up in Kansas City all day at an antinuclear power rally, and my car won't start even with a jump."

"How late, do you think?" Nessa asked, irritated he was calling so close to air, irritated that he spent his time performing random acts of environmental kindness.

He sighed. "I'm hoping by three."

"Three? Why bother coming in at all, then? I'm going to call Kevin and see if he can come in and—"

"No, no," Otto said. "I feel bad for leaving you high and dry. Let me call him. I'll offer him a six-pack or something to cover for me. I'll call you back if he can't do it. But you've seen me do my job. You know what to do. You'll be fine."

"Wow," Nessa said. "That's maybe some of the nicest things you've ever said to me."

IT WAS A starless, moonless night as she approached the station, all light blocked out by high cloud cover with a hot west wind blowing. Otto had been as good as his word and called back to let her know that Kevin wasn't available, and once again reassured her that she would be just fine.

She wasn't so sure.

Once inside, she locked the outside door of the glass vestibule, and then the inner door. On deep, dark nights like this one, the reflections of the inside light on the glass walls of the vestibule doubled and tripled and warped in on themselves until she swore she was seeing ghosts—and not the friendly kind. Until recently, she was never nervous coming here alone at night. But now, there was a burning in her chest and she couldn't keep her hands from shaking.

Without Otto here to annoy her, she started to imagine what it might be like if she were actually arrested for the murder of her almost ex-husband. Who would raise Daltrey? Of course Linda and Tony, John's folks, would swoop in and take him.

This thought gave her chills. Sure, their parenting hadn't made him bipolar. That was biology. But even though she got along with her in-laws fairly well, the thought of losing her son and them raising Daltrey the same way they had John nearly paralyzed her with fear.

By three A.M., Otto still wasn't in, and she started to worry about him. She called his cell phone four times, and it went straight to voicemail. She really hoped he was okay.

Nessa had maxed out her caffeine intake, her skull felt like it had been hollowed out, and she started seeing things: sharp-angled, barbed, darkly malevolent characters out of the deepest part of her ugly subconscious. She needed to stop obsessing and scaring herself. Enough.

She decided to play stump the music expert.

"This is Nessa, you're on the air," Nessa said, opening up the phone line.

"I have a trivia question," the female voice said.

"Shoot," Nessa said, swiveling in her chair, watching the clock's secondhand sweeping toward her release.

"Who played lead guitar on 'While My Guitar Gently Weeps'?"

"Really," Nessa said. "You're asking me a Beatles question. Is that right? You're asking me a Beatles question."

"But who played—"

"It was Clapton. Everyone knows that, even people who don't listen to music. Even the hearing-impaired."

She realized, grudgingly, that had Otto been here screening calls, this question never would have slipped through.

Nessa clicked the end button. As she could have predicted, the phone lines lit up after that. She answered another call.

"Why do you have to be so mean?" a whiny, plaintive voice asked her.

"Because my producer isn't here to screen the calls," Nessa said, and hung up, and immediately realized she'd made a huge mistake, broadcasting that she was alone at the station. Of course, most people didn't know where this show originated, but still, it was a stupid move.

"He's at a *Minecraft* convention," Nessa amended, giving herself a little thrill at demeaning her coworker. As a rule, Nessa didn't demean people who weren't there to defend themselves. But she was desperate.

"What's the spine number on—"

Nessa hung up unceremoniously. "Come on. You know the rules. No spine number or album-cover color questions," Nessa said.

"What's Elvis Costello's real name?"

"Declan MacManus," Nessa said, and hung up. "Next?"

"Four famous rap artists went to the same high school in Brooklyn, New York, called George Westinghouse Jr. High School of Career and Technical Education. Busta Rhymes, DMX, and Jay-Z are three of them. Who's the fourth?"

"Let's see . . . the fourth would be—"

Was Nessa imagining it? Was there a masker on that voice? It had the low bass line of an old Funkadelic song, almost outside of the range of human hearing. Suddenly it was as if all the oxygen had been sucked from the room. Nessa couldn't breathe, couldn't finish her sentence.

"Come on," the caller said. *"You know the answer."*

Yes. She did.

The answer was the Notorious B.I.G.

She hung up on the caller. "Oops," she said, hearing her voice shake inside her headphones. "The call dropped."

Nessa stared at the blinking phone lines, which now looked urgent and sinister to her.

She tentatively reached for the buttons and pushed one.

"This is Nessa, and you're on the air."

"*The answer,*" said the same masked voice, "*is the Notorious B.I.G.*" The same person was on two phone lines, obviously calling in from multiple cell phones. "*You look really good in that black shirt.*"

Nessa stood up so fast that her face bumped the microphone, setting off a screech of feedback.

She looked out the window, through the three consecutive panes of glass. He was out there. He could see her. He knew what she was wearing.

Nessa sat back down with a thud and clicked the next song button, then yanked the headphones off her head and ran out of the studio. Looking through just two panes of glass now, she could see nothing but the amorphous shapes made by the light reflecting back on itself into infinity.

Nessa turned off the lights as "The Prey" by the Dead Kennedys played in the background. Great. Only one of the creepiest songs ever recorded. Nessa pressed her face against the glass, her hands making a wide telescope around her eyes, straining to see into the dark nothingness of the field beyond the station.

Was he out there in the tall weeds? Nessa mashed her fists into her eyes, trying to clear her vision, distorted from light and reflection and now dark. She squinted back out into the windy night and couldn't see the figure anymore.

Nessa flipped the dead-bolt lock and crept out into the dark, looking around wildly.

"I know who you are," Nessa shouted.

Nothing but hot wind and darkness. She couldn't see anyone or anything.

"What do you want?"

Her fear was turning into something else. She wasn't afraid. She was livid, and it drowned out everything else. Who did this guy think he was, terrorizing her and her son like this? Trying to frame her for murder? This aggression would not stand.

"I'm not afraid of you," she yelled. "If I catch you, I'm going to kick your pathetic, rapey ass!"

No sound, no movement.

But someone was out there. Someone was watching.

Friday, June 17

NESSA KNEW BETTER than to call the cops for this one. What would they do? Nothing except lose a little more respect for her. But she was definitely going to call them to ask whether they could determine Nathan's whereabouts. That, she could do.

Although she slept little after the disturbing night she'd had at the station, she decided to take Daltrey and Isabeau to the Sunset Zoo in Manhattan. Spending the day outdoors, watching Daltrey delight over the animals, was just what she needed.

When they returned home after lunch, Daltrey took a nap, Isabeau worked on cataloging Nessa's music collection, and Nessa managed to bang out a blog post about the band Quasi. Then she went downstairs and looked out the back door. Isabeau was watching Daltrey run through the sprinklers.

Nessa tried to decide what to do about dinner. She was looking up the pizza delivery phone number when the doorbell rang.

This made her sad, because there was no Declan MacManus to announce an arrival. She went to the door, and there stood Otto, a cooler on the porch next to him and bags of groceries in his arms.

He looked sheepish. "Sorry for just showing up like this, but—"

"How did you know where I lived?"

He looked taken aback by her sharp tone. He stammered, "I just—I looked you up online."

"No, you didn't," Nessa said. "My address isn't online."

His face reddened and he stuttered some more. "I used to be a reporter—and I—I—I . . . covered public records and that kind of thing. I still have some friends at the courthouse and I . . . looked up your property records there."

Stunned, Nessa started hyperventilating. She leaned forward, trying to regulate her breathing. "Can . . . can anyone do that?"

"Well, yeah," Otto said. "But it's not a big deal—you don't need to—"

So anyone could find out where she lived. Why hadn't she known this? Now she cursed the day she and John had bought this huge property in the middle of nowhere.

"Hey," Otto said gently. "I'm sorry. I shouldn't have done it. I should have called you and asked if I could come by. I just . . . wanted to make it up to you for missing my shift. I'm sorry."

Nessa realized she'd just given her professional adversary a salacious glimpse into the peep show that was her anxiety and stress. Into her weakness.

She stood straight and gave him the most imperious look she could manage. "Right," she said, folding her arms in front of her. "No need to let me know that you weren't lying dead in a ditch somewhere."

He grinned a little. "You were worried about me?"

"You'd know that if you'd listened to any of the dozen messages I left you last night." She pointed at the bags. "What's all this?"

"Like I said, I want to make it up to you," he said. "I'm going to cook you dinner."

She stared at him. "But what the hell happened?" She crossed her arms again like some scolding housewife.

"Can I come in and put this stuff down? Then I'll tell you."

She rolled her eyes, but she was curious what sort of dinner he would come up with. Would it be better than delivery pizza? Maybe. But she was too tired to argue. "Fine," she said.

"Kitchen this way?" he said, walking past her with his grocery sacks. "Can you grab the cooler?"

This guy. Still trying to be the boss. She sighed and picked up the blue and white cooler and followed him into the kitchen.

"You won't believe it," he said, opening the cooler and pulling out two PBRs, and offered her one of them.

She shook her head and leaned back against the counter. PBR. Of course.

"Do they actually give you a handbook when you become a hipster?" she said. "Like you must drink this shitty beer because it's so ironic?"

"I'm not a hipster," he said, offended.

"Really. How would you describe yourself?"

"A free-thinker," he said, almost triumphantly. "A progressive with good taste."

That you had before anyone else.

She needed to cut down on the nasty thoughts. He'd extended an olive branch, and she was still being a jerk.

"Sorry," she said. "You seem to bring out the worst in me."

"Why?" he said. "Is it because you were a hipster before I was?"

"How meta of you," she said.

"Well, I brought some wine too," he said. "You have a wine bottle opener?"

"Nope," Nessa said.

"No wine for you, huh?" he said. "Let me guess. Only Cristal for the star."

The back door opened and in walked Isabeau and Daltrey, fresh from exploring in the forest out back.

"She doesn't drink," Isabeau said. "Hey, Otto." She turned to Nessa. "We had a couple of classes together at K-State."

Daltrey ran out of the kitchen when he saw Otto. Isabeau ran after him and brought him back in.

"Daltrey, this is my friend Otto. He works with Mommy at the radio station."

Daltrey covered his eyes with his hand.

"Hi, Daltrey," Otto said.

Without uncovering his eyes, Daltrey waved at Otto with his other hand, and Otto laughed.

"You want to watch *Arthur* until dinner's ready?" Nessa asked Daltrey.

He nodded, still blindfolded. She carried him into the living room and turned on the television.

"You don't have to be afraid of Otto," she said. "He's a nice man."

Nessa tried to say it without sarcasm and mostly succeeded. She returned to the kitchen.

"So, Isabeau," Otto said. "What are you doing here?"

"I'm Nessa's nanny and aide-de-camp. She told me she worked with an Otto. Didn't know it was you."

Otto cut his eyes at Nessa. "Oh, yeah? What did she say?"

"That you're a brilliant producer."

Of course Nessa hadn't said that, but Isabeau was the queen of encouragement. Maybe Nessa should try to be more like her.

Naaah.

"So no bottle opener," Otto said. "Well, no problem. I've been wanting to try this thing I saw on the Internet."

He took off his left Doc Martens boot and removed the foil from the wine bottle. Then Otto slipped the wine bottle into his boot, bottom first—*eeewww*—and said, "Which wall should I smack this against?"

"How about you go outside and do it on that oak over there?"

Isabeau made a follow-me motion and headed out the back door. Nessa watched out the window as Isabeau led him to the tree and he smacked the heel against the trunk of the oak several times. She could see Isabeau talking while Otto worked. Finally, he held the bottle up triumphantly and worked the protruding cork out of the bottle neck.

Nessa's mouth watered. She missed wine.

They came running back in like a couple of kids who'd just caught tadpoles.

"Success!" Isabeau said, her arms in the air. "That's pretty cool."

"Where are your pots and pans?" Otto asked Nessa.

She opened the cabinet and showed him where everything was.

She fought to push away her disdain for this guy that she didn't really know. When had she become so judgmental? Was it inevitable after marriage and kids? Her mother had been judgmental of everyone, commenting on people's choice of clothes, car, language, hairstyle. Maybe she'd turned out just like her mother after all.

OTTO MADE PAELLA, and it was actually quite good. He and Isa-beau drank the wine he'd brought while Nessa stuck to iced tea.

He proposed a toast. "Here's to a better working relationship."

The three of them clinked their glasses together, and Daltrey thrust his sippy cup forward. They clinked his too.

After dinner the four of them walked the property as Nessa explained the hops farm idea. Otto grew excited.

"You should totally keep going with it," he said.

"Now that my husband is . . . gone, I just don't have the time or energy."

"Are you getting a divorce?"

Nessa and Isabeau exchanged glances.

"Long story," Nessa said.

"Oh. Hey, Daltrey," Otto said. "You like playing hide-and-seek?"

He nodded, all smiles.

"You want to play right now?"

He nodded more vigorously.

Daltrey was "it" for the first game, and the three adults made sure they were just visible enough for him to find them.

Nessa was impressed with Otto's easy manner with Daltrey. Not that she'd ever tell him that, but it was nice to observe Otto out of context. When Daltrey chased him, he pretended to run fast, and Nessa caught a glimpse of Otto as a little boy before the irony bug bit him.

"Bedtime," Nessa called.

Daltrey got limp, slumping as he walked reluctantly toward her.

"Hey, Daltrey," Otto said. "We'll play again sometime, okay?"

Daltrey nodded and signed "Good night" to him.

"I'll put him down," Isabeau said.

"Let's go in too," Nessa said. "I can't take any more of this heat."

"Good call," Otto said.

They all trooped inside, and Isabeau and Daltrey went upstairs.

"Another beer? More wine?" Nessa said as she washed her hands at the sink in the kitchen.

"I'll have another beer," Otto said, pulling a PBR out of his cooler.

"Mommy," Isabeau called down the stairs. "Come say good-night!"

"Be right there," she said, drying her hands.

"Where are we going to hang out?" Otto said. "Kitchen or living room? Where do you normally?"

"Living room," she said, and went upstairs.

Daltrey was all jammied and toothbrushed and all tucked into bed.

"Good night, Daltrey," Isabeau said.

Nessa hugged and kissed him. "I love you," she said.

He held up his hand in the abbreviated ASL "I love you" sign and closed his eyes. She turned on his night-light and sound machine, turned out the light, and followed Isabeau out of the room.

Down in the living room, Otto occupied the wingback chair and Isabeau sat on the floor with her back against the couch holding a glass of wine.

"That is one cute kid," Otto said.

"Thank you," Nessa said, plugging her phone into her mini-speakers, then set iTunes to shuffle. "Ideal World" began to play.

She sat on the couch

"Is that . . . Girlpool?" Otto said, incredulous.

"Yeah," she said.

"I thought you were strictly a Led Zeppelin/Bad Company midseventies classic rock type."

"Have you ever heard me play either of those bands? Ever?"

"Well, no, but—"

"She's turned me on to a whole bunch of music I'd never heard of before," Isabeau said. "She's a very interesting person."

"Well, I wouldn't know," Otto said. "Nessa doesn't talk about herself."

"I'm a very private person," Nessa said. She didn't like where this was going.

"You can't be a private person nowadays," Otto said. "Everyone is out there and exposed, and there's nothing you can do about it. So you might as well just let it all out."

This was truer than Otto could possibly know. She needed to steer the conversation away from herself. "Right," she said. "So what about you, Otto? Where'd you grow up?"

"Mulvane, near Wichita," he said. "My dad's a farmer. Mom's a schoolteacher."

"Did everybody pick on you when you were a kid?" Isabeau said.

He drew back, shocked. "No," he said, drawing it out, which Nessa took to mean "yes." She saw in his face the younger version of himself that no one liked. And she imagined her own oddball son, and how it felt when he was shunned or shut out by other kids at the park because he didn't talk.

This and the way he was with Daltrey were what she needed to see to stop hating him.

"Everybody picked on me," Isabeau said. "I was the tallest girl in my class. It sucked." She yawned and stretched. "I can't keep my eyes open. I'm going to bed." She stood and stretched again. "See you, Otto."

"Good night," he said, looking panicked.

Nessa wanted to laugh. Was he afraid to be left alone with her? They worked alone together twice a week.

"I'll help with the dishes," he said resolutely.

"I'm going to just leave them," Nessa said.

"I'll just do them for you. You can go on to bed, Nessa."

"What, and let you dig through my stuff? Not on your life, princess."

His laugh sounded nervous, as if he thought she believed he'd really do this. He stood and walked into the kitchen.

Isabeau winked at Nessa and went upstairs.

Nessa joined Otto in the kitchen and put Otto's leftover food into his cooler while he rinsed dishes. She loaded the dishwasher.

"What do you think," Otto said. "Think I could do your job?"

"Sure," Nessa said. "A chimp could do it."

He leaned back against the counter. "That's always been the goal," he said dreamily. "To get an Altair satellite show, but I'd do it right. I'd play super-obscure stuff that only a handful of true connoisseurs would know."

"That is antithetical to the business model, which is actually to get people to listen, not to drive the larger audience away, you dumbass."

He laughed. "I know. I can't help it."

"Sure you can. You don't have to be this way. You can be a real boy."

" 'I got no strings to hold me down, to make sad or make me frown,' " he sang in a surprisingly good voice. He smacked himself in the forehead with a wet hand. "Shit. I can't believe I just made an *Ultron* reference."

"And a *Pinocchio* reference at the same time. A two-for-one! What you just said? Can't you see how many antihipster points you hit there?"

He smirked at her and dried his hands on a dish towel. "I gotta use the bathroom. Be right back."

Nessa wiped the counters, waiting for him to return, and thought about how pleasant this had been, how nice of him it was to show up and make dinner. Which didn't seem like him at all. But maybe she'd misjudged him.

When he returned, he'd obviously been mulling over their conversation.

"You know, although I don't self-identify as a hipster, I believe it comes from a sincere place," he said earnestly. "In a world that so desperately cherishes the super-popular and conformity of values, there's significance in seeking out the talent that maybe the masses don't quite recognize because it doesn't cohere to the norm, to the elite-approved idea of what's good. Our taste has been developed by corporations desperate to sell products. It's all manufactured for us and shoved down our throats. It's fast food for the soul, for the mind. It's not good for us, you know? We've lost the ability as a species to declare what we like instead of having it done for us."

"Although it's corny as hell, that may actually be the best *un*ironic explanation of hipster I've ever heard," Nessa said. "Okay, I'll grant you all that. But what really bugs me? It's the smugness. The sense of superiority. That you're better than the masses, the *sheeple*, as your people so compassionately call them."

"But isn't that what we all do, on some level? Try to elevate ourselves to drown out the chorus of self-hatred that threatens to destroy us all on a daily basis?"

"What just happened?" Nessa said, straightening and fixing him with an astonished gaze. "Did you just . . . say something real to me? Did you really just peel back your veneer of bullshit to give me a glimpse into your existential fears?"

He looked away from her.

"You'll have your own show one day," she said. "After a millennia of being the joke of humanity, the tables have turned and nerds now run the universe. Maybe the year of the hipster is coming, and you'll have your supreme day in the sun, where you run everything—organically and sustainably, of course—and turn the world into a flax-wearing, beard-growing, locavore-arama!"

Otto barked a laugh. "My real name is Jim," he said.

"Of course it is," Nessa said.

After Otto left, Nessa realized he'd never told her what had happened to him Thursday night.

Chapter Fifteen

Saturday, June 18

NESSA FELT AS though she'd been sleeping with her eyes open because it seemed like she'd been staring at the same dark object for hours. It was like the ceiling fan. Since they'd lived in this house, she'd awoken several times, and upon seeing the ceiling fan, each time she'd thought it was something different: a seagull, a cross, Superman.

But this time her mind was making it into something sinister. It was just a shadow from the window, moving with the wind, trees, maybe.

She blinked in the dark.

But the image resolved into the shape of a man.

John? And she almost sat up.

But then a strange scent met her nostrils. It was Southern Comfort and cigarette smoke. A spear of terror impaled her chest, cutting off her wind.

John was not a smoker.

Nessa did not know this person.

The man stood next to the dresser, unmoving. Nessa resolved not to move either. If she pretended to be asleep, he could take what he wanted and leave.

He turned slowly toward her.

A second sharper wave of panic rippled through her body.

Pleaseleavepleaseleavepleaseplease. . .

The man lunged toward the bed and clamped a large hand over her mouth, bearing down and mashing her lips into her gums, pressure under her nose.

A dark face lowered to hers and whispered, "Don't make a sound. If you fight me, I will kill you."

She saw that the darkness of the face was due to a black knit ski mask. His lips touched the skin of her face and the revulsion she felt was so extreme she thought she might faint. His saliva dribbled down her forehead.

A hoarse whisper. "I've got a gun, and one way or another, I'm going to use it."

He raised up and she saw a gun-shaped shadow above her face. He put it in his pocket and leaned back in. "I know you want this, bitch. You want it hard, don't you? Tell me how you want it."

Nessa felt pressure on her stomach moving southward. Everything slowed down.

It *was* happening again, this time in her own house, with her son sleeping next door.

"Nathan?" she whispered. She had to talk him out of this.

"Shut up," he said, but the shape of him was all wrong. He was shorter, had thin arms. This wasn't her rapist from California. This was a new rapist.

"Please," she said.

"Please what?" he said. "What do you want me to do? Say it!"

Her breathing came in ragged gasps and her heart battered the inside of her chest. When his hand reached her crotch, without any agency from her, her arms and legs began flailing wildly, as if restraints had just popped off of her. Her left hand caught the man in the nose.

"Ow!" he howled. "What are you doing?"

The absurdity of this question made her freeze again momentarily.

"That wasn't part of the deal!" the man yelled.

Nessa's door flew open and Isabeau stood there, all five foot ten inches of her, with a slim purple knife in her hand.

"Get off her, motherfucker," Isabeau said. "Or this knife is going right into your back."

The ski-masked asshole looked back over his shoulder, and Nessa took the opportunity to wind up and punch him right in the balls. He pitched over, gasping, clutching his crotch and groaning.

Nessa scrambled to get the nightstand drawer open and reached for the Walther PK380. It wasn't there, of course. The cops had it.

"What is this?" the man wheezed. "Some sort of femi-nazi ambush? This is false advertising!"

With the knife still in her hand, Isabeau bounded over to the bed and yanked the guy's ski mask off. Nessa switched on the bedside lamp, temporarily blinded by the light. She focused on her attacker. He had glossy black hair, smooth pink skin, and blue eyes.

She'd never seen him before.

What had she expected? That it was Otto? Detective Dirksen?

She gripped her chest, her hands suddenly freezing cold, panic rising inside her. She swallowed, willing her heartbeat to slow, but her heart ignored her and went on thundering.

"Call 911, Isabeau," she said, hoping she didn't sound quite as terrified as she felt.

"But this is what you wanted!" the man said, his voice pitched high with hysteria.

"What the hell are you talking about?" Isabeau said.

"Am I at the wrong place?" he said, still clutching his crotch.

His eyebrows were several millimeters higher than Nessa would have thought possible. The pain and fear that contorted his face made her own abate to an almost tolerable level.

"Who are you?" she demanded, her voice sounding strong in her own ears.

"Is this part of the thing?" the man asked.

"What thing? What are you talking about?"

"The ad! Your ad! If I'd known it was supposed to be a three-some, or that you had weapons, I wouldn't have—"

Isabeau stared at Nessa, then at the guy. "Okay, shitbird," she said. "I want you to tell us exactly what ad you're talking about. Where you saw it. What it said. Et cetera."

The poor guy's voice shook so badly Nessa could hardly understand him. "It was online, on that site Fantasy Island. The ad said that you—" he inclined his head toward Nessa "—had a fantasy about being rrrr . . . rrrr . . . raped in your bed in the middle of the night."

So Nathan had sent someone to do his dirty work for him.

"I knew this was too good to be true," the guy said. "I knew it."

Nessa grabbed her phone and stumbled out into the hall, closing the door behind her, confident that Isabeau could handle this guy. Nessa dialed 911. While she explained to the operator what was happening, she kept her eye on Daltrey's door.

When she opened her own bedroom door and slipped inside, Isabeau was still interrogating the would-be rapist, brandishing her knife at him with one hand and holding an unfolded piece of paper in the other.

"Here, Nessa," she said.

Nessa took the paper from her and tried to read it while her attacker blubbered in the background.

Have you always fantasized about raping someone? I've always fantasized about being raped. We should get together. Come to my house at three A.M. some morning (but don't tell me when!) and let's make our dreams come true. Nessa Donati, County Road 8, off John Brown Road.

The header indeed said FantasyIslandXXX.com on top and was dated yesterday.

"And you expect me to believe that you saw this ad online?" Nessa said. "That you didn't just type it up and print it out as an excuse or whatever to attack someone in her sleep?"

The man was crying now. "Oh, God, I didn't know it wasn't real. I'm so sorry."

Nessa was clobbered with an intense, almost overwhelming craving for a shot. Right now.

"Hey, scumbag," Isabeau said. "How did you get in the house? Slit a screen? Break down the back door?"

"No," he said.

"How'd you get in, then?"

He reached for his pocket, and Isabeau raised her knife at him.

He whimpered. "I need to show you," he said. "I'm getting something out of my pocket, okay? Take it easy!"

He pulled out a brand-new shiny house key.

"Where did you get that?"

"I got it in my post office box. The return address was this house."

Nessa and Isabeau looked at each other.

Nessa looked at the piece of paper again. The email that was from Nessa.Donati@gmail.com.

That was not her email address.

The paper floated to the ground.

Her name. Her address. Her troll had broken through the fourth wall and had invited every freak within five hundred miles to come to her house and rape her in her bed.

When the patrol car pulled up in front of the house, the would-be rapist was hauled to his feet, crying and choking out excuses and explanations to the cop, who cuffed him and took the piece of paper from him.

Once the cops left, Nessa went into her bedroom and dialed Marlon.

"I need a shot," she said, then told him what happened.

"Are you drinking now?" he said, speaking slowly and deliberately.

"No."

"Did you drink before you called?"

"No," she said.

"You did the right thing—you called your sponsor before, not after, you took the first drink. I'm going to throw another AA aphorism at you, and I want you to think hard on it. 'Man's extremity is God's opportunity.' You know what it means, right?"

"Yes," she said. But she knew he was going to tell her anyway, and that made her smile.

"It means that you can't handle this. You really can't. But God can, and you need to let him. But you still need to do your part. First, don't drink. Second, you need to get a security system out there. This is insane."

"You're right," she said.

"You can do what *you* can do, and God will do the rest."

Would He though?

"Thank you, Marlon," she said. She did feel better, especially with an action plan. "I'm going to go to the locksmith Monday and see if they do security systems too. The cop who came out here to arrest the guy told me he'd see to it that a patrol car is sent out here for the next several days."

"Excellent," he said. He yawned into the phone. "And now I'm going back to sleep."

"Good night," she said, and clicked off.

She went back downstairs and Isabeau was sitting on the living room couch clacking away on her laptop keyboard. Nessa got hers, sat down next to her nanny, and typed the Fantasy Island website URL into her browser. She searched the site for the ad the creep had brought with him.

"I can't find the ad," Nessa said.

"I know," Isabeau said. "I think whoever posted it took it down. We could try to get the owners of the site to turn over the IP address the troll's using to post this shit, but I'm guessing they're not exactly paragons of virtue."

"Can we use the email address to try to lure him out of hiding somehow?" Nessa said. "How would we do that?"

"I don't know. I'll do some research and see what I can come up with."

"By the way," Nessa said. "What you did tonight was totally badass."

Isabeau smiled at her, pleased. "Thanks."

"Where did you get that knife?"

"I have a whole collection of them," Isabeau said. "I used to throw knives competitively when I lived in Alaska."

This blew Nessa's mind. "You threw knives?"

Isabeau nodded.

"And you lived in Alaska?"

"Yup. In a tipi."

"Why didn't you ever tell me?"

"You've never asked," Isabeau said. "I keep them right upstairs in my room."

"You—what?" Nessa said.

"Don't worry," Isabeau said. "I keep them way up high in the closet where Daltrey could never get to them."

"You know," Nessa said. "Maybe we should keep them in the kitchen pantry up high. Just in case, with all this crap going on around here."

"Okay," Isabeau said. "You want to see the set?"

"Definitely," Nessa said, and Isabeau's smile widened as she bounded up the stairs.

She returned with a black nylon carrying case, which she unrolled. Six purple metal handles protruded from pockets in the sheath. She slid one out and handed it handle-first to Nessa. It was much lighter than Nessa would have expected.

"They're titanium," Isabeau said. "I can show you a video of one of my competitions if you want."

She rolled the knives back up, then got her laptop and set it on the coffee table. She typed into it and spun it toward Nessa, then clicked on the play button of the YouTube video.

The camera swung toward Isabeau, who held her knives and did an outstretched arm curtsy before turning toward six archery targets attached to an outdoor wall.

The camera focused on the targets, and one by one, each was pierced by a knife, most of them near the bull's-eye.

"Cool, huh?" Isabeau said, waggling her eyebrows, her wide smile proud and delighted.

"That's amazing," Nessa said with real admiration. "You are a woman of many talents." She reached forward and grasped Isabeau's hand. "Thank you so much. You saved me tonight. You really did."

"You're welcome," Isabeau said, then got up and went in the kitchen. Nessa heard the pantry door open and close.

Nessa realized she'd never asked Isabeau anything about herself, and it made her ashamed. She was so swept up in the drama that was her life Isabeau was just a bit player, a prop, an extra.

But by rescuing Nessa tonight, she'd earned top billing.

Sunday, June 19

AT NINE THE next morning, Nessa stuck Daltrey in front of the TV—something she was doing far too often these days—while Isabeau worked on her computer in the same room.

Nessa went up to her bedroom and steeled herself to call John's parents. Then she dialed her mother-in-law's cell phone.

"Linda, I have a problem."

"Oh?" her mother-in-law said. "What is it *now*?"

Nessa ground her teeth. "Is there any way you can push up your Kansas City trip with Daltrey? And then take him back to Russell with you for a week or so?"

Nessa was grateful that, other than cell phone usage, her in-laws were completely technophobic and had no knowledge of or interest in the Internet, so they wouldn't have read her blog and all the horrific comments.

"Need a little break, do you?" Linda said.

Nessa bit her tongue. Actually, since people were now invading her house at all hours of the night, she feared for Daltrey's safety. But she wasn't about to let slip this bit of info. She'd always had the feeling that Linda was just waiting for her to screw up so she could swoop in and take control of Daltrey's life.

"I'll have to miss my book club, but you know I'll do anything for my boyfriend." That's what she called Daltrey, to Nessa's revulsion. Linda sighed, put-upon, but agreed to pick Daltrey up in the morning.

As Nessa drove into town to Lock It Up later, she couldn't shake the feeling of the would-be rapist's hands on her, the gun pointed at her. She'd showered twice that morning, but now she felt like she needed another one. She felt like she was covered in slime.

Lock It Up Locksmith Services was housed in a converted brick home. She walked in and asked to see the owner.

"I've used your company before, but I want to talk to him to see if there's a more sophisticated system we should be using. Or maybe you could show me—"

"He should be back anytime," the receptionist said. "He went to lunch. If you want to wait, that's fine."

Nessa watched the receptionist play *The Sims* on her computer until she got bored and leafed through some old magazines. Finally, the bell over the door sounded, and an older man with thin silver hair and glasses walked in leading a younger guy who was looking at his phone. Nessa recognized him—what was his name? Brady, the kid who'd changed her locks.

She stood and introduced herself. The owner clasped her outstretched hand, and Brady looked up from his phone and started. He looked quickly away.

"Hey, Brady," she said.

"Hi," he said, without looking at her. "I have a doctor's appointment, Jerry. Forgot about it. I'll be back in a few." He turned and walked out the door.

Nessa watched him go. Why wouldn't he look at her?

The thought that struck her took her breath away. The key the would-be rapist showed her was from the new locks. The locks Brady had installed. In the trauma of the moment, this hadn't occurred to her.

"Will you excuse me for just a minute?" she said. "I want to thank Brady personally for the great job he did on our house."

She followed Brady out the door where he was sprinting toward a truck.

"Hey," she said.

He didn't hesitate or turn around. He was fumbling with the keys to the truck, and she ran toward him, overcome with the desire to kick this kid's ass. He sold her fucking keys to a fucking rapist.

"Hey, Brady," she said.

He didn't respond.

"Are you the one who placed the ad?"

He turned then, his face a mask of confusion.

"How much did you get, you little punk-ass bitch?" she hissed.

He turned back to the truck door, trying desperately to get his key in the lock.

"I don't know what you're talking about, lady," he said.

Nessa had to force herself not to start screaming and clawing at him, force herself to realize she needed to go mom on him rather than Robocop. She caught up to him and put her hand on his. "I can get you fired right now," she said, "or you can tell me who you sold my key to, and your boss never needs to know."

She grabbed his keys away from him and put them in her pocket. "Look at me," she said in the same tone she'd use with Daltrey when he was ignoring her. "I need your help. Whoever you sold my keys to came into my house in the middle of the night and tried to rape me."

Brady continued to look at the ground.

"I have a little boy," she said, pleading. "You met him. You've put him and me in danger. Don't you give a shit?"

The kid started to cry.

"Listen. Just tell me the truth and I swear I won't tell your boss. I just need to know who it was."

He couldn't stop crying.

"How much did he pay you?"

"A hundred dollars," the kid said, wiping his nose on his arm. "Both times."

"Wait—what? Both times?"

Brady started crying anew. "I needed the money."

Nessa tried to compose herself. She had to confirm that it was Nathan who'd bought the keys. "Was this guy about six-four? Blond?"

"No," Brady said.

Of course Nathan wouldn't be blond after spending twenty-three hours a day inside a prison.

"Not blond, then," Nessa said.

"And not six-four either," Brady said. The crying had stopped, but he still looked terrified. "He was—"

"Taller or shorter?"

"A lot shorter. About my height."

Brady looked to be about five-nine. She puzzled over this.

"Don't you even know how tall your own husband is? Ex-husband, whatever?"

"Kid," Nessa said. "It wasn't my ex-husband. He's—"

"But it was," Brady insisted. "He showed me his driver's license."

"His—"

"Yes! I know it was him because he has the same last name as you. Donati. John Donati."

Chapter Sixteen

AND THEN NESSA was on her back on the pavement, staring up at the sky with Brady kneeling next to her, crying again. She didn't know how long she'd been out, whether she'd hit her head, or if she'd had a seizure, or just fainted.

"Mrs. Donati?" Brady was patting her hand with his clammy one. She yanked her hand away and sat up. "Are you all right?"

Her hands were scraped up from the gravelly surface beneath her. John was alive.

"When did this happen?" she said. "When did . . . Mr. Donati buy the keys from you?"

"Are you sure you're all right?"

"Just answer the question," she snapped. "When did this happen?"

Brady startled, then looked up, obviously trying to remember. "It was, like, a week ago. He said you'd locked him out of his house, and he just wanted to get in there and get his stuff. That's all he wanted to do. His name was the same as yours, so I figured it was legit, you know?"

She couldn't breathe, felt like she was going to pitch over again. The world was not real, not at all, it *couldn't be.*

John was alive.

Brady held up a Vulcan "live long and prosper" hand. "I swear to God," he said, sniveling again. "I never thought something like this would happen. I swear to God."

She tried to stand.

Her legs turned to water and she fell to the ground again, her bones and muscles no longer capable of supporting her weight, her brain unable to support this fact:

John's alive.

Brady chattered away like a monkey, but she couldn't understand anything he said because she was trying to adjust her worldview.

"I'm going to go get you some water. Stay right where you are."

As if she could do anything else at this moment.

He ran back inside the locksmith office while she sat leaning against his vehicle's tire in the shade.

She'd never known John at all, not really. And he was so much sicker than she ever realized.

Her mind lined up all the events of the past three weeks, and it was now so obvious. Of course it was John. He was punishing her for keeping him away from *his* stuff, *his* wife, *his* house, *his* son. He'd smeared the pickup truck with his own blood, fired her gun into the bed, and called the cops . . . he'd done all of it. And then tormented her with the details of her past.

Why had he never been that ambitious about jobs?

Brady returned, paper cone in hand, with about thimbleful's worth of water in it. She threw it back and swallowed.

"You can make it up to me," Nessa said to the quaking locksmith.

"If he approaches you again after I change the locks, I want you to text me. Tell him you'll give him the new keys, set up a meeting, then tell me. This is really important. John's a crack addict. He wants to hurt me and my son, my three-year-old boy. I don't know if you know anything about addicts, but they don't care about anything but rock. The drugs rot away their brains so that they lose their connection to the people they once loved. It's like the rabies virus. It just wants what it wants and to propagate itself without regard to its host. That's what's going on here. Will you do that for me?"

Brady sniffled and wiped his eyes and nose and nodded.

"I will," he said. "I'm really sorry. I honestly thought he was just trying to get his stuff. I didn't know."

"Well," Nessa said, "now you know." She tried to stand again, and this time succeeded. She got in the Pacifica and headed for home.

The temporary photo of Daltrey with X's over his eyes bubbled up in her brain. *He Will Die* scrawled across it. John had meant what he'd said—he'd rather see Daltrey dead than with her.

She wept as she drove, thinking about everything that was lost. The only man she'd ever loved, the only one to whom she'd bared her soul and then some, had not only not loved her enough to remain drug-free, but was also now trying to drive her crazy or get her killed. Or drive her to addiction again. How had she been so thoroughly fooled?

A little at a time, John was going to tell everything he knew, like skinning her alive, one inch at a time. Which meant that sometime soon he was going to out her to the cops.

She needed to tell the police that John was alive, and that he was behind all the incidents she'd reported. But that would have to wait until tomorrow, since she knew that Detective Treloar didn't work weekends, and she had no intention of getting stuck with Detective Dickhead.

When she returned home, she was shocked to find Marlon on the top rungs of her collapsible aluminum ladder, leaned against her house.

He wore shorts and a sleeveless T-shirt, a tool belt around his waist, and he was covered in sweat in the hot late morning. He was bolting something to the back of her house.

"There you are," he called down.

"What are you doing here?" Nessa said, shielding her eyes from the bright sunlight, and was suddenly horrified at what she must look like after just a few hours of sleep, her puffy, tear-smeared face, her hair a greasy rat's nest.

Thank you, Joyce Gereben, for this lovely maternal legacy you've bestowed upon me. What did it matter how she looked? Marlon was her sponsor, not her . . . whatever . . .

He appeared as uncomfortable as she felt, perched up there, screwdriver in hand, looking almost as if he'd been caught egging her house.

"Listen," he said. "I just couldn't let another day go by without getting you some security out here. I went ahead and bought a system for you, and I hope you're not offended—it's not that I don't think you're a capable human being, can't take care of yourself. In fact, I think you're one of the most competent people I've ever met, not to mention ballsy, but—"

"Can you come down here? I need to tell you what happened this morning. Where are Isabeau and Daltrey?"

"Inside," he said, tightening a bolt. "Give me just a sec."

"What are those?" Nessa asked, pointing.

"Video cameras," he said, "so every area of the house will be covered. I also got a keyless computer entry system for you; Isabeau is putting that together. This has just gotten so insane. We can't let it happen again."

Nessa bit back an apologetic reply and instead said, "Thank you."

Marlon came down the ladder and onto the covered deck, where he dropped wearily into a patio chair. Isabeau came out the back door carrying an instruction sheet.

"So let me tell you about your new security system," she said.

Nessa held up a hand and said, "First let me tell you what I just found out."

Isabeau and Nessa both sat, then Marlon and Isabeau listened with open mouths and wide eyes as she told them about Brady the locksmith.

"So the person who's been behind all this is—"

"John," Marlon said in an awed voice.

Nessa nodded, starting to cry again. Isabeau rose and squatted by Nessa's chair, wrapping her arms around her.

"I'm so sorry," she said.

"What am I going to do?" Nessa said.

"Well, first thing we're going to do is flame that fucking locksmith on Yelp," Marlon said.

This was so unexpected that Nessa burst into a howling laugh fueled by hysteria and anguish.

Marlon looked pleased. "And then you have to go to the police," he said. "You have to tell them."

"But I promised the kid I wouldn't get him in trouble."

"Without him, the cops will not believe you," Marlon said.

"John must be watching the house," Nessa said. "Brady's coming back out here tomorrow to install new locks again so John'll approach him again to get the keys."

Isabeau and Marlon glanced at each other, confused.

"And then what?" Isabeau said.

"I'm going to tell the cops I have reason to believe that John's still alive," Nessa said, "and that he's responsible for all this. But I want to catch him myself."

"That is ludicrous," Marlon said.

Nessa couldn't explain that she was trying to keep the police at arm's length while still getting their help—but on her terms. She couldn't have them fingerprint her, or they'd find out who she really was, and there would be dire consequences. She would lose Daltrey. But she couldn't tell these people any of this. John, however, knew everything. And she would not let him destroy her. She would do anything to stop him. Anything.

"Just—please," Nessa said. "I want to do this my way. With these new video cameras, we'll be able to catch him in the act, right? Then I can take the video to the cops so they won't think I'm any crazier than they already do."

Marlon and Isabeau glanced at each other again.

"And my in-laws are taking Daltrey for a while, so I can concentrate on tracking John down, and Daltrey will be safe."

"You don't suppose they're helping John?" Marlon said. "Maybe the three of them have set this whole thing up?"

"Oh, no," Nessa said. "They've been putting up with John's bullshit for more years than I have, and I guarantee you that they would never do anything to hurt Daltrey."

This was the only thing she was sure of.

"Well," Marlon said slowly. "This new system should keep John—and any other potential rapists—out, regardless of the key situation."

"You're the boss, boss," Isabeau said.

"You better keep me in the loop," Marlon said. "Because I will go to the police and out this locksmith kid if anything goes wrong."

"John is mostly interested in hurting me emotionally, financially, reputationally."

"That's not a word," Marlon said.

"Hurting me physically is just a bonus," Nessa said.

Isabeau looked from Marlon to Nessa and then down at the instruction sheet she'd been holding the whole time. "So let's find out more about the new security system."

Nessa could tell she was excited to share.

Isabeau read from the instructions. " 'Encrypted locking technology is keyless and codeless—all you need is your smartphone and the app. Will automatically lock your door behind you when you leave. Compatible with most standard cylinder dead bolts, including Lock-tite, and blah, blah, blah. Your regular key will still work if you don't have your phone.' "

Marlon seemed reassured by what he was hearing. "It was the highest-rated system I could find," he said.

Isabeau continued reading. " 'Instant invites let you give custom access to friends and family.' " She smiled widely at Nessa and pointed a thumb at herself.

Friends and family. Is that what these two were now? Nessa found herself choked up at all this work Isabeau and Marlon were doing for her.

"I had no idea you had any real skills," Nessa said to her sponsor, frowning to cover up her uneasiness at being the object of such affection.

Marlon stood, obviously ready to get back to work. "We all have our secrets."

Monday, June 20

BRADY THE LOCKSMITH was only too happy to come out on Sunday to replace the locks. He was obsequious and contrite and she actually felt kind of sorry for him.

"Now remember," she said. "You call me the second he tries to buy keys from you. Understand?"

Brady swore he would do so.

Before Nessa's in-laws arrived, she looked at the video camera footage to see if John had lurked around the house the night before. She read the directions of how to play the video, then played it at accelerated speed, figuring she'd notice an intruder's appearance.

It was difficult to keep watching, since nothing happened.

When she was done looking at video, Nessa called Lauren to tell her they wouldn't be able to go to the splash park the next day because Daltrey's grandparents were taking him to Kansas City. Lauren was disappointed, of course, but at least Nessa didn't have to lie to her.

Nessa sat outside to intercept her in-laws before Daltrey saw them. At exactly eight A.M., Linda and Tony Donati drove up and got out of their car. They were in their late sixties and dressed like tourists.

Linda gave Nessa perfunctory air kisses, and Tony hugged her, avoiding her eyes.

"Before I let Daltrey know you're here," Nessa said, "I need to tell you what's been going on."

Linda and Tony looked uneasily at each other.

"All right," Linda said.

Nessa told them about the online harassment, the abandoned truck, the poisoned dog, everything. With each addition to the list, Tony and Linda seemed to shrink, to fold under the weight of what their son had done. The final blow, the story of the almost-rape, made Linda cover her mouth with her hands.

"I'm sorry to have to tell you all this," Nessa said, "but that's why I need you to get Daltrey away from here. I've installed a security system at the house, but I want my son safe."

Tony was nodding, staring at the ground, his hands in his Bermuda shorts pockets. Linda smoothed her hair and straightened.

"We'll keep him as long as you need us to," she said, a quaver in her voice.

"Thank you," Nessa said. "Now let's go get Daltrey."

They went inside, and Linda wiped her teary eyes.

"Where are you, darling boy?" she called out. "Where's my grandson?"

Daltrey came toddling in, all smiles, fat arms held out to his grandma.

"Hello, Daltrey," she said in a loud slow voice usually reserved for the elderly and the IQ-challenged. "Grandma and Grandpa are here. Are you ready to go? Are you ready to go to Worlds of Fun? Can you say Worlds of Fun?"

Tony turned from the TV and, on seeing his grandson, began to cry, his mouth covered with his big meaty hand. To Nessa, he said, "He looks so much like his daddy. So much." He pulled a handkerchief from his pocket and wiped his eyes and blew his nose. Then he picked Daltrey up and squeezed him.

Daltrey put his hands on either side of his grandpa's face, which made Tony cry harder. Nessa teared up, watching this. If Tony could get his hands on John right now, he'd break him in half.

Linda, on the other hand, turned her pink-lipsticked face toward Nessa, a big fake smile on, her eyebrows high on her forehead, breaking the harmonious spell of the earlier confab in the yard. "Have you started talking yet, sweetheart? Has Mama taught you how to talk?"

This was her way of interrogating Nessa—by asking Daltrey things he could not possibly answer. But now, Nessa was actually grateful for Linda's habit. Nessa's irritation helped things to seem normal, if only for a moment.

Nessa ground her teeth under her forced smile. "He's all packed and ready to go."

"Did you have a bath last night?" Linda said to Daltrey, her manicured hand on his head. "Did you have a bath?"

"Yes, Linda, he had a bath. And yes, before you ask him, I washed all his clothes before putting them in his suitcase."

"Did she?" Linda said to Daltrey. "Did Mama wash your clothes? I'll bet she didn't iron them!" She poked him in the tummy like the Pillsbury Doughboy, and like that corporate mascot, he giggled.

The sooner they got out of here, the better. It would be many years before Daltrey felt the tension between them. Hopefully Linda would be dead long before then.

"Can I offer you some coffee?" Nessa asked, praying they'd say no.

"No," Linda said, "Grandma and Grandpa and big-boy Daltrey need to get on the road! It's two hours to Kansas City the way Grandpa drives! We've got to go. Do you need to tinkle, Daltrey?"

He shook his head.

"You'd better try," she said. "We don't want to have to stop, do we, Dolly?"

Nessa clenched her teeth again and said, quietly, "Please don't call him that."

"For God's sake, Linda," Tony said, his irritation drying his tears.

"Don't call you what?" Linda said to Daltrey. "I was just calling you by a cute little old nickname!"

"Linda," Tony said. "His name is Daltrey. Not Dolly."

"Of course it is! All right, go on. Go tinkle."

Tony squeezed him again before putting him down. Daltrey ran to the bathroom and closed the door behind him.

Linda pulled a lined piece of paper from her purse and handed it to Nessa. "Here's where we'll be staying and the phone number." She pointed to a neatly printed address. "And this is our itinerary. We're going to the Royals game on Monday against the Cardinals, and then we'll go to the amusement park on Tuesday. The toy and miniature museum on Wednesday and we'll have dinner on the Plaza. Then we'll take him back to Russell with us. What a treat!"

Tony put his arm around Nessa. "You want us to keep him until the end of the month? Can you spare him that long?"

Ten days. Nessa wasn't sure. "Why don't we play it by ear? Let's say until the thirtieth, but I may just have to come down and get him before then."

He nodded and kissed the top of her head. "I understand, sweetheart."

Daltrey reappeared, and Linda bent at the waist to address him. "Did you wash your hands? You need to wash your hands after you go potty. Otherwise, you'll be sharing germs with everyone. And you don't want to share your germs, do you?"

Daltrey held up his hands for inspection, and she kissed them. Daltrey signed, "Wash," but Linda turned away from him. Her in-laws were not interested in learning ASL to communicate with their grandson.

"That's just encouraging you not to talk," Linda had once said to Daltrey, who was two at the time. "They just don't want you to talk . . . at . . . all!"

Daltrey held his arms up to Nessa, and she scooped him up and buried her face in his velvety neck, kissing him and making him squeal. "I love you, Daltrey."

He put both hands on either cheek and pressed his forehead to hers, his long-lashed eyes boring into her. Then he held up his little hand in the shorthand ILY sign. She mirrored it with her right hand. Then she kissed and hugged him and set him on the floor.

"You be good, little man," she said, and he looked over his shoulder with a "Duh" expression that made her laugh.

"Have fun, you all," she said to her in-laws, and hugged them both. "Thank you so much for doing this. It's been a tough couple of weeks."

Linda surprised her by laying her hand on Nessa's cheek and giving her the most sincerely sympathetic look she'd ever given Nessa.

"I know it has, honey," she said. "I'm so sorry."

Then she hugged Nessa tight, and Nessa began to cry again.

After they left, Nessa went into the kitchen to get coffee, and Isabeau wandered in, still wearing shortie pajamas, her hair disheveled.

"Why didn't you come down to meet the grandparents?" Nessa said, smiling.

"I heard them," Isabeau said, pulling juice out of the refrigerator. "That awful voice the old lady uses when she's talking to Daltrey just made me want to spew!"

"Yeah, me too. But they're not that bad," Nessa said. "They're just weird and neurotic. But so am I. Neurotic, I mean."

"Well, you're a better woman than I," Isabeau said.

Nessa wondered what kind of grandparent her own mother would have been. While her in-laws drove her crazy, at least they weren't like Joyce.

Thinking about her mother, Nessa was again struck by the similarities between John and Joyce—how far he was willing to go to punish her for punishing him. When he felt wronged, he would hold on to his indignation like a precious treasure, clasped tightly to his chest, glaring out at Nessa with wounded eyes, daring her to ask him what was wrong. Just like her mother.

If she did ask, her mother would say, "Nothing. I'm fine."

So would John, just like that. And then he'd lift his chin, with that hurt but brave posture like her mother's.

The difference? When John did these things, Nessa would push back by pretending she didn't notice that anything was wrong. She'd get louder and jollier, acting as if they'd never been so happy, just to goad him. And he'd get chillier and icier and more long-suffering, and she'd want to clock him in the face. And finally she'd lose her shit and scream at him, and he'd finally spill what his fucking problem was and they'd end up laughing, and then they'd tumble into the sheets and have make-up sex—when he could get it up. The medication had put a damper on that, but the fact was she hadn't minded that much.

With her mother, the silences were more dangerous. Scarier. Because as a kid, when Mom pulled the love away, you knew you were lost. You knew you didn't exist anymore. She had made you disappear with her anger and disappointment.

But enough navel-gazing. She had work to do. Nessa sat at the table with her laptop and opened her email. She had several Google alert notices. DeadJohnDonati had been a busy boy.

She'd tried to talk Isabeau out of looking at the alerts anymore, but to no avail. Today, on Nessa's blog, DeadJohnDonati had posted this:

Nessa trivia question: What was her secondary hobby as a teenager? Was it A) played in a band or B) charged $5 per blow job, $10 per lay, at the corner of Santa Monica Boulevard and Highland Avenue?

Isabeau read over her shoulder before Nessa could close the browser.

"Now it's just getting ridiculous," Isabeau said. "I wonder if all this is having the opposite effect of what John intends. Oh, Nessa Donati, she's from outer space! She's got three heads! She was a hooker!"

If only it *was* ridiculous.

Nessa had to find him and stop him before *everything* came out. Now that her boy was gone, Nessa had work to do. She was going to find John. And she was going to stop him.

Chapter Seventeen

SHE WAITED AN hour before driving to the police station. She wanted to make sure Linda and Tony wouldn't come back before she left.

At the station, she talked to the desk sergeant. "Can I speak to Detective Treloar?"

"He's not in."

She hated to ask for Dirksen, but she didn't have any other choice. She sat in the waiting area, fidgeting, for fifteen minutes before Dirksen appeared.

She stood. Her voice shook. "Can we go somewhere private to talk?"

"Sure," he said, and led her down the hall to an interview room. He pulled out a chair for her on one side of the table, then sat on the other side.

"I think my husband is alive," Nessa said.

He wasn't expecting that; it was clear from his surprised expression. "What are you talking about?"

"I have reason to believe that John staged his disappearance."

It sounded even crazier when she said it out loud, and the contemptuous twist of the detective's mouth reflected this.

"Really," Dirksen said. "And why do you believe that?"

She swallowed. "I also think he's the one who put the ad on FantasyIslandXXX.com. I assume you know about that."

"Yeah," he said, and he actually looked sympathetic, although maybe she just hoped he did.

Nessa explained most of the things that had been going on, unable to think of certain nouns, using too many words, sounding like a flustered hausfrau. It was humiliating and frustrating.

She handed the detective her file folder of screenshots: the comments, the website (without the naked photos, of course), the social media accounts—everything she and Isabeau had found online. She hoped this would speak for her.

As the stack of paper clunked onto the desktop and rattled the ice in the detective's fountain Coke, his mouth dropped open. "Are you kidding me with this?"

"This isn't all of it," Nessa said.

He riffled through it, not really looking, and pushed it aside, probably to set in a pile along with all the books everyone says they've read but never quite get through, like Joyce's *Ulysses*.

"Do you have a department that investigates cybercrime?"

He laughed. "No."

"Can you contact the FBI, get their help? They probably have more resources to do this sort of thing than you guys do, right?"

"We'll consider that."

Nessa stared at him. "No, you won't. I can see it in your face. You're not going to do anything."

"We have our hands full with real crimes, Mrs. Donati."

"Like attempted rape?" she said. "Like that?"

"There's no indication that your husband is responsible," Dirksen said.

"But *someone* is. Someone came into my home. Held a gun on me. Threatened my life with my three-year-old son in the next room." She shouldn't have said that last bit, because she was afraid she was going to cry, and she could not cry in front of this asshole.

"Lady, that's not my case. Your husband's disappearance is."

Lady. Baby. Honey. Dismissive terms for hysterical women like her.

She'd promised herself she wasn't going to turn Brady in, but if ever there was a time to break a promise, this was it.

"Listen," she said. "I found out that the locksmith who changed our locks actually sold the keys to John. Twice."

Dirksen again leaned back in his chair and crossed his arms but said nothing.

He didn't believe her. Or maybe, more accurately, didn't want to.

"Detective Dirksen," she said, trying to keep her voice even and reasonable. "Do you have some sort of problem with me?"

He regarded her. "Listen, Mrs. Donati. I skimmed some of your blog and I can see why you kind of irritate some people."

"I'm sorry," she said. "What?"

"You're pretty sarcastic. Some people find that offensive."

Sarcastic like Howard Stern? Like Perez Hilton? If she were a man, this attribute would be a million-dollar asset. But since she was a woman, she was shrill, abrasive, bossy, strident, high-maintenance. Nessa would not rise to this bait. She would stay on topic. She would be the rational one. "But what does that have to do with—"

"My point is," Dirksen said, warming to his lecture, "that if you're going to put yourself out there with a superior attitude and everything, you're going to attract some negative attention. If you were a little nicer, I'm sure this just wouldn't even be an issue."

"Nicer."

"Yes," Dirksen said, a smile curling his lips. "More . . . ladylike."

Her skin prickled with heat. Rage bubbled up inside her. No. She wasn't going to just sit here and take this. He'd gone way too far. "You know, a blow job isn't very ladylike, but I'll bet you never complain about that."

His fleetingly shocked expression gratified her. But then he masked his response and parried. He leaned forward, his hands on the table. "This is exactly why you will never get any respect. You come on all rough and tough, but the minute someone says something you don't like, you come crying to the men."

"Wow," she said, so incensed her anger doubled back on itself, making her calm once more. "I don't even know what to say, except that I'm guessing you're not really going to be any help here."

He threw his hands up. "If you want to report the locksmith, you need to talk to Detective Treloar. Not me."

"You're not going to look for John?"

"We did. In the lake. His body is probably caught in the trees and buildings over by the cove," he said. "We can't send divers down there. Too dangerous. But I can pretty much guarantee that Mr. Donati is dead. No credit card activity, no phone activity. He's dead as a doornail." He narrowed his eyes at her. "Is it possible, Mrs. Donati, that you're just throwing crap at the wall, hoping something will stick to . . . cover something else up?"

"Like what exactly?" Nessa said.

"Like . . . when we finally get the DNA tests back, you know what we're going to find? We're going to find that your son's DNA is a familial match to the blood and tissue we found embedded in the side of the pickup truck along with the bullets from your gun."

He sat back and watched her face, waiting for her to shrivel up, to react. But for once, she was stone. No sweat, no tears, no shaking. Because she hadn't shot John.

Dirksen leaned forward again and lowered his voice. "We're going to find out that you killed your crackhead husband, and even though you did the whole world a favor, you're going to prison for a long, long time."

She stood, willing herself not to wobble or swallow. "John's alive, Detective Dirksen, and I guess I'm going have to find him myself. I'm going to look in the crack houses in Manhattan and Junction City, and when I find him, I'm going to blog about how the Riley County Sheriff's Office wouldn't help a desperate single mother." She turned and walked out of the interview room.

She was a suspect, she knew that for sure now, but since they wouldn't find a body, it would be very difficult to prosecute her for murder. If this guy had anything to say about it though, they would convene a grand jury, and she would be tried and convicted. Nessa would not only lose custody of her son, she would spend the rest of her days in prison for something she didn't do.

Oh, the irony.

Tuesday, June 21

NESSA RECEIVED AN email from Ella the KCMA receptionist:

Package here for you . . . should I lock it up or do you want to come get it?

Normally, Nessa would've waited until her next shift, but

she wondered if this was yet another message from John. And if maybe it had some fingerprints on it that she could give to the police to prove it was from him.

She hadn't been to the radio station during the day since she was hired, so it felt strange to drive out there in the middle of the afternoon. It looked different in the daylight—smaller and shabbier. Inside, she peeked through the window into the on-air studio and saw a short round middle-aged man wearing her headphones and sitting on her chair, spitting into *her* microphone.

Possessive much?

Nessa turned to Ella, a girl no more than eighteen, who was typing on her keyboard.

"Hi, Nessa," she said, and finished what she was doing before reaching under her desk and retrieving a padded envelope. She put it on the desk in front of Nessa, who picked it up.

"No return address," Nessa said. "Just says 'A Fan.'" She turned it over and saw that there was no postmark either. "Did this come in the mail?"

"Nope," Ella said. "It was just lying against the door when I got to work this morning."

Nessa thought about leaving to open it. But then again, a witness might be a good thing to have.

So she sat in the reception chair and felt the envelope, but whatever was inside had plenty of insulation around it. Was it too small to be a bomb?

The envelope was lined with two layers of bubble wrap. She tried to tip whatever was inside out, but it wouldn't budge, so she started to reach inside. But then she had visions of a poisonous snake. It wasn't out of the realm of possibility.

"Do you have a pair of scissors I could borrow?" Nessa asked.

Without looking away from her computer, Ella reached into a drawer, withdrew the scissors, and put them on the desk.

Nessa sliced off the three remaining edges, then carefully folded back the front of the envelope.

"What the hell?" Nessa said.

Taped inside of the bubble wrap was a full hypodermic needle.

Nessa gasped, and Ella looked up from her keyboard.

"What is it?"

Before Nessa could do anything, Ella stood and looked.

"Oh, my God," she said.

Nessa stared at the syringe in horrified fascination. John had taped it with the needle pointing up. Had Nessa reached inside without looking, she would have been punctured. There might have been enough pressure to inject her with the liquid inside the chamber.

Did John really want her dead? She stared at the hypo and wondered.

Ella picked up the phone receiver. "I'm going to call the police."

Nessa was still staring at the syringe. She could have been killed. She could have died, and Daltrey . . .

Nessa snapped out of her trance. "No," she said. "You don't need to do that. I'm going to take it to them right now."

"I can testify if you need me to," Ella said.

"Thanks," Nessa said. "Do you have some Scotch tape?"

Ella handed her a roll and Nessa taped the envelope back together.

She could have been dosed. Germs. Hepatitis. Rabies. HIV. This was starting to remind her of some wack-job conspiracy theory stuff. This was straight-up crazy.

"You should totally post this on Instagram," Ella said. "It's not every day you see this kind of thing."

"Really, Ella?"

"Sorry," she said, shame-faced.

What was it with this generation wanting to document every single thing they saw, from bloody car accidents to their own reflections? Of course, she was part of that cloud culture now. She was part of the problem. But it would never occur to her to take a picture of a weapon.

Nessa carefully stowed the envelope in her bag. She hadn't touched the hypo, so she hoped John's fingerprints could be lifted from it.

Once in her car, she started driving toward the Riley County Sheriff's Office to get the syringe tested. All of a sudden, she realized that if she walked into the cop shop, they were going to take her fingerprints. There would be no stopping it.

Nessa turned off into an abandoned warehouse parking lot to think it through. Could her doctor's office do the testing? They probably could.

She removed the envelope from her purse and opened it to examine the hypo.

Since it was still taped to the envelope, it was hard to determine the color of the liquid in the syringe, but it looked very familiar, and she suspected she knew what it was. Heroin.

A scene from *Nightmare on Elm Street 3: Dream Warriors* came to mind, the one where the ex-junkie girl's tracks open up like hungry mouths, desperate and dying of thirst.

Nessa actually started salivating, painfully. Her eyes watered. The syringe seemed to have its own gravitational pull. She tried to resist it. She didn't know for sure that it was heroin. *But of course it's heroin*, said the little voice in her head. *One little shot won't hurt. Just one, and then never again.*

That voice had spoken to her many times, insistent, seductive, convincing as hell.

Just one more time.

Nessa snatched up her phone and hit the speed dial for Marlon's number. It rang as she stared, salivating, at the plastic cylinder.

"This is Marlon. I'll call you as soon as I can."

Beep.

Fuck.

She dropped her phone, panting, tense, literally almost preorgasmic. Every hair on her body stood on end.

Just once.

It blared in her brain, and in her mind's eye she watched herself let go of the rope.

And then she was clawing through her purse to find something, anything, to tie herself off with. She was nothing but a starving animal hell-bent on survival. Nothing would get in her way now, between Nessa and her smack-lust.

And then her eyes were drawn to her wallet, through the plastic window of which shone Daltrey's smiling face.

All the oxygen left her body. Horror paralyzed her.

Oh, dear God. What had she almost done?

The Dickies played on her phone.

She hit the button and shrieked into the phone, "Where the fuck were you? Where were you?" Sobbing, frantic.

"Whoa, whoa," Marlon said. "What's happening? Where are you?"

Nessa couldn't speak for a moment, crying so hard she couldn't get a breath.

"I called as soon as I could, Nessa," he said, calm. "Where are you?"

"I almost—I almost—" She couldn't say it. Couldn't, because Marlon didn't know.

He thought she was an alcoholic, like him. She'd never told him her real problem, and she knew this was all wrong. She wanted to tell him, but she just couldn't.

"You almost," Marlon said. "But you didn't."

"No, I didn't." She kept her eyes on the photo of Daltrey.

"You're going to be okay," Marlon said. "Just for today. You just have to get through today."

"Yes," she said.

"Do you need me to come to you? I can cancel my class if I have to."

She took a deep, shaky breath, still looking at Daltrey. "No," she said. "Go teach. I'm okay now."

"Go to a meeting, and I'll call you tonight. You can do this, with God's help. Expect the miracle. Expect it."

"I will," she said. "Thank you, Marlon. Talk to you tonight."

After Nessa clicked off, she wrapped the syringe back up and shoved it in her purse. She put the Pacifica into gear and drove toward her doctor's office.

She should go to a meeting, needed to, but she didn't have time.

She parked in the lot outside the medical building. Inside, she approached the receptionist and said, "Would there be any way to squeeze me in to see Kelley this afternoon?"

"What seems to be the problem?" the receptionist said.

"I want to discuss a personal matter with her."

"You can tell me."

"I'd rather not, thanks."

"I'll take a look at her schedule. What's your name?"

"Nessa Donati."

"Have a seat."

Nessa did and dialed Isabeau's cell but got her voicemail.

She made her voice breezy as she could. "Hi, girl, I may be late, but I'm hoping to be home in time for dinner. I'll let you know if it's going to be later than that." She clicked End.

She waited a little more than an hour, silently repeating the Serenity Prayer before a nurse stepped out and called her name. Nessa rose and followed the nurse back, where she was left in an examining room.

The doctor's PA, Kelley, whooshed in with a clipboard. "Hi, Nessa," she said. "What's up?"

She explained what had happened and then said, "Can you test this to see if it's what I think it is?"

Nessa pulled the envelope from her purse and opened it for the PA.

Kelley put on latex gloves and removed the hypo from the bubble wrap. She held it up daintily. "You need to contact the police."

How could Nessa explain? After her exhausting morning, it seemed impossible. Was it irrational to believe that Dirksen would find some way to turn this against her? Or would it prove to them that John was alive and harassing her? She couldn't decide. She felt like she had vapor lock.

"Listen," Nessa said. "I've had a lot of contact with them lately— and I mean a lot—and they don't move very fast. So if I came into contact with something toxic, I'd rather know now than in six weeks."

Kelley sat thinking, looking back and forth from the syringe to Nessa's pleading face.

"My contract is with you," Kelley finally said. "Not with the police. Your health is my top concern. I think we have some Herosol. Let me go see."

"Okay," Nessa said.

Kelley left the room, taking the syringe with her, and Nessa sat staring. Her brain began to work again, now that the relapse danger had been removed. And she wondered what John's plan was. In his drug-twisted mind, he must think that getting her back on heroin would in some way help him. But it was fruitless to try to puzzle out a bipolar crack addict's thought processes.

Kelley returned without the hypo, but with a little purple-stained square of paper. She showed it to Nessa.

"It's heroin," Kelley said.

"That's what I thought," Nessa said. "I can't thank you enough."

"I hope I don't regret this," Kelley said. "Don't make me regret this."

"I won't."

Nessa left the office, shaky and exhausted, still wondering about John's intention. Was it to get her hooked back on heroin?

Or was it to kill her?

Chapter Eighteen

6/21

Hi, I'm Nessa, and I'm an alcoholic. Okay, that's not true. Why do I lie even to my own personal journal? Is it because I want it to be true, as if being an alcoholic is that much better than being a heroin addict? I guess in one respect it is, because normally it takes booze longer to kill you.

I've been sober six years, five months, and two days.

More regret: the first time I did heroin, I did it by accident.

My mom was working at a crappy downtown bar as a cocktail waitress when I was seventeen, and Candy and I used to go down there and hang out and try to get old guys to buy us drinks. Mom ignored all this, pretended we were drinking Shirley Temples and doing our homework.

Candy was, but I'd pretty much stopped going to school by then. It was summer though, and one night I was there without Candy. She had something else going on, I don't remember what. Late that night, a guy with impressively long hair—down to his hips, clean and dark and shiny—asked me to dance. He had a mustache and big brown eyes, and wore a wifebeater and faded jeans, and he was probably late twenties.

Without a word, he took my hand and pulled me out onto the dance floor.

He leaped around, making me think of "Spill the Wine" by War—"an overfed, long-haired leaping gnome" because that's what this guy was.

When a slow song came on, he took me in his arms but shockingly didn't try anything.

He shouted into my ear, "You want to . . . ?"

"What?" I yelled.

"You want to . . . ?" He held out one hand palm up and then positioned his thumb and forefinger under his nose as if he were holding a straw and theatrically snorted.

Cocaine.

Yes, I definitely wanted cocaine.

I was already drunk and stoned, but I smiled and nodded. He grabbed my hand and we headed toward the door. I stumbled after him, his hand surprisingly large around mine as he pulled me outside to a yellow sports car, opened the passenger's side door, which lifted upward, and helped me in. He went around to the other side and got in himself.

I sank into the buttery leather seats and smelled money. I'd never been anywhere near anything this luxurious and expensive.

Who was this guy?

"What's your name?" I said.

"Hoover," he said with a smile and a wink.

He took a small mirror from the console, unfolded a tiny

envelope, and poured powder from it onto the mirror. He used an American Express platinum card to cut lines into the powder, periodically smiling over at me in the dark with his gleaming straight teeth. Then he withdrew a prerolled hundred dollar bill from behind his ear, twirled it in his fingers like a baton, and handed it to me. I felt a tingle of excitement as I clamped one nostril shut, stuck the bill up the other, and snorted a line.

It diffused into my brain as I snorted another line with the other nostril, then handed over the bill and leaned back in the soft seat. He slid the moon roof open, reached across me, and tripped my seat's recline button. I fell through the layers of night, my eyes rolled back, my body shuddering in silky, euphoric waves. I blinked, and then I watched the stars overhead reveal themselves one by one, coming into sharper focus until I could see minute details, rings and space dust and nebulae and supernovas.

"How you feel?" Hoover purred in my ear. I anticipated his hands on me but they never came.

"I feel sooooo good," I said. My own voice sounded too slow.

He reclined his seat too, and pointed at the sky. We said nothing as we watched it rotate around us. I had never felt so connected to the planet, to humanity, to God himself.

What the hell was this stuff?

About thirty minutes later Hoover closed the moon roof and brought my seat to its full upright and locked position.

"You gotta go now," Hoover said.

I raked my hair back and nonsensically said, "Me too."

"When will I see you next?" Hoover said.

"What's today?"

"It's Thursday."

"Tomorrow night," I said dreamily.

"See you then."

He chucked the tip of my nose, pulled me out of the car, and turned me toward the bar.

I floated back inside, and whatever that shit was, I wanted more, because I hadn't once thought about Nathan, or the trial, or my mother's upcoming reality show.

I wanted more. And I got more, much more.

But not from Hoover. What I couldn't have foreseen was that my mom would start dating him shortly after that night. She never asked him what he did for a living, what he did to have a fancy sports car and take her to nice restaurants and on tropical vacations. She was famously antidrug, but if drugs paid for all the luxuries in her life, so be it. She would just cover her eyes and act as if she didn't know.

I only found out later that it was heroin. So of course, I wanted my best friend to feel the same things I had. And she did.

Friday, June 24

RIGHT AFTER WAKING up, Nessa made a quick run to the grocery store. The sky hung oppressively close to the ground, with heavy, dark clouds bearing down like a steam press, threatening thunderstorms and even higher humidity.

By the time she returned home, the rain had blown in.

A blue sedan sat idling in front of the house.

What now?

Nessa parked the Pacifica in the garage and went in the back door. She heard the doorbell ring, missing the old happy Declan MacManus "Friends are here!" bark.

She'd had more strange visitors in the last four weeks than the entire time they'd lived in this house.

Nessa opened the front door to a middle-aged woman in a damp skirt and blouse with a disheveled bun, holding a dripping red umbrella over herself with one hand and a leather briefcase in the other.

"Mrs. Donati?"

"Yes," she said.

"I'm Shanae Klerkse from Child Protective Services."

"Child . . ."

"Protective Services," the woman said.

"How can I help you?" Nessa said. She briefly pretended Shanae Klerkse was here to interview her about Lauren, the mom who refused to use sunscreen and had no air-conditioning. But by now, Nessa knew better. This was about her.

"May I come in?" Shanae said.

"What is this regarding?" Nessa said.

"Well, Mrs. Donati, we received a phone call reporting that your home may be an unsafe environment for your three-year-old son."

"From whom?" Nessa said.

"It was an anonymous call."

"Of course it was," Nessa said.

"We are obligated by law to investigate every report. Is your son at home, Mrs. Donati? I'd like to interview him."

"Do you know American Sign Language?"

"No," Shanae said. "Is your son deaf?"

"No. He doesn't speak."

"Is he home?"

"Nope," Nessa said. "He's in Kansas City with his grand-parents."

"When will he return?"

"In a few days."

The rain fell heavier, and lightning flashed. The CPS case-worker flinched. "May I come in, Mrs. Donati?"

Nessa debated. It was common courtesy to ask someone in out of the rain, but what would this mean? Was it better to cooperate? Should she call a lawyer?

Another lightning strike followed by a quick explosion of thunder finally made Nessa motion Shanae inside. She had noth-ing to hide, of course, so she might as well get this over with.

"Thank you," her guest said, stepping inside and collapsing her umbrella.

"Would you like a bottle of water?" Nessa said. "I'm going to get one for myself."

"Sure," Shanae said.

"Why don't you take a seat in the living room, and I'll be right back."

Nessa grabbed two water bottles from the fridge, and won-dered if this would be seen as environmentally irresponsible, if this would count against her. Ridiculous thoughts for a ridiculous circumstance.

Back in the living room, Shanae sat on the wingback chair and was holding a clipboard and a pen on her lap. "What are you growing out back there?" She wrote on her clipboard while Nessa explained the hops-for-local-craft-brewers concept.

Nessa sat on the couch, cracked open her water bottle, and took a drink, watching the weather rampage out the window behind Shanae. Even though the sky was gloomy, there was still enough light behind her to make her interrogator's face hard to read as she was asked all the usual questions. Nessa tried her best not to answer tersely, sarcastically, or defensively.

"So you've taken Daltrey to the doctor about his speech delay."

"Yes," Nessa said. "Our pediatrician, Dr. Blatter, says it's nothing to worry about."

"Does he say what the cause might be?"

"Since *she's* not worried about it, we haven't discussed causes."

"Do you read to him? Do you work on ABCs with him?"

Nessa thought her head might pop off like a champagne cork. "Yes."

"You might want to have his hearing tested."

"We have," Nessa said. "Several times."

"And you'll want to start reading out loud to him on a regular basis."

Nessa just nodded.

Then came the really fun questions:

"Do you keep pornography in the home?"

"Do you drink? Use drugs?"

"Have many sexual partners?"

"None, since my husband left," Nessa said.

"How many abortions have you had?"

This one caught her off guard. How was this relevant? How was it anyone's business? And the wording of it was interesting. Not have you had *any* but how many? Nessa wondered if the questions were asked in a specific order to rile up the interviewee.

"None," Nessa said.

She couldn't see the expression on Shanae's face as she wrote down the answer, so Nessa impulsively rose and strode toward the window behind her, pulling the curtains closed and switching on the lamp to Shanae's left. Nessa turned toward the couch and her eyes lit on a lump between two of the magazines on the end table next to her bottle of water. White, oval, an inch wide.

China white heroin.

The sight paralyzed her, stopping her forward progress. Sweat immediately popped out on her forehead. The bag held a magnetic pull, and her eyes watered with the effort of not looking at it.

Shanae glanced up at Nessa and reacted to the expression of horror no doubt distorting her face. "Mrs. Donati? Are you all right?" She swiveled her head toward the end table.

Nessa threw herself to the ground, clutching her left calf. "Muscle cramp," she said, drawing Shanae's attention. How could she keep it there? And how could she get her out of the house?

Who knew what other goodies had been hidden around here for this person to find?

Nessa groaned loudly.

"Let me grab your water," Shanae said, rising, and Nessa screamed.

Shanae turned her attention back to Nessa.

"I know this is weird, but would you mind . . . massaging my leg?" Nessa said.

"All right," Shanae said. She lowered herself to the floor and tentatively rubbed Nessa's calf.

Nessa looked around for a heavy object to smash the caseworker's skull with. Would that be worse than Child Protective Services finding drugs in the house?

A deafening peal of thunder sounded right on top of a brilliant lightning flash and the lights brightened, then went out.

"Oh, that's better," Nessa said. She stood and walked to the end table. Nessa sat on it, hoping she wouldn't crush the glassine bag and send a burst of heroin powder into the air. With shaking hands, she picked up her water bottle and took a drink. "I think I'm okay. Thank you."

"You're welcome," Shanae said, rising and sitting on the chair.

The lights came back on.

"I just have a few more questions," the caseworker said.

"Okay," Nessa said, straightening her phony spasming leg. She felt as though she were sitting on a blazing coal, burning through her dress and flesh. It was all she could think of during the final questions, and she wasn't sure any of her answers were coherent. Finally, Shanae rose and turned toward the chair to pack up her questionnaire and clipboard. Nessa quickly pulled the top magazines over the glassine bag, which was intact, then turned back around.

Shanae was gazing at her, unmoving.

Nessa attempted a friendly smile.

"You probably need more potassium in your diet," Shanae said.

"Yes," Nessa said.

"I'll return when your son is here to interview him," Shanae said. "When do you expect him back?"

"On the thirtieth," Nessa said.

Shanae made a note of it on her clipboard. "I'll give you a call and let you know when I'm coming this time." She pulled back the curtains and looked out the window. "The rain's letting up," she said. "I better get out to my car before I'm stuck here overnight."

"Well, thank you," Nessa said, her desperately beating heart making her vision blur.

"Don't get up. I'll let myself out."

Nessa didn't move until she heard the sedan drive away. Then she peeped out the window to be sure Shanae was gone before lifting the magazines. The glassine bag flexed, seemed to come alive and stretch. Nessa picked it up and saw that it was stamped with a red sunflower.

In big cities, dealers proudly branded their wares. She was surprised this practice took place in small-town America too. But because of this, she could use the stamp, the brand, to try to find where the heroin had come from and who had purchased it.

Nessa took a photo of the glassine bag with her phone and flushed its contents down the toilet before she could think too much about it. She didn't want a repeat performance of Tuesday's near-disaster hypo breakdown. When that was done, she cut up the glassine bag and flushed the tiny pieces.

How long had that bag sat here, just waiting to be discovered? She'd faithfully gone over the security camera footage and there'd been no trespassers since the new security system.

It was time to find John. She was going to find him, and then she was going to kill him for bringing this shit into her house.

Chapter Nineteen

Saturday, June 25

SINCE DALTREY WAS gone, Isabeau was going out with friends to Aggieville the next evening. "Don't wait up for me," Isabeau told her.

Nessa wasn't sure she'd be home any earlier than Isabeau would. She had plans of her own.

When Nessa had caught John doing crack in their house, she'd known that somewhere was a card with his dealer's name and phone number on it. She'd searched his pants' pockets and found what she was looking for, holding on to the card like a souvenir, like a treasured memento. She even kept it in a special box with John's six-inch braid—the one she'd tossed into the Big Blue River—and the tickets from their first concert together: Rodrigo y Gabriela at Red Rocks.

Now she retrieved that card from the decorative box. The dealer's name was Tyler.

For the first time in a while, Nessa wasn't wearing long sleeves.

Today, the faint scars from her left-arm tattoo sleeve were exposed by the tank top she wore. Temporary brown dye covered her blond hair, and she hadn't straightened it but let it fall into natural waves. But her skull and crossbones nose stud took a few tries to get in since the hole had almost closed up.

After dressing, Nessa used smudgy black kohl liner around her eyes, then found Daltrey's Halloween face-paint crayons and sponged on some of the white base, mixing some green into it to make her look dope-sick. She also blacked out some of her back teeth and made fake sores on her arms and cheeks. The last part was the hardest—picking and biting at her fingernails until they were broken and gnarly and then digging her hands into the soil around her potted fern and getting the dirt deep under her fingernails.

The reflection in the mirror this time didn't look anything like her mom, but it wasn't an improvement. Nessa had transformed from country housewife into punk in under an hour.

The clock in the kitchen said it was eleven P.M., so Nessa left the house and drove to a Conoco station to use the pay phone there.

Her heart pounded as she walked toward the phone. She picked it up, inserted a quarter, and punched in the numbers on those old metal buttons.

"Yup," said a male voice.

"I need a quay," she said in a low voice, even though no one was around.

There was a pause. "Who is this?"

"Nessa Donati. John's wife."

Another pause.

"Meet me at the McDonald's on Sixth Street in JC," he said. "I'm in the blue Toyota."

The line went dead.

She thought about not going, but she had to find John and put a stop to all of this. If the cops weren't going to look for him, Nessa would have to do it.

She drove over to the McDonald's in Junction City and got there at eleven-thirty. The place was pretty lively, plenty of cars to get lost in. She drove past it, parked a block away, and walked the rest of the way. She saw lightning on the horizon and watched it illuminate the darkened street. What would she find when she got to Tyler?

These were familiar feelings. She remembered walking the LA streets in one of the seedier parts of town with Candy, looking to score. The sensation that someone would jump out of an alley and cut her followed her down those nasty, reeking streets. That was where she learned to look tough, look like you belonged in this world and the people who inhabited it would believe you.

She hoped that rule still held seven years later in this little town.

When she got to the McDonald's, she went and sat on the curb of the parking lot, pulled out her vapor pen, and smoked. She heard music coming out of some of the cars parked there and knew just to wait.

She waited for twenty-five minutes, watching cars go by, trying not to make eye contact with anyone, although she kept an eye out for the Toyota. She was about to give up hope when a blue Toyota pulled into the parking lot and slowed in front of her. The passenger's side window rolled down and she heard a voice but was unable to see the face it came from.

"You looking for someone?"

Nessa stood and walked purposefully toward the car, not bothering to bend over and peer in. She didn't want to look like a hooker to anyone who might be watching.

The dealer was not what she expected, although it made sense that Kansas drug dealers wouldn't resemble South Central dealers. This guy was a kid, maybe twenty-one. She'd be surprised if could grow a beard. If his balls had dropped yet.

"Hi, Tyler," she said.

"You want a cigarette?" he said to her.

She scratched at her arms and made herself shiver. She coughed. "I was hoping you'd say that."

He held the pack out to Nessa, and she hesitated only a minute before taking it and accepting a light. She drew the smoke into her lungs, sirens going off in her head at the unfiltered tar and nicotine blasting into her system. She coughed for real this time and for a moment she thought she was going to throw up. Just as she was able to get it under control, Nessa realized that it would have been a good thing to ralph right now—it would've sealed the deal and made her look even more like a junkie.

Tyler was driving them out of the lot now, and Nessa despaired of getting back to her car.

"You a cop?" he said. "You have to tell me if you are."

Nessa almost laughed and she would have if she hadn't been so scared. She couldn't believe that people believed this urban myth. Cops didn't have to identify themselves.

"I told you," she said, "I'm John's wife."

He looked at her sideways.

"I didn't know he was married."

She looked out the window and said, "I'm not surprised."

"Well, I was surprised when you called," he said. "I haven't seen John in a couple of weeks."

"Really?" she said. "How many weeks exactly?"

He stared at her. "I don't *exactly* write this stuff in my diary."

Nessa tried to do the math in her head, tried to think of when John would have planted the heroin in her house. Had it really been sitting there all that time? It didn't make any sense.

Goose bumps rose on her arms as she considered the possibilities.

Was John *not* doing crack? Was this some sort of setup?

The feeling that overcame her had a hallucinatory quality. She remembered when she was a child, long before drugs, when all of a sudden, for no reason, she'd have no idea what day it was, what season it was, how old she was. It would be as if she'd pierced the veil between this dimension and whatever lay just outside it. She had that feeling now.

"He must have jumped to one of my competitors," Tyler said, wistful.

Nessa shook off her déjà-whatever-it-was. Of course John was doing crack. She'd caught him *in flagrante delicto*. Of course he was.

Because she could not contemplate the alternative.

She focused on Tyler. "I was hoping you could tell me where I could find him."

"Nope."

"Can you give me contact information for your competitors?"

He gave her an incredulous look. "Seriously? I'm not Macy's in *Miracle on Thirty-Fourth Street*. I don't send dissatisfied customers to my competitors." He went on driving and then said, "So are you going to buy shit from me or what?"

"Actually," she said, "I'm looking for someone who sells this."

She held up her phone and the image of the glassine bag.

He pulled his hands off the wheel as if she'd just presented him with a fresh dog turd.

"Well, that explains it," he said, shaking his head. "I don't do that shit. John's moved on to the hard stuff."

"As opposed to crack," she said. "You can't be serious. Do you know who sells this brand?"

"I might," he said. "Let's go see if he's home."

"Great," she said.

"Sunflower," he said.

"Yeah."

He shook his head.

Tyler drove to a little yellow house that seemed to sag and stopped in front of it but didn't turn off the car.

"There you go," he said.

"Aren't you coming in too?"

"Fuck, no. I don't want anything to do with that shit."

This was not good. Nessa remembered the old days and the nonchalance with which she had approached apartments and abandoned parks in order to score dope. She hadn't had a son then. She'd had no reason to be afraid. Now she did. But she had to find John and she had to stop him.

"Could you call the guy to let him know I'm coming and that you, like, vouch for me?"

The guy sighed deeply and pulled out his phone and called. He squinted out the window at the house, which was dimly lit from the inside.

The phone rang several times.

Finally someone picked up. Nessa could hear the person on the other end of the line. His voice was gravelly.

"Yeah, hey," Tyler said. "I have a friend here who needs something. You think you could help her out?"

There was silence. Nessa figured the guy had nodded off or just wasn't interested in "helping."

"All right," the voice said. "Send her on over."

"We're out front. She's coming in now, so don't shoot."

"You're out front? Get the fuck out of here, man! You don't idle in front of a man's house!"

"Sorry. She's coming now." He clicked off his phone.

"Thanks, Tyler," Nessa said, feeling light-headed.

"Listen," he said. "You need to brace yourself. Don't stare at him. He hates it when people stare."

"Who does? What do you mean? Why would I stare?"

"Just do what I say. You'll see what I mean when you get in there. I have to go."

She got out of the car and dropped the cigarette to the ground before crushing it out. She made her way quickly up the walk, pulled back the screen door, and knocked lightly.

The front door opened and standing there was a woman in her fifties or sixties with long, thinning, oily hair, the color of peanut brittle. She wore wire-frame glasses and was shaped like a giant bowling ball with stick arms and legs.

Nessa had thought the person on the phone was a man, with that low voice.

"You Tyler's friend?" she said. Not in the voice Nessa had heard on the phone.

"Yeah," Nessa said.

"Well, come on in, you're letting all the cool out."

Nessa stepped inside and the dark smells of unwashed bodies in the Kansas heat combined with tobacco smoke and rotten food to give the place a very specific ambiance. The bacteria colony in this place could take over the world.

Nessa rubbed her arms.

"You look in bad shape," the woman said, putting her icy, spidery hands on Nessa's shoulders and shaking her a little bit. Then she laughed, her voice cracking and hissing thanks to a thirty-year three-pack-a-day habit.

The only light in the living room was a flat-screen TV. A guy sat in a chair staring at it, watching an infomercial, his right knee drawn up under his chin, rocking like a mental patient. He didn't acknowledge Nessa or even seem to notice she'd entered.

Her guide made a forward motion with her hand, and Nessa followed her into the kitchen.

Two men sat at the table playing cards, an overflowing ashtray in front of them, beer cans and a half-empty bottle of whiskey surrounding it. One of the men sat facing the doorway, the other opposite him. He didn't look around when she entered.

"You want a beer?" the old lady said.

She thought about making some excuse, saying she was allergic to hops or something like that, but didn't want to make them suspicious. "Sure."

The woman pulled a Pabst Blue Ribbon out of the filthy refrigerator and handed it to her. What do you know. PBR, the choice of drug dealers and hipsters everywhere. Otto would be impressed. As much as a hipster can be impressed anyway. She got a kick out of thinking about Otto in a place like this. He'd shit himself.

She popped open the can and took a long swallow. It tasted so good and went down so smooth she couldn't help but think, *It wouldn't be so bad to go back to this.*

The man facing her stuck his cigarette between his teeth and held out his right hand to her. "I'm Allen," he said in the voice Nessa recognized from Tyler's phone call. She tentatively reached for his hand and he yanked her forward and spun her toward his card partner. "And this here's Smearface."

She stifled a scream as Allen laughed uproariously.

"What, you never saw someone with a shot-off face before?"

"Allen," the old lady said. "Cut it out."

The bottom half of Smearface's face was sheared off, his nose just two slits in his head like Voldemort. He wore mirrored sunglasses and he whistled and wheezed when he breathed.

"Hi," he said, and Nessa saw that his tongue was about half the size it should be with few teeth. It was like looking at a horrible Halloween mask.

Allen turned her loose, and she staggered to the counter and leaned against it, her arms crossed tight against her stomach. She was afraid she was going to throw up.

"So, yeah," Allen said to Smearface, "so this security guard at the school, he was born with a fucked up hand, and they had to amputate it up to the elbow, and he wore his sleeve pinned up like this, and so we called him the long arm of the law."

Smearface laughed, or at least she thought he did—the grunts and snuffling must have meant amusement. "Long arm of the law!" he repeated. He could speak incredibly well, although his missing nose provided a nasal quality to his speech.

Just then, Allen brought his booted feet down on the ground

hard and started. "Did you hear that?" He looked at Nessa. "You heard it, right?"

She shook her head.

He jumped to his feet and knocked over his chair, pulling a shotgun off the top of the refrigerator. He went to the window and looked out, the shotgun dangling at his side. Nessa's heart beat like a rodent's, fast and shallow.

"Those fuckers come around here again," Allen said, "that's it. I'm gonna blow a hole in them."

He sat back down with the shotgun across his lap.

"Mom, would you look out front?"

The old lady appeared in the doorway with a matching shotgun. "Can't see anything," she said.

So it was a family business.

"Look again!"

"Hey," Nessa said.

All three of them turned their paranoid gazes to her.

"Are you the guys who sell sunflower?"

They looked at each other.

She reached for her phone and they pointed their guns at her.

"Just getting my phone," she said, digging in her pocket with her right while holding her left aloft. She thought she might faint. With shaking hands, she scrolled to the photo of the glassine bag.

"This?" she said. She held it in front of Allen's face, then Smearface's.

"Yeah," Allen said.

But Smearface said, "Let me see that."

Nessa froze, couldn't make herself hand it over.

He snapped his fingers and she gave it to him. He pinched the screen outward, enlarging the image.

"Did you sell to a guy named John?"

They looked at each other.

"John," Smearface said.

"I know lots of Johns," the other said.

"Wouldn't have been one of your regulars. He's more of a rock man. He's about five-ten, dark brown hair and blue eyes."

"Yeah, we had a guy—remember the guy like five days ago, maybe a week? Came in here acting all squirrely?"

"Beard?" Smearface asked her.

Well, he hadn't had one when she'd thrown him out but he'd have no reason to shave now.

"Can I show you a picture of him?" She held out her hand. Smearface handed her the phone, and she scrolled through the photos until she found one of John and Daltrey, then held it in front of their bloodshot eyes.

"Is that the squirrelly guy?"

Smearface held up a thumb over the lower half of John's face. "Could be him, I guess."

Allen nodded, losing interest.

"What did you mean by 'acting squirrelly'?" she asked.

The guys looked at each other, suspicious, the default setting of most dope dealers.

"You know, squirrely," Allen said. "You say he was more of a rock man, and I can see that. He was really jumpy, you know. Didn't look like someone who would be interested in sunflower, unless he's a Belushi."

She wasn't about to explain that he hadn't been buying it for himself. "So you remember him. And this was about a week ago?"

They both nodded enthusiastically.

She put the phone back in her pocket, and finished off her beer. "Well, thanks," she said, turning to go. Mom blocked the doorway out of the kitchen.

"You're not going to make a purchase?"

Nessa stammered. "No. I just wanted to find out if John had been here. I'm trying to find him."

"You drank one of our beers."

"Yeah," she said. "Thanks." Nessa tried to get around Mom, but she stuck out a bony arm and caught Nessa by the elbow.

"That's not how we do things around here."

All the blood in Nessa's body drained to her feet, making her feel like she might just lift off of the ground.

"What do you mean?" her voice came out as a squeak.

"You come in here, don't make a purchase, we might think you're an informant or something like that," Mom said. "Might be wearing a wire."

She grabbed the front of Nessa's tank and pulled. Nessa grabbed her wrists, but the old lady was shockingly strong and managed to use both hands to rip Nessa's tank right in two.

"No wire," Mom said, turning her toward the men. Nessa tried to cover herself with her arms, but Mom held her fast.

"Might be somewhere else," Allen said with a gleam in his eye.

"Maybe you ought to look," Mom said. "Put your wallet on the table. Keys, phone, everything you got. Need to make sure you don't have pepper spray or some damn thing."

"Please," Nessa said. "Don't."

"On the table," Mom repeated.

Nessa emptied her pockets, and Smearface grabbed up the wallet while Allen rose from his chair, licking his lips and fingering his belt buckle.

Oh, shit.

While Mom kept Nessa's elbows pinned together behind her back, Allen got on his knees in front of Nessa and started to unbuckle her belt. She wanted to knee him in the face, but there were two shotguns in the room, and who knew how many other weapons were within arm's reach.

"What have we got here," Smearface said, opening Nessa's wallet. "Sixty-seven bucks cash."

Allen looked up into her face as he slowly unbuttoned her Levi's.

Nessa began hyperventilating.

"Platinum Amex," Smearface said. "Wow. How many junkies you know got that?"

Allen slid her jeans off her hips.

"Please," she said. She turned her head and tried to catch the old woman's eye but she was having none of that.

"Kansas state driver's license. 'Donati, Nessa.' Business card . . ."

Allen rubbed his palms together before reaching inside her pant legs to feel her calves and then slowly travel up to her thighs and in between her legs. His other hand snaked up to peel her panties off.

"Altair Satellite Radio?" Smearface said, reading the card. "You're—holy shit. You're Nessa of *Unknown Legends*!"

Allen froze, his index finger hooked over the elastic band of Nessa's underwear, and turned his head toward his buddy. "Are you shitting me?" Then he looked up at her. "Is that you?"

She couldn't decide which would be worse for her. Maybe they hated the show. Maybe they thought she was a pompous blowhard or a know-nothing. Maybe they were Beatles fans.

But she said, "Yes. That's me."

Allen rocked back on his heels and slapped his thighs. "This is unreal. We listen to your show every week."

Mom loosened her grip on Nessa, who pitched forward onto her knees, painfully. Then she pulled up her underwear.

"I am so sorry," Allen said, hoisting her from the floor and yanking her pants up, which hurt. Mom let go of her. She buttoned her jeans, buckled her belt, and swallowed back the vomit that was crawling up her throat.

"Mom, get her a shirt, will you?" Allen said. "And make sure it's clean."

Mom left the room, and Nessa pulled the remnants of her tank together.

"I can't believe it," Smearface said. "It's really you."

"It's really me," she said, blood finally pumping through her body. She had been convinced just moments ago that it never would again.

Mom appeared in the doorway with an oversized T-shirt that looked like it was from the eighties.

"Not that one, Mom," Allen said.

She handed it wordlessly to Nessa, who held it up and looked at it. *Harley's Best, Fuck the Rest*, it said. She pulled the shirt on over her head.

"Let us make it up to you," Smearface said. "We can give you a dose for free, but you gotta shoot it here."

God grant me the serenity to accept the things I cannot change, to change the things I can, and the wisdom to know the difference.

She pictured Daltrey's face.

"No, thanks," she said. "Can you give me a ride to the McDonald's? I left my car over there."

Allen drove her and talked the whole way about his favorite band. The Beatles. She couldn't tell if he was being ironic or not, but thought he probably didn't have the brain power to pull it off. When he pulled up to the McDonald's, he said, "Hey, that guy you're looking for—your husband or whatever? Does he have, like, weird eyes? Different eyes?"

"When he's on crack, he definitely has weird eyes," Nessa said, remembering the way his eyelids seemed to disappear when he was high. The bloodshot sclera had shone all the way around the iris, giving him a demented appearance.

"Yup. That was him." Allen scratched his head.

"If John gets in touch with you again, could you call me during my radio show?"

"Sure," he said, looking her up and down. "You want to go out sometime?"

"Still married," she said, trying to keep her face from contorting with disgust. "But thanks."

Nessa walked away from the car. She now had the locksmith and the dealer on the lookout for her. Not a bad night's work.

Then she found a bush and threw up her dinner. She'd been sober six years, six months, and six days. The PBR wasn't quite as smooth coming back up as it was going down.

Chapter Twenty

WHEN NESSA PARKED her car in the garage at one-fifteen, Isabeau came charging out of the back door and stood with her arms crossed over her chest until Nessa closed up the garage.

"Where the hell have you been?" Isabeau said.

"Well, I—"

"I've been worried sick! I tried to call you, text you, everything but Pony Express! Where were you?"

Nessa held her hands up in front of her. She felt terrible for upsetting her nanny. "Take it easy, Isabeau."

"*You* take it easy! Where. The hell. Were you?"

She looked into Isabeau's sweet face, this face that was filled with pain and anxiety—that Nessa had caused. And not just by worrying her. By keeping her at arm's length.

Isabeau didn't want anything from her. She truly cared about Nessa.

Nessa felt a surge of protectiveness and affection.

"It's a long story. Let's go inside."

Once they got into the living room, into the light, Isabeau's jaw went slack.

"What happened to your face?"

Nessa's hands flew up to her cheeks and she remembered her druggie stage makeup. "I needed to make myself look like a junkie."

"What?" Isabeau was incredulous.

"Sit down," Nessa said.

Isabeau sat rigid on the couch, her expression demanding an explanation. Nessa told her all about her evening, leaving nothing out, including the visit from Child Protective Services the day before, which Isabeau had missed.

"Wow!" Isabeau said. "I can't believe you did that. I would have gone with you. It would have been safer."

"Well, it's done now, and I have confirmation that it was John who bought the heroin."

Isabeau pressed a finger to her lips and shook her head, staring off at nothing. Then she looked over at Nessa. "Hey," she said. "I just realized that you're not wearing long sleeves. You always wear long sleeves."

Nessa looked into Isabeau's honest eyes and thought of everything Isabeau had done for her. Loved Daltrey like family. Saved Nessa from the rapist. Helped set up the security system. Did absolutely anything Nessa asked. Held nothing back, ever.

Isabeau was the real thing. A friend. What might it be like to open up to another human being? What would it be like to have a real friend? But what if Isabeau betrayed her somehow? Nessa could never know for sure that she wouldn't. That was the chance you had to take. With trepidation, Nessa held her breath, braced herself, and jumped off the cliff.

"It's to cover up my lasered-off tattoos," Nessa said.

"It looks like you had a full sleeve on here," Isabeau said.

"I did," Nessa said.

"I'm sorry, but I'm a little drunk." Isabeau looked at Nessa guiltily. "It must be hard to be around people who drink, huh?"

"No," Nessa said, melting back into the couch, weariness overtaking her. "Booze was never my real problem."

"What do you mean?"

Nessa hadn't even told Marlon about this. But a weird thing had happened tonight. She'd tracked down John's dealers and lived through it. She'd done something courageous, though stupid, and it made her feel brave.

"I mean it was just a gateway drug for me," Nessa said. "I could kind of take it or leave it—no addiction there. It just led to other things."

"So—wait. You're not an addict?"

"I didn't say that."

"Crack?" Isabeau said.

"Oh, hells no," Nessa said. She gulped. If she let this out now, there was no taking it back. But she was so exhausted from trying to hold up this wall, this wall that threatened to flatten her, that had nearly stolen her humanity.

"It was heroin."

Isabeau looked shocked, and her eyes filled with tears. "Oh, Nessa," she said.

"That's why I got these tattoos here." Nessa pointed to where the blue stars of the constellation Phoenix used to be tattooed. "To cover my tracks."

"That's intense," Isabeau said. "How long ago was that?"

"A lifetime ago," Nessa said, imagining the girl she used to be, the one who took any drug anyone handed her, who would never get married, let alone have children. The one who busted headlong into any and all situations like a blind girl crashing into a plate-glass window with zero regard for who got hurt.

Nowadays, she saw women writing letters online to their younger selves to dispense imaginary advice.

Dear me, she would write. *Don't drink and drive. Don't try to grow up so fast. Don't believe you're invincible, because you're not. Don't confuse careless with cool.*

Don't go to that party.

Isabeau scooted closer and looked at Nessa's left arm, tracing the remnants with her finger. Nessa held still, allowing her to puzzle out the faint markings, their secrets, their codes, the story of Nessa's life in ink.

"Okay," she said. "You have to tell me what all the tattoos were, because knowing you, there's a story behind every one."

Knowing you. This phrase struck Nessa because Isabeau was the first person since John who could honestly say that, at least to a limited extent. Nessa realized the fact that Isabeau had been drinking was the only reason she was emboldened enough to ask such personal questions.

"You can still see parts of them," Nessa said. She pointed to the top of her shoulder, where the light green pigments of a flower stem were still visible. "That was a rose, my favorite flower," she said.

"This one here," Nessa said, pointing at the faded yellow markings below the rose, "was two cave women sitting on thrones holding stone scepters."

"Why?" Isabeau said. "What did it mean?"

"It was the name of my favorite band in high school."

Isabeau thought. "Hanson?" she said, and had a little giggle fit.

"How could that possibly mean Hanson?" Nessa said, laughing.

"I don't know. I'm not the music person you are."

"It's Queens of the Stone Age," she said.

Isabeau pointed to Nessa's arm again. "This one looks like it was graffiti."

"Right," Nessa said. "That was under a bridge I used to live near."

"What did it say?"

"Who knows? It was just gobbledygook, like other taggers. It was just to remind me . . ."

"Remind you of what?"

"Of how far I've come, and how I'm never going back."

"Is that why you tried to have the other ones removed?"

"What do you mean?"

"Because you're not that girl anymore."

Wow. That was more insightful than Isabeau could ever know.

Nessa took a deep breath, then held her left arm out so that Isabeau could see the tattoos she'd kept. In purple script, *Candy* with two dates side by side.

"What does this mean? Who's Candy?"

Nessa couldn't speak as Isabeau's gaze traveled from the tattoo to Nessa's eyes, which were filling with tears. "Are those dates?" Isabeau said. "Like a tombstone?"

Nessa laid her head back on the couch cushion and closed her eyes. Exactly like a tombstone. If Candy could have known that Nessa would be carrying this sack full of guilt with her wherever she went, she would've lightly slapped Nessa, like she always had whenever Nessa was acting stupid. Somehow, Nessa hadn't been able to stop Candy from doing it, hadn't been able to help laughing. She'd loved and hated it.

"Oh," Isabeau said. "She was your best friend, wasn't she? The one you mentioned?"

"Yes," Nessa said.

"She died seven years ago," Isabeau said, looking at the date. "I'm so sorry."

"Things happen to you," Nessa said, opening her eyes and looking at Isabeau. "And there's nothing you can do about it. You can't go back. You can't change it."

Isabeau hugged her, and Nessa let her. "I'm sorry," she said again.

Isabeau looked closely at the remnants of the script tattoo below that one. "The Glimmer Twins," she read aloud.

"Candy and I got matching tattoos, same place, same size," Nessa said, wiping her eyes.

"And what's this date here?"

"My anniversary."

"I thought you and John were only married five years ago."

"We were. It's my sober anniversary." In spite of everything, Nessa was proud of this one. She'd made her way out. Stayed sober, no matter how much stress she was under.

Isabeau stared. "Hey. That's the same date that Candy died."

"I went cold turkey," Nessa said, shivering in remembrance. "The absolute worst. Worse than childbirth, but you get a prize at the end of both."

"Oh," Isabeau said, but didn't ask any more about it.

They sat in companionable silence for a bit, then Isabeau said, "That heroin confession was a pretty big one, so I'm going to tell you my big secret."

"You don't have to do that," Nessa said, not sure she wanted to hear it. Being entrusted with other people's secrets carried a heavy price, one she wasn't sure she was ready to pay.

"But that's what friends do," Isabeau said. "Right?"

Nessa was humbled by this. She nodded.

"When I was in high school," she said, "I had an affair with my dad's best friend."

"That's awful," Nessa said.

"I know," Isabeau said. "I've never been able to forgive myself for it."

Nessa was horrified at that misinterpretation of her comment. "Not awful of you. Awful *for* you. You were a kid. It's the guy who should be shot. It's called statutory rape."

"His name was Dusty Matthiasen. I wrote about him in my diary, and looking back, I really think I wanted my mom to find it and read it. I think I wanted her to stop it. I so wish she would have."

"I had just the opposite problem," Nessa said.

"What do you mean?"

"My mom snooped through everything of mine, from the time I was little. No privacy at all. But really, that wasn't the worst of it. It was the reason she did it."

"What do you mean?" Isabeau said again.

Nessa thought for a moment. She'd never actually put this into words, and it was a revelation. "I wrote about everything in my diary—sex, drugs, shoplifting—all kinds of stuff. But that wasn't what bothered her. No. She wasn't snooping to find out what I was up to. She was snooping to see what I was saying about her. What I thought about her."

"That is bizarre."

"Isn't it?"

"I even wrote about a suicide attempt," Nessa said. "Another thing Marlon and I have in common."

"Marlon tried to commit suicide? I thought he loved himself too much!"

Nessa covered her mouth with her hand. Oh, this was bad. She had just broken the cardinal twelve-step rule. What's said in confidence stays in confidence, and she'd just tossed out this information as if she were disclosing his favorite ice cream flavor.

"Oh, shit," she said. "I assumed you knew. I don't know why I assumed that. I'm sorry I dumped that on you."

Isabeau made a locking motion in front of her mouth and pantomimed throwing away the key. "I'd never hurt him. He's been such a great mentor to me."

"Me too," Nessa said.

A low moan sounded, making her jump. "What was that?" Her heart was racing again. She realized it was the wind outside.

Isabeau looked up at the ceiling. "Ghosts," she said, raising her eyebrows up and down.

"Or is it skeletons in the closet?" Nessa said.

The wind suddenly whipped up and lightning flashed outside the windows. "Storm's a-comin'," Isabeau said as the thunder boomed. "Supposed to get, like, two inches of rain and heavy winds." She stretched. "So how did you and Marlon meet?"

"Through AA, of course," Nessa said.

Isabeau grimaced.

"You didn't know that either," Nessa said.

Isabeau shook her head.

"Oh, shit. I have such a big mouth."

And this was why she shouldn't have friends—getting close to people produced pain. But then again, she'd experienced pain in her loneliness. Sitting here with Isabeau, sharing stories, the pain of the last few weeks seemed to lessen a little.

"No, you don't," Isabeau said. "This is the most I've ever heard out of you." They sat in silence for a moment. "So how does a girl get hooked on heroin anyway?"

"It's a long story."

"I'm not going anywhere."

Nessa looked at her. *This is what friends do.* So she told Isabeau all about it.

"So you thought you were doing coke," Isabeau said.

"Yeah," Nessa said. "And H was so great, I just had to turn my best friend on to it too." She gestured to her constellation tattoo and said, "Obviously we started shooting it. Stupid. Really stupid. And yes. I started turning tricks to support my habit."

The judgment, the disengagement, the revulsion she feared seeing on Isabeau's face failed to materialize. The tightness in Nessa's chest loosened further.

Isabeau leaned her head back against the couch and gave Nessa a sorrowful smile. "I'm sorry you had to go through all that."

"I'm sorry your dad's best friend was a rapey douchebag."

"I'm sorry your best friend died. That's never happened to me. I can't even imagine."

She probably couldn't imagine causing a friend's death either.

Chapter Twenty-One

Sunday, June 26

THE NEXT MORNING, Nessa called Lauren's husband, Mac. They'd only spoken in person before, when she'd drop Daltrey off to play with Tosh and Ziggy, so he sounded surprised to hear from her.

"I wonder if you can track some IP addresses for me." She resisted offering to pay for his time. "I have a very persistent troll on my blog who's made some nasty comments."

"Some reason you think the guy's local?"

"Possibly," she said. "So you can trace an IP address? Find out where it originates?"

"Sure," he said. "And it's not even illegal. Why don't you email me a list of the IPs and I should be able to pinpoint the basic location within a mile or so, unless he's using proxies."

"Thank you, Mac," Nessa said.

He gave her his email address and said he'd get back to her as soon as he could. She hung up and emailed him Isabeau's spreadsheet of IP addresses.

Tuesday, June 28

NESSA TURNED OFF her alarm for the morning after her Monday night shift. Otto had been unusually cooperative and helpful, which made her suspicious. But she was too bone-weary to think too much about it. It was all she could do to get through the shift.

Daltrey wasn't coming home until Thursday, the same day as Isabeau. Nessa felt like part of her had been missing for the past week, and she couldn't wait to see him. And who knew? Maybe Linda really would have gotten him to talk.

Nessa went upstairs to change Daltrey's bedsheets and lingered at the bookcase by all the little people treasures John had hidden for their son, picking them up one by one. She had the urge to smash them all, to destroy any good feelings she had left for her sick, increasingly disturbed husband. But if the treasures disappeared, it would devastate Daltrey and wouldn't do her any good.

As she walked downstairs, her phone pinged. It was a text from Mac.

Found the origin of the IP address. There are actually two of them. Manhattan Public Library and the Hilton Garden Inn down on Third Street.

Nessa stared at her phone. John was staying at the Hilton Garden Inn? She thought again about what Mac had said, wondering if a crack user could do all the things her troll had done. And if he could, where had he gotten the money to stay in the Garden Inn? She hoped she was going to find out in less than an hour. She grabbed her purse and drove to the hotel, where she parked on the street. When she got out of the Pacifica, she had to stop on the sidewalk to get it together. The most bizarre thoughts swam through her brain.

How do I look? Do I look good?

What difference did it make? Nessa had more important things to worry about than her appearance.

She strode into the hotel and up to the front desk. "Can you tell me if a John Donati is registered here?"

The clerk typed into her computer. "No, ma'am," she said. "No one by that name."

Nessa pulled up the photos of John on her phone. "Maybe you've seen this man?" she said.

The clerk shook her head.

"He doesn't look familiar to me," she said.

"Thanks."

She went to the concierge desk and asked the two women there if they'd seen him. They had not. She repeated the same rigama-role in the restaurant and the bar. No one had seen him. After walking the halls of the hotel, looking around and finding nothing, she drove over to the library and repeated the whole process. No one recognized the photos, but how closely did anyone look at the shadows of humans who passed in and out of their lives on a daily basis? Still, it was frustrating. She'd thought that finding the IP addresses meant she would be able to confront John, but she felt like she was chasing a ghost.

As she headed for the door, she heard someone call her name. She turned and saw a familiar face, a man with two elementary school girls in tow. It was Kevin, her ex-producer. And these must be the kids he wanted to spend his evenings with.

"Hi, Kevin," she said. "How's it going?"

"Great," he said. "Girls, this is Nessa Donati. We work to-gether."

They waved uninterestedly, clasping books to their chests.

"We *used* to work together," Nessa said. "So what did Otto offer you to cover for him the other night? If I know him, he didn't actually offer anything."

Kevin looked confused. "Cover for Otto? When?"

"Thursday before last, I think."

"Otto didn't call me to cover for him," Kevin said.

"Dad," one of the girls said.

"Just a minute, honey," Kevin said, then turned his attention back to Nessa. "You mean he didn't show up for work?"

"No," Nessa said, confused herself. "He said . . ." Now she couldn't remember—had Otto actually said that Kevin couldn't come or . . .

"Well," Kevin said, "I'm going to check his time card, because if he didn't work when he said he did, then—"

"I think it was just a misunderstanding," Nessa said. But was it? Or had Otto left her at the station alone on purpose?

DRIVING HOME, NESSA tried to put Otto together with the information she had. Yes, Otto was jealous. Yes, he was a whiny hipster. But it just didn't fit.

When she got home, a police car was parked in front of her house. This was beginning to be a regular occurrence. Nessa parked in the garage, dread building up in her stomach, and went in the back door. The doorbell rang, and Nessa opened the door to Detective Treloar, looking grave and apologetic.

They must have lifted some of her fingerprints from the truck and run them through NCIC. They knew who she really was, what she had done. She was about to be arrested.

Her throat started to close up. But she walked out the front door and met Treloar on the front porch anyway.

"Detective," Nessa said, crossing her arms tight over her chest. "How are you?"

"Mrs. Donati," Treloar said. "May I come in? There are some things I'd like to discuss with you."

So this wasn't an arrest house call. This was something else.

"Please," she said, mirroring his manners. "Come in."

They went into the living room. She sat in the wingback chair and Treloar sat on the couch.

"I'm here to give you some news," he said. "We've recovered a body from Tuttle Creek Lake that matches the description of your husband."

Nessa doubled over. It was as if he'd just pitched a brick into her midsection, knocking the air out of her.

John couldn't be dead. He was too real. His imprint on her life and the world was too deep, too DNA-altering. She knew that other widows—ex-widows? What would she call herself?— probably had that same phantom limb feeling, that itch that couldn't be scratched because it was separated from her but still somehow connected, through fiber and sinew, soul and spirit, body and bone.

She stood, trying to remember how to inhale, then found herself walking in a tight circle. She wanted Treloar to reach out with a comforting hand so she could break the bones in his fingers and then tear his eyes from their sockets. She was desperate to inflict pain both on someone else and on herself, because if she let her brain wrap around the thought it was circling, she would fall down a hole and never stop falling.

As if thought caused action, she dropped to the ground, her head smacking the coffee table, the exquisite agony of it giving expression to what she couldn't put into words.

She rose to her hands and knees and smashed her head into the coffee table again.

Treloar's hands were on her shoulders, struggling to restrain her, to keep her from crushing her own skull like a melon.

John was dead, and now knowing this, she was dead too. He'd been pulled from the lake, but she was still down there, tangled in the trees beneath the surface of the water by the cove. And she'd never surface again.

It was as if she'd always known he was dead, since the beginning, and all her railing and fist shaking at him and his imagined abuse of her had only served to beat back the truth, to delay her recognition of the fact that she couldn't live without him.

She couldn't live.

She couldn't, didn't want to, wanted to shut her eyes and sink beneath the surface of the water forever.

"Mrs. Donati," Treloar said from a far distance, from the other side of a chasm that had opened up in the world and that she'd never be able to cross again.

What seemed to be many hours later but was probably only minutes, Nessa reentered her body. Her head pulsated and she came to herself in the middle of whatever Treloar had been saying while she'd been away.

"The storm on Saturday night knocked a couple of the tethered boats loose," he said, "and they were just trashed over in the cove. The wind was so strong it must have shoved the boats into those submerged trees and actually broken some of the branches, because the body floated up to the surface. He must have been trapped."

She took a deep breath. She was coming out of an acid trip, the worst one imaginable. And she was the soccer mom again, composed, calm, normal.

Sweet denial blossomed in her head. It wasn't John.

She gazed at Treloar, feeling a detached sense of pity for him. "So you're saying that John is dead," she said, and was overcome with the urge to laugh. Poor guy. He just didn't know any better.

"If it's him, then yes," Treloar said. "Now, it's procedure to request that a family member view a photo of the deceased for identification purposes, but the . . . body has been in the water for quite a while, so it's unrecognizable."

She further came back to herself, the impulse to laugh extinguished. "Was he . . . shot?"

His eyes ticked away from her. "An autopsy is being performed right now. We should know the cause of death soon. We'll need Mr. Donati's dental records."

"You have DNA though, right?" Nessa said.

"That's right, but it takes much longer. If we got his dental records, it would speed things up considerably."

She nodded, trying to breathe, her hand pressed against her chest to prevent her heart from bursting through her skin.

"Can you call today and get those records couriered over to us?"

"Yes," she finally said.

Once again, her worldview had shifted. Once again, she was having to adjust to a new reality. How many times could a person do this without losing her fucking mind?

"Mrs. Donati," Treloar said. "I need to let you know that this is being treated as a homicide. I know that's no surprise, but you're most likely going to be arrested. Probably on Friday."

The bottom dropped out of her stomach. "Are you supposed to be telling me this?"

"No," he said, looking away from her. "But you've been through a lot lately, and I wanted to make sure you had the chance to make arrangements for your son before it happens. Do you understand what I'm telling you?"

She nodded. "Thank you, Detective."

"Do you have an attorney?"

"No. But I'll get one."

Treloar stood to leave.

Nessa stood also and swayed on her feet. She grabbed hold of the chair arm to steady herself. The detective made a move toward her and she said, "I'm fine."

And her brain returned to normal, just as if the previous minutes hadn't happened.

Had John been shot? With her gun?

She was almost certain that he had been.

But by whom?

Back to wondering, puzzling, but with a difference. Nothing mattered anymore. Again, that detached, floating feeling, of going through motions that signified nothing.

As soon as Treloar's car drove away, Nessa got on the phone to the dentist and ordered his records to be sent to the Riley County Sheriff's Office.

Then she sat in the wingback chair and stared at nothing.

Whoever you are, she thought, *you win.*

WHEN SHE AWOKE, she didn't know where she was. The house was dark and silent, and her head ached, which brought back memories of Treloar's visit. She flicked on the lamp, sending spears of pain through her head.

John was dead.

It was now a fact, etched in granite.

How much time had passed? She looked at her phone and saw

that it was eleven-thirty P.M. She had to talk to someone, so she dialed Marlon.

"I have some news," she said. "The detective came here earlier to tell me—"

"Did you talk to John about me?" He said it as if he'd been waiting for her to call, waiting to bark out this question.

Confused, she looked at her phone to make sure she'd dialed the right number. "Marlon?"

"Did you?" His accusatory inflection scared her.

"I'm sorry, I just woke up," she said slowly. "Of course I did. I always told him about the insights you gave me and how many times you saved me from—"

"Because I got a call this afternoon from a reporter for the K-State campus newspaper wanting to write a story about my suicide attempt back in 2002, and how I overcame my substance abuse problems with the help of Alcoholics Anonymous."

This shocked her out of her stupor. Why did he think she'd called the reporter? "I don't think I ever—I can't be the only person who—"

"*Anonymous.* It's right in the name. Alcoholics *Anonymous.* It's supposed to be anonymous. You get that, right?"

"Of course I—"

"The reporter said it would be nice to get a comment from me, but she's running the story regardless."

Nessa tried to think. Had she ever told John this story?

John.

She was certain she hadn't.

John's dead.

But even if she had, why would John call the student newspaper about it?

"Marlon, John's—"

"She received an email from NessaDonati@gmail.com."

"That's not my email address, Marlon. You know that."

"I know. It's John. But you told him. You broke a confidence."

"But John's . . ." Nessa trailed off, shaky. "I don't think I did. It must be someone else."

"It can't be," he said. "Because you're the only one around here that I told."

This stunned her. Why had he told her, of all people?

"And what about those other things," Marlon said. "The things I've read in the comments on your blog recently?"

"I need to tell you—"

"Prostitution. Auto theft." He paused meaningfully. "Heroin."

He couldn't hear her. Maybe she really was already a ghost.

So she didn't say anything.

"Are you a heroin addict?"

She hesitated. "I was, yes."

"It's never *was*, and you know it," he said. "Once an addict, always an addict. You're only in recovery. You're not cured."

She knew her lines. She'd go ahead and say them, because nothing mattered anymore. "I'll never use again."

"It's that kind of overconfidence that will make you slip and fall. That's how it happened for me."

"I'll never use again," she repeated.

"Good God. You sound like you're high right now. Since you can't even be honest with yourself, I know you *will* use again. This program only works with complete honesty. You know that."

A little spark bubbled up, a hint of her former self. Maybe she could still pretend to be alive. "It's semantics. What difference does it make what I call myself?"

"It does make a difference. If you say you're an alcoholic when you're a fucking heroin addict that makes you a liar. I told you everything. And you told me nothing."

She couldn't speak.

"Step number four: 'Make a searching and fearless moral inventory of ourselves. This step requires self-examination that can be uncomfortable, but honesty is *essential* in this process.' Honesty is essential, Nessa."

"I know," she said.

"Step number five: 'Admit to God, to ourselves, and to another human being the exact nature of our wrongs.' "

It all flooded in. Nessa began to cry silently.

"Have you done that?"

She couldn't answer out loud. No, she hadn't.

But it didn't matter.

"Well, you haven't done it with me. Until you do, Nessa, we have nothing more to say to each other."

He hung up.

Yes. Perfect. This was right. It was all being taken away.

But not by John, because John was dead.

Something rose in her gut: anger. And it began to outweigh the nothing that had hijacked her psyche.

Whoever was doing this was not going to take one more thing away from her. Not one more person. She had to make this right, because she didn't want to live without Marlon.

Not one more.

She had to fix this. Right now.

She ran out of the house and across the yard to the garage. In the Pacifica, she drove toward town, her heart and head pounding, and played "Use Once and Destroy" by Hole at top volume, screaming along with Courtney Love, fierce and furious, even though it felt like her head would shatter.

It was nearly midnight, and Marlon's street was dark and quiet. Too bad. She strode up to his door and rang the bell. No answer. She rang it again. Nothing.

She went around to the living room window and looked in, her hands cupped around her face. It was too dark to see anything. She went back to the door and rang the doorbell four more times, then knocked on the door.

"Marlon! I know you're in there. I'm going to keep ringing and pounding until you let me in or until the police get here, whichever comes first. Open the door! Marlon!"

When he still didn't open the door, she backed away from his house and scrolled through the music on her phone until she found the song she wanted—"Animals" by Nickelback—and blasted it.

"Your favorite, Marlon," she shouted.

Several dogs began barking, and a light came on in the house next door, followed by Marlon's porch globe light. His front door flew open, and there he stood, looking possessed in his rancor.

"Get in here," he hissed.

She ran inside and he slammed the door behind her.

"What the hell is wrong with you?" he shouted.

Nessa was out of breath and frantic. "I'm here," she said, "to do step number five. I'm here to admit to God, to myself, and to another human being—that's you—the exact nature of my wrongs."

"It's too late for that," he said.

"Why?" she said, her fists clenched at her sides. "Why is it too late?"

"Because I'm sick of the chaos that follows you wherever you go. I'm sick of your lying. I'm sick of being held at arm's length."

"Didn't you hear what I said? I'm here to—"

"I heard you. I just don't believe—"

"John's dead."

Time stopped as they stared at each other, and Marlon's exasperation deflated into bewilderment.

Nessa collapsed on the couch and began sobbing.

In her desolation, she only dimly felt Marlon curl himself around her, his arms shielding her, his face in her hair, murmuring to her as if she were a tiny child.

After a while, her sobs devolved into whimpers, and the story leaked out of her in fits and starts.

When she finished, she felt light as fog, and a merciful quiet enveloped her aching soul.

"Are they sure it's him?" Marlon asked.

"*I'm* sure it's him," she said.

He nodded. "I know what you mean. I knew the minute Lori was gone. Felt it in my guts."

He brushed the hair back from her face and wiped her tears away with his fingers. "Can I get you a glass of water?"

"Thank you," she said, suddenly shy at finding herself in his arms.

He padded into the kitchen and she heard him putting ice in glasses and running the tap. She looked around the room, at the sparse furnishings and decor, except for a large framed portrait of Marlon's late wife.

He returned with two glasses, one of which he handed to her, then sat next to her on the sofa.

She took a long drink of her water and cleared her throat. "Okay," she said. "Step number five."

"Oh, no," he said. "You don't have to do this now. Not after—"

"I'm doing it now," she said.

He didn't argue.

"When I was sixteen, I was raped by a football player at my high school."

Marlon's face crumpled, but she didn't allow him to say anything.

"In high school, my best friend was Candy, and we could have been twins. This is important. Same eye color, same hair color, hairstyle, same build. They called us the Glimmer Twins after—"

"Mick Jagger and Keith Richards," Marlon said, nodding. "Please continue."

"So Candy and I were at a party, and I got so fucked up that Candy had to practically carry me upstairs to one of the bedrooms where I could lie down until she sobered up enough to drive us home. I found out later she went to the basement to watch a movie with some other girls. So I was practically paralyzed, you know— vodka, E, pot, and who knows what the hell else.

"I don't know how much later Nathan the football player came into the room, locked the door, and got up on the bed." Nessa cringed, remembering how her one fucked-up thought at that point had been that she didn't look very good—Nathan was the hottest guy in school, and she'd had a crush on him, like everyone else.

"I tried to talk but my mouth didn't work. None of me worked at that point, but that didn't seem to matter to him. Because he stripped completely naked and got on top of me."

Nessa's breath hitched and she had to stop talking, squeezing her eyes shut and crossing her arms over herself, as if it were all happening now.

The only other person she'd talked to about this in her current life was John. She sneaked a peek at Marlon now, and he was look-ing at her in the same heartbroken way that John had.

Nessa cleared her throat and let go of herself. "So, yeah, so I was no virgin. What was weird was that I would have loved to have sex with him. But this was something else. If he'd ever spoken to me before that, or even made eye contact with me, that would have been one thing. But I might as well have been a knothole in a tree, you know?"

Marlon remained silent, but his posture and expression made him look ready to launch out of his chair and track Nathan down.

"I threw up on his letter jacket," Nessa said, "so he punched me in the face and broke my nose." She pointed at the bump on the bridge of it.

Marlon flinched.

"So Candy and some other guy finally got the door open. Long story short, Nathan was eighteen, so he was charged with felony rape. He got thirteen years in Chino, and there went his college scholarship. So up until about nine days ago, I thought Nathan was the troll. He was paroled last year. I thought he'd tracked me down and was going to make me pay for ruining his life."

Marlon sat digesting this story, and Nessa let him process it while she shivered in the air-conditioning and relived past terrors.

What she hadn't told Marlon was that even after she was sober and married to a man she loved, sex was always hard thanks to that night. Not all the time, but she'd never again know what it was like to have sex without the rape hanging over her bed like an anvil from a fraying rope.

Marlon stood. "More water?"

She nodded and he left the room. Marlon returned with the refilled glasses and handed one to her, then gripped her shoulder.

She reached up with her opposite hand and squeezed his, then let him go.

"What made you think . . . he was the troll?" Marlon asked as he sat down.

"Couple of things," Nessa said, taking a long drink and setting the glass on the coffee table. "I found some things around my house with BIG on them."

"I don't understand."

"The song that was playing while he was raping me was 'Dead Wrong' by Notorious B.I.G. He had it on repeat. I guess it was his jam, like all the wannabe homie white boys. I used to love rap, but that was pretty much ruined for me. To this day I can't listen to Tupac or Biggie because of this guy."

"You said there were a couple of things."

"Right. The other one was that the troll posted a trivia question to my blog. The answer to it was 'Rosie.'"

"And what does that mean?"

"That's my real name. Well, my nickname. My birth name was Gypsy Rose Lee Gereben. So that's another thing I haven't told you, but I'm going to tell you why it's not my name anymore, which is where I confess the exact nature of my wrongs. But first I'm going to cry for a minute."

And she did. This was something about Nessa that had always driven John crazy. She never just cried—she announced her intention beforehand. Marlon rose again and left the room while Nessa sobbed hard. He returned with a box of tissues. He held it out and she pulled several Kleenex out before he sat down again.

Nessa let herself finish while Marlon sat quietly stroking her hair. She blew her nose and took a drink of water.

"Okay," she said. "Candy also went by a nickname. Only hers

was cooler. She chose it, she said, because Candy was the ultimate rock name: 'Candy Shop' by 50 Cent. 'Sex and Candy' by Marcy Playground."

" 'Candy-O' by the Cars," Marlon offered. " 'In Candy's Room' by Bruce Springsteen . . ."

Nessa let a smile break through her tears. "Right. Anyway, I've never known anyone who picked their own nickname and had it stick. But Candy was that kind of person.

"She lived with her grandma because her own mom had abandoned her when she was an infant. When we weren't out at the Smell, we were at her grandma's house. She'd seen all the legendary acts in the sixties at the great old clubs like the Troubadour, Whisky A Go Go, and Pandora's Box. She saw the Doors, the Byrds, Led Zeppelin, and Janis Joplin live. We'd sit and listen to her stories for hours."

Marlon obviously couldn't help smiling at this bit. "She sounds great," he said.

Thinking of Candy's grandma brought Nessa to tears again. Being around her, Nessa had gotten to see what real maternal love should look like. Thanks to Grandma, and thanks to Candy's own drive and ambition to be successful and get out of LA, Candy had had top grades and planned to go to college, unlike Nessa, who'd been completely out of control.

"Candy and her grandma kept me grounded," Nessa said. "Until she had a stroke and died. It was shortly after that I got Candy hooked on heroin too."

Through her tears, Nessa watched Marlon struggle to refrain from throwing out more AA sayings.

"It wasn't long before we were shooting every day. Since it

was summertime, Candy said she'd just do it until school started again, because she was going into her senior year and wanted to keep her grade point average so she could apply for scholarships. Because we were eating into Candy's college savings, we started telling each other, *We'll just do it on the weekends.* Which then became *only after dark* and finally, *just until I start college, and then we'll never do it again.*"

Marlon was nodding his head vigorously with obvious recognition of the addiction pattern.

"Then it became the first thing I thought of every morning. *Just a little taste.* It circled my brain like a catchy but horrible song that looped and looped with no way to stop it."

More crying, more nose blowing, more water gulping. When did the feeling better part start?

"My eighteenth birthday came up, and Candy and I discussed for hours that we were going to quit right after that. Just one more time. So that night, we were going to go downtown and score, then go shoot up. But that morning, my brother, Brandon, gave me a little gift-wrapped package, which he said was from Hoover, this guy who gave me my first hit. After that, he became my mom's boyfriend, but that's another story. Anyway, I opened it because I wanted to see what kind of shit he was bribing me with this time. He had a thing for me, see, and I used it to get drugs and booze and whatever else, while my mom looked the other way.

"I locked myself in the bathroom and opened it. Inside was a brand-new works kit—syringe, cotton, spoon, lighter. And a bag of beautiful black tar heroin. I couldn't wait to show Candy.

"So we had the H and at sunset we trespassed and got into the atrium under the Seventh Street Bridge, which is just disgusting—trash, graffiti, and all kinds of crap. But when you're a junkie, it's a wonderland. We were getting ready to shoot heroin for the very last time. We'd promised each other that this was it. We were done with drugs."

As with describing the rape, Nessa began to tingle as if it was all happening again. She could picture the maze of pipes, the brilliantly colored graffiti, the smell of rot, and garbage, and death.

"We settled in and I said, 'Happy birthday to me.' And Candy said . . ." Nessa's throat closed up again. She cleared it and went on. "She said, 'You first. It's your birthday.' " Nessa cried silently for a while, folded in on herself, the psychic pain nearly unbearable. "But I always went first. I sat there thinking, *I'm eighteen today. I need to not be so selfish. I need to act more mature*, so my first act as an official adult would be to let my best friend go first."

She could see Candy sitting against the concrete wall, her shining eyes, the love she had for Nessa, the kind of love she'd never experienced before that.

"I tied off Candy's arm and we hunted for a vein. I saw the one I wanted, a fat, blue, virgin. I filled the syringe and flicked the bubbles out of it, then slid the needle into my best friend's arm."

Nessa stood, desperate to be moving, to shake the memories loose and spit them out and examine them. She walked to the window and looked out so she wouldn't have to face Marlon.

"Candy's eyes rolled back and her face turned to the ceiling. I watched and released the tube from Candy's arm. As I slid out the syringe and tied my own arm off, from the corner of my eye I saw Candy go stiff. I thought maybe she'd seen the cops, but I looked around and saw no one. But when I looked back at Candy, there was foam on her lips and coming out of her nose, and she'd bitten into her bottom lip."

Nessa was shouting now, wailing the words. Her saliva flecked the window before her. "The syringe fell out of my hand. She began to convulse and fell over, her back arching, her head banging over and over on the ground. I grabbed for her and looked around for something to jam in her mouth, but I couldn't find anything. Candy kept on biting her lips and her tongue, and there was blood everywhere. Everywhere."

All Nessa could do was watch until Candy stopped convulsing just as quickly as she'd started. Her skin was gray and her lips were blue. Her eyes were open, but she couldn't see anything anymore.

"I slapped her face. Her breathing was shallow, and I tried to sit her up. Candy needed to walk around to metabolize the junk. I tried to stand her up. I really tried. Her breathing got slower and slower, foam and blood dripping from her mouth and her nose."

Nessa had screamed at Candy to quit being such a selfish bitch and wake up. She kept dragging Candy back and forth, the toes of her worn tennis shoes scraping along the trashy cement.

Still standing at the window, Nessa wiped her own nose and looked at Marlon.

"I didn't know what to do. I needed to call 911, but I didn't have a phone. I'd sold it to buy junk. Besides, I had a police record— DUI, grand larceny, possession . . . prostitution. Now that I was legally an adult, if I called the cops I would go to jail and never get out again.

"I didn't know CPR, but I had to try. I pushed on Candy's chest and put my ear to her lips. No sound. Not a pulse. Nothing. Candy was gone."

Nessa stared out at nothing, feeling emptied out, bereft, alone.

She turned away from the window, sat back down, and wiped her eyes and nose.

"I panicked. I couldn't think straight. I just knew I was about to be in the biggest trouble of my life. I'd killed someone. Even though it was an accident, even if it would be considered manslaughter, I didn't think I could handle prison. I had to get out of there. Candy was dead. It was over for her, but I couldn't go to prison."

Then Nessa realized there had been another reason to flee: she'd known that Joyce would somehow capitalize on Candy's death, turn it into an opportunity to be on television again. Suddenly, Nessa could get away from Joyce and her schemes, her boyfriends who wanted to molest her, the bizarre home she'd never thought she would escape. This was her ticket.

"So I switched purses with Candy," Nessa said. "I put mine next to her body, hoping that the cops would think she was me. She was actually wearing one of my outfits—we were always sharing clothes—and I switched jewelry with her. We had matching tattoos." Nessa rolled up her left sleeve and showed Marlon the Glimmer Twins tattoo.

"So I took her purse with her driver's license and I ran from the Seventh Street Bridge. I didn't even go back to the apartment to get my stuff. I went to the train yard and jumped into a graffitied box car that was headed east like a fucking hobo, dopesick and in shock, so grief-stricken I wanted to die. But I didn't. I ended up in Denver, in a homeless shelter that had a rehab program. Cleaned up my act, because now I was living for two of us.

"Thanks to Candy's good grades and spotless police record, I was able to get my GED, then I got a bachelor's in communications from Metro State. If I hadn't stolen Candy's identity, I'd have kept on using, because my record would have followed me around forever. If it weren't for Candy, I'd be dead now."

They sat in silence a moment.

"So you started using after the rape, is that right?" Marlon said.

Nessa nodded. "Actually, after the trial. During the reality show. But I'll tell you about that another time."

"That," Marlon said, "is an extraordinary story."

"I know. Thank you for listening."

She looked down and saw that their hands were entwined. Marlon noticed this too, but he didn't let go. He smiled at her.

"So what was Candy's real name?"

"Vanessa Angela Frye," she said. "Which was my name until I got married. But I've always gone by Nessa."

"It suits you," Marlon said.

"Now you know everything," Nessa said. "I am sincerely, deeply sorry that I talked about you to John. Please forgive me. I need you to be my sponsor. But I also need you to be my friend."

Marlon squeezed her hand. "As it turns out," he said, "I need you too. After our phone conversation, I was completely wrecked, even though you are a monumental pain in the ass."

Nessa lunged toward him and threw her arms around him, burrowing her face into his neck. He held her tight.

"Thank you," she said.

They looked at each other, and Nessa was nearly overwhelmed with the urge to kiss him, with the urge to sleep with him. Looking into his eyes, she could see he had the same urge. But it would ruin everything. Even though she hadn't felt this close to another person since . . . John, in the beginning, when they'd had their whole lives ahead of them.

Instead, she laid her hand on Marlon's cheek, stood, and walked out the door.

Chapter Twenty-Two

Wednesday, June 29

SHE'D READ ABOUT this, this autopilot feeling that comes after a loved one dies and there are things to do.

Nessa got up the next morning, showered, dressed and called Lock It Up. The receptionist said that Brady was off that day, so Nessa looked up his address online and drove to a town house on Todd Road. She wanted to talk to him about when exactly John had bought the keys, make sure it *was* John.

Brady's town house was nicer than she would have imagined. Although selling keys to criminals on the side probably helped.

She pounded on the door, praying that he was home. He was, and he opened the door shirtless with a bottle of Pepsi in his hand. When he saw Nessa, the look of happy anticipation drained away from his face.

"Mrs. Donati," he said, clearly terrified that she'd changed her mind and was going to turn him in.

"Brady, I need to ask you a question."

"What is it? I haven't sold any more keys, I swear."

"No," she said. "It's not that. I'm going to show you a photo of my husband, and I want you to tell me whether he's the man you sold the key to. All right? Can you do that for me?"

Brady looked wary, as if she was setting some sort of trap for him. "I guess," he said, hunching his shoulders and crossing his arms to shove his hands into his armpits.

She pulled up a photo on her phone of John with Daltrey on his shoulders, but the light was good and you could clearly identify his features.

Brady took the phone from her hand and scrutinized it. "This is your husband?"

"Yes."

"That's not the guy."

A shrill of terror bloomed in her gut. "You're sure?"

"Definitely. That's not the guy. The guy I talked to had a beard."

"Well, picture this guy with a beard. What do you think now?"

Brady shook his head. "Still not him. Definitely not. His coloring's all wrong. This guy has brown eyes, right? The guy who bought your keys had darker hair and he had . . . different eyes. Weird eyes."

"Weird how?"

"I don't know. Just weird."

That was the same word Allen the drug dealer had used.

"Is there anything else you can tell me about the guy?"

"I don't think so."

"Thank you, Brady. Sorry to have bothered you."

He closed the door and Nessa shivered, even though it was in the low nineties. She drove home and made a list of everything that needed to be done. She decided not to tell her in-laws about John until they returned with Daltrey. This was news better given in person. She then spent the day trimming and tending to the hops vines. She'd been following the advice on a hops-growing website she'd found, and they seemed to be doing well. It did her good to work outdoors, which she did until late afternoon, and she found her thoughts straying to Marlon all day long, thoughts she kept batting away. It was probably quite normal after a spouse's death to obsess about the first semi-suitable mate that crossed your vision.

But that wasn't fair. Marlon wasn't just some guy. She knew him, she respected him. She trusted him.

Her phone rang, a number she didn't recognize, and she let it go to voicemail. Then she listened to it.

"Mrs. Donati, this is Shanae Klerkse from Child Protective Services calling to make an appointment to interview Daltrey. Please call me back at your earliest convenience. Thank you, and have a nice day."

That could definitely wait.

About five, her phone dinged with a text from Isabeau.

Consider this my two weeks' notice. However, I will stay on until you find a replacement because I'd never leave that poor little boy alone.

What the actual hell? Nessa texted back, *What's going on? Is something wrong?*

No reply.

Nessa resent hers. Still no answer, even fifteen minutes later. So she called Isabeau's phone but it went straight to voicemail.

"Isabeau, it's Nessa. Can we talk about this? I'm worried that something has happened. Can you please let me know? Please. Oh, and by the way, Detective Dirksen came by to let me know they think they've found John in Tuttle."

Nessa was sure that last bit would pique Isabeau's interest enough to call and find out the details.

But it didn't. There was no return call.

It was an awfully strange coincidence that the only two people semi-close to her had been turned against her in less than twenty-four hours. And there was only one person Nessa had accidentally told about Marlon's suicide attempt.

But Isabeau idolized Marlon. Didn't she? How well did Nessa really know her?

Goose bumps covered her skin.

But what had she done to Isabeau to anger her so much? Was there some connection between the two of them that she was un-aware of?

Had Isabeau called the student newspaper?

Seething, infuriated, Nessa called Isabeau's number again, and as she expected, it went to voicemail again.

"Hey, Isabeau, you lying sack of shit," Nessa said. "Just so you know, I know why you're quitting. It's because your work here is done. It's because you're the fucking troll. You called the K-State student paper and told them about Marlon's suicide attempt. I know it's you, because you're the only one I've ever said anything about it to. I don't know what we did to make you want to destroy us, but I'm on to you. And I'm going to the police." She hung up and waited.

Immediately her phone rang.

"I'd never do anything to hurt Marlon," Isabeau yelled into the phone.

"Well, you did," Nessa said.

"I didn't call the paper, for God's sake. I'm not the troll. *You* are. You set this whole thing up to get attention. You killed your husband because he was a pain in your ass. You emailed my dad's best friend's wife, you bitch."

Nessa was speechless. For a moment, she didn't know what Isabeau was talking about, but then she thought back to their heart-to-heart talk on Saturday night. Which was the same night she'd let the information about Marlon's suicide attempt slip.

The same night.

"Wait a minute," Nessa said, her brain buzzing as if she were receiving an incoming transmission.

"I'm hanging up now," Isabeau said.

"I think . . . hold on. Please just hold on for a minute."

She looked up at the sky, listened to the insects droning, and it morphed into a cacophony of electronic static.

"Isabeau. The troll has bugged the house."

"Oh, of course he has," Isabeau said, sarcasm dripping from every word. "Because you're so important that—"

"Just listen! We talked about both of those things on Saturday night. In the living room. Remember? Your affair and Marlon's suicide attempt."

Silence on the line.

"Isabeau?"

"Yeah, I'm here," she said, her voice empty of the earlier venom. "But—wait. Is there anything else that's come out that might have only been mentioned in the house?"

"Let me think," Nessa said, looking out over the hops vines. It came to her almost immediately. "Remember when you found the Facebook and Twitter accounts, and how on one of them, the troll said that Daltrey didn't speak because of vaccines?"

"Yeah."

"I've never mentioned that in my blog, that Daltrey hasn't

started speaking yet. I've never talked about it on the radio either, because . . ." Because she wasn't her mother, using her children to get attention, to try to become famous, to get sympathy. "I've never mentioned those things."

"When was that?" Isabeau said. "What day was it that the troll made that comment?"

"I'll look it up." But this wasn't really the issue at hand. Not really. It was the fragile, delicate trust she'd given and received with Isabeau, and she had to rescue it. "But—you really thought I'd get in touch with that wife and rat you out? Did you really believe that?"

"Well," Isabeau said slowly. "You were the only one I'd told. I was so shocked to get that email after all this time, and I'd just talked to you about it a few days ago."

"I want you to know that I would never betray you. You're—" Nessa gulped, but forced herself to go on. "You're the best friend I've had since I was a teenager."

There was a beat of silence as Nessa's heart lay naked and quivering on the ground, unprotected, exposed. What would Isabeau do with it?

"Wow, Nessa," Isabeau finally said. "That means a lot, coming from you. You've become one of my best friends too. I really mean that. I know it's hard for you to let people get close to you."

"Thank you, Isabeau," she said, her eyes tearing up.

"I'll be home tomorrow."

"See you then."

After Nessa clicked off, she went back into the house. It felt different to her, as if her sanctuary, the house itself, was listening, digesting her for the nourishment of the troll. She tiptoed into the living room, and then realized how ridiculous she was being. No one would care how hard her feet hit the floor when she walked.

She looked around the room, trying to imagine where a person might hide a bug, and what would it look like? She'd seen them in movies but didn't know how accurate her vision of such a thing would be.

She started with the bookcase, pulling each book off one by one, looking inside front and back, riffling the pages. She felt along the surfaces of the bookcase. Felt and looked underneath. Scrutinized each knickknack. Tipped over the floor lamp and looked at the bottom of it. Turned over the wing chair. Pulled out the cushions. She repeated this process with everything in the room, methodically looking over every surface.

And then she came to the coffee table, which she cleared off and looked beneath it. Stuck to the underside was a one-by-one-inch flat black square. She stared at it, her nerves on fire. If she touched it, would the troll know?

Nessa sat back on her heels and thought. Then she pulled out her phone and snapped a photo, which she attached to a text message that said, *I found this on the underside of my coffee table. Is it a bug?*

She waited, staring at her phone, watching the dancing dots that signaled Mac was texting her back.

Yes. Attach portable speakers to your phone and turn on some loud music. Then get a knife and remove it carefully. Bring it to our house, keeping the music with you and loud. You'll lose the signal from the transmitter about ten yards from your house. We'll worry about finding the transmitter later.

Nessa was almost overcome with the desire to start whispering obscenities into the device, to assault the ears and guts of the asshole listening in. She fetched her speakers and plugged them into her phone, then cranked "Fuck You" by Cee Lo Green, hoping the sheer volume of the song left the listeners' ears bleeding. She left it playing near the bug, went to the kitchen and got a knife, then returned and eased the blade beneath the edge of the bug. It popped off into her left palm. She set the knife down, then picked up the speakers and her phone with her right hand and went out the back door.

Nessa estimated that the garage was about twenty yards from the house, but she kept the music going as she set the bug on the passenger seat and started up the Pacifica.

And then something insane happened. Green's jubilant bravado and the tune's funky groove infused her with a defiant, carefree joy that transcended this shitstorm she called her life. A joy she hadn't felt in many months outside of her son's presence. She drove under the shield of this joy all the way to her neighbors' house with the windows down, the heat and humidity and smells of the woods and the fields filling her senses.

Just for this moment, she was in control. She was acting instead of reacting. Just for this moment.

She pulled up to Mac and Lauren's house and turned off the music, and she had to calm herself down so she wouldn't look like a complete wack-job. Ziggy and Tosh were jumping on the hosed-down trampoline, their shorts and dreadlocks dripping.

"Hi, Nessa," they both called as she got out of the car.

Nessa just waved, even though she assumed that the bug was no longer transmitting. Better not to take chances.

Mac came out of the back door. He beckoned her to the Adirondack chairs and held out his hand. She put the black plastic square in it.

"Wow," Mac said. "I've never seen one like this before." He turned it over. "I'll take it apart and see if it has a SIM card. The bug might be tied to a cell phone number, in which case, we can find your troll, or at least his cell phone number. Then maybe the cops can track him through his phone." He looked up at Nessa. "Are you all right?"

"If you can figure all that stuff out," Nessa said, "I will be."

Thursday, June 30

NESSA SPENT THE endless day working on her computer, waiting for Daltrey and Isabeau to reappear. At three P.M., she heard tires crunching dirt and gravel outside and looked out the window. It was Linda and Tony, right on time.

She ran outside and saw that Daltrey was dead asleep in his car seat. Then she remembered what she had to tell her in-laws.

Nessa stuck her head in the driver's side window and told Tony to keep the car running so Daltrey could keep napping because she had something to tell them.

Tony paled as he got out of the car. She hugged them both and broke the news about the body in the lake. Tony cried, of course, and Linda even teared up.

"It's going to be a couple of weeks before they can determine if it's John," Nessa said. "So I know this is hard, but if you want to start thinking about arrangements, I think we should have the memorial in Russell, don't you?"

The grateful expressions on their faces broke Nessa's heart. They hugged her again.

"I'm so sorry," Nessa said, and cried. "I tried to keep him clean, I just—"

"It's not your fault," Linda said, smoothing Nessa's hair.

"Do you want to come in?" Nessa said.

"No," Tony said. "We want to get home before dark. Would you call us when you find out . . . anything?"

"Yes," Nessa said, then got Daltrey out of the car. He opened his sleepy eyes and grinned at her.

"Hi, baby, how are you?" she asked.

He signed "Fine," and Linda sighed.

"I tried," she said.

"It's okay, Grandma," Nessa said. "Thank you for everything."

Tony wrestled the car seat out of the car and deposited Daltrey's little suitcase on the ground. They got back in the car and drove away.

"I missed you so much," Nessa said. "Did you miss me?"

He nodded energetically.

"Are you hungry?" she said.

He shook his head and squirmed to get out of her arms. She put him down and he ran to all the outbuildings, touching each one. He stopped at the hops vines and pointed before coming back to her.

They went inside and Isabeau drove up half an hour later. The joyous reunion between Daltrey and Isabeau did Nessa's heart good. Then Isabeau threw her arms around Nessa. She talked about her camping trip to Waconda Springs and said they should take Daltrey there before the end of the summer, because he would love it.

The three of them watched a Disney movie until Daltrey's bedtime, and then Nessa tucked him in. "See you tomorrow, sweetie," she said.

He signed "Good night."

Downstairs in the living room, Nessa beckoned to Isabeau to join her out back.

"I don't want to talk about this inside in case there's another bug in there," Nessa said. They sat on the deck chairs.

"So what did you find out?" Isabeau said.

"First tell me what happened with your dad's best friend."

"Well," Isabeau said, "they ain't best friends no more. Dad punched him in the nose."

Nessa actually laughed.

"Yeah. My folks are pissed. They're trying to talk me into pressing charges against him, but I don't know."

"You should consider it," Nessa said.

"Okay. I will. So what did you find out?"

They discussed the body in the lake and what it could mean. Nessa told her about her exchange with the locksmith, saying it wasn't John who bought the keys, and about the bug—that Mac was taking it apart to see if he could figure out who it belonged to.

"Wow," Isabeau said. "That is so messed up."

"I know."

Nessa looked at the clock on her phone, dropped it into her purse, and stood. "I've got to go," she said. "But I'm really glad you're home. And that you're not quitting."

Isabeau smiled.

NESSA DROVE UP to the dark station parking lot and killed the engine. Otto's Vespa was parked there.

It was a starry night, and Nessa threw her head back to take in the constellations, Cee Lo Green's voice growling in her head, and she smiled. The wind blew hot and steady across the field.

She used her key to get into the station, which was dark—just how Otto liked it. Her phone pinged as she relocked the front door from inside. She pulled her phone from her purse and looked at it.

Got the phone number from the SIM card, the text said, and for a minute she didn't know what that meant until she saw it was from Mac. Another text followed it, displaying a phone number. She didn't recognize it, but she didn't recognize a lot of phone numbers. On a whim, she decided to call it. If it was John's final phone number, maybe she would hear his voice on the voicemail.

The satellite feed was playing the indie-alternative station. Nessa opened the on-air studio door, and there sat Otto in front of the glowing board and computer monitors.

She tapped the number and pressed her phone to her ear.

Over Robbie Robertson's "Somewhere Down the Crazy River," she heard—was it an accordion? What the hell? An accordion playing "Smells Like Teen Spirit." She started to laugh, as Otto turned toward her and pulled his own phone out of his pocket.

"Hello?"

The voice echoed on both her phone and Otto's.

They stared at each other.

"Why are you calling . . ." Otto said into his phone, then pulled it from his ear and looked at it, his smile vanishing. "Oh, shit."

She walked, fists clenched, toward him.

"You fucking hipster douchebag," she said. "You. You're the troll."

How could she not have figured it out? How had he slipped right by her? Because she'd never credited him with enough brains to do something like this. Fucking bastard, threatening her child and . . .

Chills covered her body.

Killing her husband.

"Listen," Otto said, holding his hands up. "I couldn't pay my electricity bill. My rent's past due. I needed the money. They told me you lied to get the job. They said they needed to bug your house to get the evidence—"

Nessa grabbed the lapels of his jacket.

"Who told you that?"

"—and all I had to do was plant the bug in your living room and transcribe what I heard on the—"

"*Who told you that?*"

"The FCC."

"The FCC?" Nessa spat. "How stupid are you? Do you really think the government asks private citizens to put bugs in other people's houses?"

His eyes seemed to clear. She could almost see dawn breaking on his face.

Nessa pressed down on Otto's shoulders until the office chair back was at a forty-five-degree angle. "My husband is dead. I'm going to be arrested. A rapist came to my house, and you—"

"Whoa, whoa," Otto said, frantic, shoving her backward until he was upright again. "I seriously do not know what you are talking about. All I did was put that bug under your coffee table! That's all I did! I don't know anything about that other shit. They said—"

"They? Who? Who are *they*?" she screamed. Then she launched herself at Otto and tightened her hands around his throat, holding nothing back.

"Hello, Candy."

A painful jolt of adrenaline accompanied the voice that came over the in-studio speakers, and she let go of Otto immediately and stumbled backward.

Candy?

"Them," Otto said, his voice chafed and raw, pointing at the speaker.

Nessa looked up as if *they* would be perched atop it.

"Thanks, Otto. You've fulfilled your obligation." The voice cut out the satellite feed, a low-pitched, electronic voice, like Stephen Hawking, only without the British accent. It was the same voice that had called the station to let her know it could see her inside the studio a few weeks ago. That voice filled not only the studio, but her whole consciousness.

"Okay," Otto said toward the ceiling, "but can I just be the one to—"

"You're not going to do your show, Candy. Otto's going to take over for you tonight, because you need to get home."

Without the voice even saying it, Nessa knew. They were in her house, where her little boy was sleeping.

Right now.

Her phone pinged, and she looked at it. A photo appeared of Daltrey in a blindfold, his little hands tied behind his back.

And a gun pointed at his head.

Nessa gasped so hard she felt something tear in her throat. Then a mewling sound dribbled out of her mouth as queasiness nearly overcame her, her stomach convulsing in terror. Her son.

They were going to take him away from her, one way or the other. If they killed him, she would die too.

The phone dropped from her hands and landed faceup on the ground. The photo disappeared. That damned self-deleting photo app again.

Nessa hissed to Otto, "You have no idea what you've done."

Otto panted, clearly horrified.

"Candy!" the voice said sharply. "Do not say another word to Otto. Leave immediately and go home. I'm going to call your phone, and you'll stay on the line. Do you understand?"

"Jeep's Blues" played, and Nessa picked the phone up off the ground and answered it.

"Now go out to your car and drive home," the troll said over the phone. "If you're not there within fifteen minutes, the boy dies. And be careful driving. If you're pulled over by the police, he dies."

Brilliant. The troll would keep her on the phone so she couldn't call the police.

Where was Isabeau? Was she part of this? Had she so thoroughly fooled Nessa?

As if the troll could read her mind, her phone pinged and she looked at it. Another photo appeared on her phone.

Isabeau. On the ground. Her head surrounded by a pool of blood.

Oh, God. Oh, help me, God.

Nessa's legs were suddenly dream legs: heavy, rubbery, useless. Moving in slow motion, threatening to give out completely. And everything around her became crystalline, magnified and in sharp focus, so much so that her eyes hurt. Outside, the bug-covered outdoor light was blinding in its brilliance, the insects themselves as if she were seeing them under a microscope, the planets and stars above her. It was as if she'd never truly seen until now.

Her legs became solid again and she ran to the Pacifica and got in. Her hands shook so much she dropped her keys on the floor mat, then smacked her forehead on the steering wheel.

"Shit!" she yelled.

"What are you doing?" the troll said, suspicious.

"I hit my head," Nessa said through gritted teeth.

"You didn't really think you'd never be found out, did you?" The voice was tinny but familiar somehow.

"No," Nessa said, "I didn't." And she meant it, because the day had come. It was today.

She put the car in gear and drove toward home.

"I'm going to put you on speaker so that I can drive carefully."

"Great idea," the troll said. "There's a GPS tracker on your vehicle, and we can see exactly where you're going. And if you don't go straight home, the boy dies."

Nessa brought up the keypad on her phone and texted 911. The return message was *Error Invalid Number.*

Damn Manhattan. They'd get this service in the next fifteen years or so. Too late for her. Too late for Daltrey.

Maybe she was having an acid flashback. Maybe she was hallucinating. Maybe whoever had been tormenting her and trying to drive her insane for the last month had finally gotten the job done, because this was not happening.

"What do you want?" Nessa said. "Why are you doing this?"

"Because you killed my daughter."

"I—what?" Nessa said. Her brain felt like it was going to snap in half. So this was . . . Candy's birth mom? The one who abandoned her, left her to live with her grandmother? *Now* she gave a shit? What the actual fuck?

"And you're going to die tonight just like she did. If you do what I tell you, I'll let your son live. If you don't, he dies. "

"Are you—are you Candy's mother?" Nessa asked.

"No, of course not," the voice said. "I'm Rosie's."

Chapter Twenty-Three

NESSA DROVE OFF the road, onto the gravel and weed-strewn shoulder, unable to hold on to the wheel, her head roiling. The Pacifica rocketed toward a guardrail but Nessa was paralyzed with terror, couldn't take her foot off the accelerator. Finally her left foot found the brake and stomped it to the floor, sending Nessa's head into the steering wheel again. She jammed the gearshift into Park.

Her mother? Her own *mother*?

In Nessa's inflamed brain, a B-roll of snippets from Joyce's appearances and roles on TV and film played on a screen, bearing down on her like a bullet train until Nessa had to throw the door open and scream into the indifferent night. *"No!"*

She screamed until she ran out of breath.

So this was all meant for Candy?

When Nessa finally inhaled, she heard Joyce's unmasked voice coming from the speaker phone. "Candy!"

"Mom," Nessa said, gasping. "Mom." Nessa's own voice sounded like her five-year-old self, small, terrified, alone.

"What did you say?" Joyce said.

"Mom," Nessa gulped. "It's me. It's Rosie."

There was a pause on the line.

"Rosie is dead," her mother said. "But I know who you are. You're the white-trash girl who got my daughter hooked on drugs and—"

"Mom, I swear. It's me. It's Rosie!"

"Oh, stop it," Joyce said. "I had to identify Rosie's body. Do you think a mother doesn't know her own child? You're Vanessa Frye, the girl who ruined my family forever, took my child from me."

"Mom—"

"Stop calling me that!" Joyce shouted, throwing out a shrill of feedback because the phone couldn't handle the volume.

Joyce wept, beautiful, melodic, practiced sobs. This was the role of a lifetime for her, and she was giving it her all.

"You left Rosie there alone to die. What did you care? I tried to get the police to go after you, to find you and punish you, but they don't care about finding a junkie. In LA, they only care about junkies if they're actors' children."

She said those words bitterly, biting them off one by one. Then she broke down crying again.

And Nessa wept with her, remembering that day, remembering her attempts to keep Candy conscious, the foam and blood dripping from her nose and mouth, the half-shut eyes, her soul and spirit so far receded into her body that it would never return. That face had haunted Nessa's dreams ever since and would until the end of her days. And she deserved that. It should have been her who died that day. She should have taken the first shot.

Her mother said the words that described exactly what Nessa was feeling: "You're so selfish you didn't think twice about the trail of devastation you left behind, did you? You just went on and lived your life, your perfect, charmed life."

Nessa was now crying so hard she could barely see.

"I see that you've stopped. You have three minutes to get home."

Nessa pulled the gearshift into Drive and pulled onto the road again. She tried not to speed, tried to clear her eyes. Lucky she'd driven these roads so many times. She turned off the highway onto the county road that led home.

"There's no point turning you into the police because the statute of limitations has run out for several of your crimes. For murdering Rosie, you'd only be charged with second degree murder or manslaughter."

But it had been an accident. A tragic, stupid accident.

"When you get home," Joyce went on, "I'm going to give you the chance to write about all of this on your blog. You're going to write a suicide note confessing to Rosie's murder. And then you're going to do what you should have done seven years ago. You're going to kill yourself the same way you killed Rosie."

Nessa was less than a mile from home now, and she was filled with the desperate and threadbare hope that her own mother would recognize her, would realize her mistake. That it could be true that her mother loved her this much that she would commit murder to avenge her.

"I've tried and tried to help you redeem yourself on your own," Joyce said. "To do the right thing. I set up circumstances that I thought would put enough pressure on you so that you'd self-medicate—"

"You murdered John," Nessa whispered into the phone.

But Joyce couldn't go off-book. "But no matter what we did,

you wouldn't start using again. We called Child Services anonymously. Sent you the syringe. Put the heroin in your living room."

We?

But before the word had fully formed itself in her head, Nessa knew who the other half of *we* was.

BIG on the guitar pick.

Weird eyes. Not just weird eyes, but different. *Different from one another.*

Heterochromia. One blue eye, one brown.

BIG. Brandon Isaac Gereben.

Her brother.

She had to stop the car again because she couldn't see, couldn't handle the steering wheel, she was so racked with sobs. Her brother. Her family. Her blood.

"Don't stop," Joyce said. "You have less than ninety seconds to get to your house, and you're stopping? You obviously care as little about your son as you do about—"

A roar arose from Nessa's throat, filling the car and deafening her own ears as she jammed the Pacifica into gear and spun out the tires. It was the roar of a mother lion. The tires threw dust from the dirt road into the air, and the Pacifica fishtailed toward the house as she savagely wiped away her tears.

She raced toward her home and almost plowed into the side of it. Nessa jammed the Pacifica into Park, threw open the door, and ran without closing it or turning off the car. A clock ticked in her mind as she stumbled in the yard, willing herself not to fall or drop the phone, her son's lifeline.

"I see you've arrived," Joyce said into the phone as Nessa opened the back door. "Welcome home, Candy."

Chapter Twenty-Four

NESSA WOULD CONVINCE her mother of who she was. She had to. This thought steadied her as she walked inside, until she saw Isabeau dead on the floor.

She covered her mouth with her hands to keep a scream from escaping. Daltrey was in the house somewhere, and she didn't want to scare him more than he probably already was.

More tears flowed for her only friend since Candy, dead like Candy.

"Candy?" called Joyce from the living room. "In here, dear."

Even in the midst of this nightmare, Nessa couldn't help but hear everything Joyce said as a poorly acted, badly written script.

She tried not to track any blood into the living room.

How stupid! *Who gives a shit?* Isabeau was dead, and Daltrey had a gun to his head.

Nessa ran into the living room, and there sat her mother on the couch, like the soap opera queen she was. Beautifully coiffed, manicured, still gorgeous after all this time.

And suddenly Nessa was like a little girl, seeing her mother for the first time in years, and she had to throttle the compulsion to run to her, to throw herself into Joyce's lap.

Because this woman was threatening her son. Had killed her husband. Had tried to destroy her.

"Where's Daltrey?" Nessa demanded.

"Oh, he's fine," Joyce said. "He's up in his room with Brandon."

The initial stab of pain for her poor, stupid brother was overcome by her new and fresh hatred of him for holding a gun on her son. The first thing she was going to do, once they knew who they'd been harassing all this time, was to kick the shit out of her brother. He was having a ball, apparently, in Joyce's good graces.

"Well, let's get right to it," Joyce said briskly, rising from the couch, as if welcoming a talk-show guest. "Give me your phone."

Nessa did. Joyce powered the phone down and put it in her pocket.

"Mom, it's me," Nessa said. "I'm Rosie. Look at me."

"My child is dead," Joyce said. "*My* child would never leave me unless she was dead." She straightened her blouse hem and put her hands on her hips, looking around the room. "Now, you sit over there," she said, pointing at the wingback chair. "The light is best there, I think."

Joyce was directing. This was the ultimate reality show to her.

She recomposed her face into a pleasant smile. "From that chair you can also see the TV. So that you have continued motivation to follow my directions, I'm going to leave it on, so you can see what's happening upstairs."

There on the screen was Daltrey, lying on his bed, motionless, a gun to his head.

"He's not moving! What have you done?" Nessa shrieked. "He's already dead, isn't he?"

"Oh, no need to worry. I need him alive. I gave him some Nyquil to help him sleep."

Nessa prayed that this was true.

"How are we doing up there?" Joyce called up the stairs.

Nessa stared at the screen as the gun withdrew from it and a gloved hand gave the thumbs-up sign. Nessa watched Daltrey and finally saw his chest rise and fall. He was alive. And Nessa would do anything to keep it that way. Anything. Whatever Joyce wanted.

Anything.

"Please, Candy, have a seat," Joyce said, indicating the wing-back chair.

Nessa sank into it, and Joyce knelt before her, and a waft of Chanel No. 5 overwhelmed her, activating an olfactory memory of long ago.

"Mommy," Nessa whispered, watching Joyce tie her ankles to the chair legs with bungie cords, but seeing instead Joyce tying four-year-old Rosie's tennis shoes.

Joyce hesitated for a fleeting second, almost looked up into Nessa's face, but then she took a larger cord and tied it around the chair at waist level, leaving Nessa's arms free. Joyce tucked a blanket around Nessa so that the bungee cords wouldn't show.

"We're going to videotape this," Joyce said. "It's going to make amazing TV. The grief-stricken junkie confessing on screen to accidentally killing her best friend. And to killing her nanny with a frying pan in a fit of drug-fueled aggression."

With a shock, Nessa realized what this was. Joyce was auditioning. This was a talk show, a Lifetime movie, and a reality show all rolled into one. Her magnum opus.

Joyce stood back from Nessa's chair to evaluate her set decoration. She nodded, satisfied.

"Mom," Nessa said, focusing on Joyce's eyes, willing her to see her daughter, "remember that time when Brandon was in the hospital, and we went down to Dana Point and pretended to be movie stars? You were Sigourney Weaver and I was Dakota Fanning. Remember?"

"And then, Candy, for the finale," Joyce said, as if Nessa hadn't spoken. She held up a length of rubber tubing and a syringe wrapped in a Kleenex, presumably to keep her fingerprints off them. "You're going to give yourself this shot of heroin."

Nessa's salivary glands doubled their output at the sight of the hypo. Damn her own body for continuously betraying her.

Nessa held her breath to make her face turn red and then pointed at her forehead, where a pink V always appeared when she did so. "Remember this, Mom?" she said, her voice frantic. "You used to call it a stork bite, but you also used to say it made me look like a Klingon. Remember how much it would stand out when I got mad? You'd stand me in front of the mirror and say—"

"Now, I've gone ahead and written your suicide note," Joyce said, setting the syringe and tubing on the coffee table, all business. "So all you'll have to do is cut and paste it into your blog. Let's go ahead and do that now."

A bead of liquid gathered at the end of the needle and dripped onto her coffee table, and Nessa salivated, her veins pulsating.

Nessa swallowed. "Mom," she pleaded. "Look at me."

"Stop calling me that," Joyce said, her voice full of acid. She turned her face toward the staircase. "Come down here, Brandon," she called. "Bring down the video camera."

Nessa's brother appeared in the doorway, and her heart leaped in her chest. Her first friend. Her mentor. He would know her. He would see their mistake. He loved her.

Brandon looked heavier and older than his Facebook photo. He had the beard Brady and Allen had talked about, wore a wife-beater and shorts, and he was carrying a pistol and a video camera on a tripod.

Brandon handed his mother the gun.

"Hi, Candy," Brandon said to Nessa with a grimace, not looking at her.

Oh, Joyce had been stoking his hatred for a long time. Had it burning at a white-hot passion now. He was looking forward to watching his sister's killer die. Had been dreaming of it.

"Brandon," Nessa said. "It's me. It's Rosie. Look at me, and you'll know it's me."

He looked uncertain for a moment, but then his expression hardened.

"Hand her the computer and have her log in to her blog, and then you copy and paste the text."

"Brandon," Nessa said.

"Stop talking to him," Joyce said, "or your son dies right now."

"Stop yelling, or we'll go home right now."

"Stop pouting, or you're going to bed right now."

"Stop crying, or the cameramen will leave right now. Is that what you want?"

Nessa did as she was told—logged in to her blog. She absolutely believed that they would hurt Daltrey, and that could not happen. If he was dead, she wanted to be dead too. There was no point in going on without him.

The hypo on the coffee table was two feet from her. Could she throw the laptop at it and break it? But before she could do anything, Brandon took the computer from her and put a flash drive in the USB port. He sat on the floor and took care of business.

"It's posted, Mom," he said.

No. This wasn't happening. Her heart thrashed in her chest, seemed to be skipping beats, and a painfully hot flush covered her face.

"And now, Brandon, set up the camera. Obviously, Candy, it will do you no good to ask for help, because it's video. It's not live. I know you understand how this works—"

"Because of all the shows we did together, right, Mom?"

"So all you have to do is confess to what you did. And then tie yourself off and inject yourself with heroin."

"You'll want to do a close-up on the hypo, Brandon," Nessa said, "and then fade it out so they can cut to commercial."

Brandon's eyebrows drew together and he finally looked at her. Then he couldn't seem to look away.

"Unless, of course," Joyce said, "you'd rather your son die in your place."

Nessa's whole body twitched, hearing this. Even considering the possibility.

"Brandon," Nessa said.

He didn't respond, just kept staring.

Seeing this, Joyce clamped her hands on either side of Brandon's face to make him look at her. "She'll say anything. Didn't I tell you she'd do anything to get out of it?"

"It's me, Brandon," Nessa said again. "It's Rosie."

"Rosie's dead," Brandon said, on script. But he'd never been an actor.

"No," Nessa said. "*Candy's* dead. The little boy you were

pointing a gun at? That's your nephew. *Your* nephew, Brandon. His name is Daltrey."

This made another dent, Nessa could see it.

"That's enough," Joyce said.

"Brandon, listen to me. I'm Rosie, and I can prove it."

Joyce said, "You know she's not Rosie."

"Yes, I am," Nessa said. "I stole Candy's identity when she died, because she didn't have a police record like me."

"Shut up," Joyce said to her.

"Where were you the night Dimebag Darrell was shot onstage?" Nessa said to Brandon. "December 8, 2004. Do you remember where *we* were?"

Brandon didn't move, didn't look at her.

"We were at the Muse concert at the Wiltern LG Theater in LA, and Matt Bellamy announced it from the stage. Do you remember? It was just you and me."

"I'm not listening to you," Brandon said, uncertain. "Rosie could have told you that story."

"Brandon. What Mom has made you to do is—"

"Shut up!" Joyce thundered. "Brandon. Will you give Candy and me a few minutes alone? Go on upstairs and I'll call when we're ready to go."

Brandon did as his mother told him. He always did. Nessa heard one of the bedroom doors upstairs click closed.

"Mom, how can you possibly not know it's me?" Nessa pleaded.

Then Joyce turned her face toward Nessa, and smiled.

"Of course a mother knows her own child," she said. "Hello, Rosie."

Chapter Twenty-Five

VERTIGO OVERCAME NESSA, and she felt faint.

Her own mother had *knowingly* tormented her, smeared her name, and almost gotten her raped . . . and had killed her husband.

Nessa had always known that Joyce loved Brandon more than her. But now she knew that Joyce had never loved her at all. Never. Had always been willing to sacrifice her on the altar of Brandon's health and her own fame.

Nessa was alone in the universe, floating in space, cut off from the rest of humanity, and she'd done it to herself.

With her mother's help.

Only one person left alive loved her, and he was in danger of dying tonight.

"We had a deal," Joyce said quietly. "And then you stopped coming home, right in the middle of the season. There was no show without you. You knew that. What was I supposed to do?"

Nessa was delirious with a combination of déjà vu and vivid fear, and underneath it all, the chattering of her veins' rapacious desire to absorb what was in that syringe, to drink it up, to be filled and let this nonstop agony of fear and anxiety and desire finally end. With each passing moment she felt her grasp on the rope of her life loosen. It was slipping through her hands, and what a relief it would be to just . . . let . . . go.

But Daltrey. She had to fight the encroaching nothingness. She focused on her mother, on finding a way out of this.

Joyce turned on her like a tiger. "Your fame was supposed to be *mine*. Not yours, not after what you did to me."

"I didn't do anything to you, Mom," Nessa said, hiccuping with sobs so violent she could barely get the words out. "The only person I did anything to was Candy. And that was an accident."

"No," Joyce said. "It wasn't."

"Of course it was, Mom! I never—"

Joyce's expression struck a memory. The parted lips, the lifted chin and eyebrows. Waiting for one of her children to sound out a word, or interpret a figure of speech.

As understanding broke in Nessa's mind, her blood felt unbearably hot in her veins, melting her from the inside, paralyzing her limbs.

"It wasn't Hoover who gave Brandon the heroin to give to us," Nessa said.

Joyce brushed some imaginary lint off her blouse.

"It was you," Nessa said in a whisper, the air leaving her body and threatening to never return.

Nessa's mother sighed and looked up at the ceiling.

"You were as good as dead already," Joyce said. "I knew it was just a matter of time before you overdosed, or were stabbed to death, or who knows what else." Now she looked Nessa in the eye. "At least this way, I knew we could make something positive come out of it. And I would have control over what happened. So I was ready when I got the call from the coroner." Her proud and shrewd expression clouded. "But then he showed me photos of . . . Candy. Dead. I screamed and nearly fainted. I didn't have to act shocked, because I was shocked. *You* were supposed to take the first shot. It was your birthday! But you know me. I am nothing if not quick on my feet. I identified Candy's body as yours, and that was that. Because I knew it wouldn't be long until you actually killed yourself anyway, one way or another."

Her expression turned sour. "But then we find out—you have a radio show! You're rich and famous, have a beautiful house, acres of land, nice car. A fabulous life. You were supposed to die."

Of course. Because how could Nessa actually go on living, prosper, thrive, without Joyce? How could anyone?

"Brandon's the one who figured out 'Nessa Donati' was really Candy," Joyce said. "Something you said on the air one day—I don't remember what it was. Then it took some time to track you down. I have to give Brandon credit. He's very handy with computers. Anyway. We took the money we had left and came out here to . . . Kansas." She said it as if the word was a mouthful of moldy bread.

"We started watching your house. Watched the locksmith change the locks. Bought the keys from him. Then we waited, and you and the boy left for the weekend. And that husband of yours—another addict, of course!—drove up to the house in a pickup, went into one of your sheds. And he hung himself in there."

Nessa gasped. Her intuition all those weeks ago had been accurate—he had killed himself, but not in the tragic romantic-lead manner her mind had conjured. No. He'd killed himself on her property, so she'd find him like an Easter egg. *See what you've*

*done to me? See what you drove me to? This is your fault. All your
fault.*

Never thinking that his own son might find his swinging
corpse. Never thinking about anyone but himself. And this was
yet another knife in Nessa's heart.

"So," her mother went on, as if describing a mundane but
arduous task like cleaning out the gutters, "we cut him down.
Went in the house, found your gun, shot his corpse and then—
it's actually harder to make a dead body bleed than you'd think."
She shuddered at the memory. "Anyway. We drove down to the
river and put him in the water. We were sure he'd be found, and
all the evidence would point to you. The police will discover
that gunshots didn't kill him, but—well, it's a moot point now,
isn't it?"

She looked at her watch. "I know you want to know how the
story ends—you never could wait. You always read the ends of
books first. Had to know how the movie ended before you'd watch
it. So I won't keep it from you now. The long-suffering mother
finds out that, unbeknownst to her, all these years, she's had
a grandson. And now she can be part of the charming, though
mute, little boy's life."

How heartwarming it would be for the viewers. She could just
hear the *awww*s coming from the audience.

"And his uncle will be overjoyed to discover he has a nephew."

"But once Brandon realizes—"

"He'll get over it," Joyce said. "I knew it would be easier on
him if he thought you were actually Candy. But he knows we need
money for treatment. His lymphoma has come back."

"What?" Nessa said.

"That's right. If he doesn't get chemo, he's going to die."

"So I have to die instead."

Joyce looked away from her. "You're dead already."

"Mom," Nessa said. "You don't have to do this. It's going to ruin your life and Brandon's. It's not going to turn out like you think."

"It's going to turn out exactly like I think."

"I'll pay for Brandon's treatment."

Joyce's lips curled in a derisive smile. "Oh, no, you don't. You're not going to just swoop in now at the eleventh hour and get to be the hero. Absolutely not."

"Right," Nessa said. "That's your part—'hero.' My part is 'bad seed.' It's 'black sheep.' I don't get to change roles in the middle of the show."

"What's done is done."

Of course. Joyce needed to control everything.

"Mom," Nessa said. "There's a problem with your plan. It's not perfect. Because how are you going to explain that I stayed away all these years? That I never came back to you?"

Joyce's expression didn't change.

"You have no idea what I've been through in the last couple of years," she said. "Once all the work dried up, your brother suffered. The things I had to do to make sure he had his insulin. If you'd have just continued to come home, I wouldn't have been mad about the heroin. I would have understood."

A part of Nessa was desperate to believe this. "But I didn't want you to see me like that."

"I know, honey," Joyce said, starting to reach for Nessa's face, but then pulled her hand back and looked away.

"I just couldn't do the show anymore," Nessa said. How could she make Joyce understand? That allowing producers and cameramen and writers watch her every move and comment on it and try to shape it was exquisite torture.

"We did what we had to do," Joyce said, her expression hardening. "But then you decided to throw it all away, walk away and leave your brother and me with nothing."

The words themselves were full of Joyce's patented melodrama. The manipulation, the emotional blackmail, were achingly familiar. But something about the *way* Joyce said it, in a fragile, tremulous voice, summoned a shocking impulse within Nessa—to mother her own mom.

"Oh, Mom," Nessa said, swallowing, hoping that Joyce could hear the authentic emotions behind what she was saying. "I know it's been hard. Dad screwed you over, no question about it. You got left with a chronically sick kid that you had to take care of and worry over all by yourself. You gave him the injections. You watched his diet, drove him to all his appointments."

Nessa watched her mother luxuriate in the praise like a cat in a patch of sunlight and realized that she meant what she was saying. Joyce really had been alone. She really had been the only one who took care of Brandon. And she was mentally ill, a borderline personality or a narcissist. What she really needed was help. She was twisted up inside because she'd been abandoned, and she couldn't protect her children from illness or predators or death.

As a mom, Nessa felt in her heart that her mother, in her own deranged way, had done the best she could. But somewhere along the way, she'd fallen off the deep end, and there was no water in the pool to catch her.

Maybe Nessa only imagined it, but for a moment, she felt like her mother saw her.

"But, Mom," Nessa said. "You and Brandon weren't the only

ones who suffered. I was *raped*. I was a kid. A baby. And you turned me into a sideshow. Don't you understand? I started using heroin because of that."

"I *know*!" Joyce screamed it into her face, so loud and suddenly that Nessa rocked back in her chair. "Why do you think I sent that incompetent rapist here? Then practically put the drugs in your hand? You see, I came up some new show ideas. Show A was 'Mother of a Murderer.' That one didn't work out because Brandon's plan was so ridiculously complicated that all it did was confuse the detectives. So then as usual, *I* had to come up with the workable idea. Here's the logline: 'Famous radio personality turns out to be dead girl, commits suicide out of guilt before her mother can stop her.' The synopsis: Long-suffering mother of ill son and dead daughter discovers the daughter is still alive. But in a cruel twist, the daughter commits suicide before the devoted mother can get to her side."

Something had been removed from Joyce. A protein, an enzyme, a hormone, a neural connection. All Joyce could do was *act* like she loved, *act* like she was happy, *act* like she was in love. Had she been born this way? Or had her parents and circumstances made her this way?

In her mind, Joyce put people into two rooms—one for good people (the list was short and sometimes nonexistent) and one for bad people, which included nearly everyone else. Sometimes Nessa was allowed into the warm room, but rarely. Brandon had twisted himself into pretzels insinuating himself into it.

Nessa had read a novel once in which a character dreamed he was watching the entire human race holding hands and marching around the planet in a circle. But he couldn't figure out how to become a part of the circle.

Nessa had once been part of that circle, but had let go of it.

Joyce, on the other hand, couldn't even *see* the circle. And she'd wrenched Brandon from it so she wouldn't be alone.

"Mom," Nessa said. "Just walk away, and I'll leave you alone. I won't report this. I'll tell the cops that an intruder killed Isabeau, and I came home to find her dead. You and Brandon can get in your car and drive away."

Joyce almost seemed to consider this. Nessa reached out a hand.

"I love you, Mom," Nessa said, tears running down her face in an endless stream. "You're sick. I can get you the help you need."

Now Joyce fixed her eyes on Nessa and for a brief second Nessa thought maybe she'd broken through the layers of Joyce's mental illness.

But then Joyce gave her that superior, haughty look Nessa knew so well. "Oh, the heroin addict is going to help me. Oh, happy day. Lucky me. No. You're not going to fool me again. Not ever again."

Joyce rose from the couch and walked toward Nessa, and Nessa was certain Joyce was going to strike her. But she didn't. She leaned over and kissed Nessa's cheek. She pulled back and looked into Nessa's eyes.

And smiled.

Nessa's breath died in her lungs.

"Your son is very photogenic," Joyce said, and laid her hand on Nessa's cheek. "And don't worry. He's going to love living in California. I'll take good care of him."

Like fucking bloody hell she would.

It was as if someone had lit a fire beneath her chair. Nessa launched herself at her mother, throwing all her weight forward onto her feet, bringing the chair with her. The momentum and weight of the chair knocked Joyce to the ground, and Nessa grabbed a handful of Joyce's hair as she rolled the chair on its side.

Joyce repeatedly slapped Nessa's face, but Nessa wouldn't let go. When one of Joyce's fingers strayed toward Nessa's mouth, she bit into it and whipped her head back and forth like a dog with a chew toy.

Joyce screamed and scratched at Nessa's eyes. "You're not going to ruin this for me. Not again." Joyce reached toward the coffee table.

Nessa clutched at her mother's hair, but Joyce was so determined she dragged Nessa and the chair toward the syringe, the handful of hair tearing loose with a moist ripping sound.

Joyce grunted and lunged for the coffee table, plunging face-first into the floor.

Nessa dug her fingernails into Joyce's leg, and Joyce kicked Nessa in the temple. Joyce's hand scrabbled over the tabletop and tipped it.

Nessa tried to wrench the bungie cord from around her chest, tried to slide free, but it held firm.

Joyce turned back toward Nessa with a victorious smile, the hypo in her hand, blood dripping from her torn scalp. Nessa flailed, trying to grab hold of Joyce's arm to knock the syringe loose, but Joyce was intent on seeing it all through.

She bulldozed the chair with Nessa in it and knelt over her, panting, triumphant, holding the needle high over her head.

And part of Nessa yearned to let Joyce plunge it in. Would welcome it. Nessa closed her eyes and surrendered.

Then she heard heavy, quick footsteps come down the stairs.

"Mom!" Brandon said.

Nessa's eyes flew open as Joyce's head turned. Without thinking about it, Nessa got hold of her mother's arm, the one holding the needle aloft. But Joyce threw all of her body weight behind it, trying to stab downward. Self-preservation overrode Nessa's desire for heroin, and she clawed at Joyce's face with her other hand.

Joyce shouted, "Brandon, shoot him! Go shoot him! Now!"

The sound of running feet echoed away from Nessa. She couldn't see Brandon but knew he was headed to Daltrey's room.

"Brandon, no!" Nessa howled. "Don't do it!"

A sound like an envelope tearing sliced through the air.

Joyce screamed and jumped up, running from Nessa, who was left strapped to the chair. She heard a heavy thump, then a sharper thump, and Joyce wailing, "You killed my boy! You killed my son!"

Then Isabeau was crouching over Nessa, cutting the bungee cords with one of her purple knives. Her hair was bloody and matted to her face, her eyes glazed. But she was alive.

Joyce tackled Isabeau, simultaneously trying to get the knife away from her and stab her with the syringe.

Nessa ran to the stairs where Brandon lay crumpled at the bottom, one of Isabeau's throwing knives in his back. Nessa picked up Brandon's dropped gun and ran for the living room.

"Let her go, Mom," Nessa said. She cocked the pistol and aimed it at her mother's head.

Joyce kept trying to stab the weakened Isabeau.

"Go ahead, Mom, just give me *one more* excuse to pull this trigger."

Joyce stopped fighting, and Isabeau disentangled herself before yanking the syringe from Joyce's hand.

It was then that Nessa heard the sirens.

Isabeau sat on the couch, holding her head, and Joyce ran to Brandon's side. "Oh, my son," she said. She pressed her fingers against his neck. She turned to Isabeau. "You're lucky that my son is still alive, but you're still going to prison."

"You first," Isabeau said.

"And you," Joyce said to Nessa. "You're nothing. I did everything for you, and this is the thanks I get."

"Shut up," Nessa said, her voice and hands shaking with rage. "Say another word and I will kill you. Now go sit on the couch. Now. Do it."

Joyce did, reluctantly, and Nessa handed the gun to Isabeau, who pointed it at Joyce. Nessa ran up the stairs, terrified of what she would find in Daltrey's room.

There he was, lying on the bed, his breathing shallow, and Nessa feared they'd overdosed him with the Nyquil. She carried him downstairs, breathing him in, crying and shaking, wanting to never let go of him again.

A loud banging sounded on the door. "Mrs. Donati? Police. Please open the door."

Nessa ran to the door and opened it.

Joyce began shrieking, "She stabbed my son! That girl over there stabbed him! Arrest her!"

Two uniformed police officers looked at each other. "Mrs. Donati?" one of them said.

"Yes," Nessa said. "There are two people in my house who drugged my son, held me hostage, and tried to kill my nanny." She pointed to Isabeau, who waved.

"That girl," Joyce yelled, "threw a knife at my son!"

Two EMTs arrived at the door, and Nessa beckoned them inside. "We've got three people who are going to need to go to the hospital," she said. Then to the officers, she said, "Can you get Detectives Treloar and Dirksen out here? I think they might be interested in what happened here tonight."

One of the uniforms got on his radio and called the station.

It was chaos as the EMTs loaded Brandon and Isabeau onto stretchers. Nessa went to Brandon's side and put her hand on his face. "It really is me," she said. "It's Rosie."

"I know," he said behind the oxygen mask. "I'm sorry." A paramedic rolled Brandon out the door to a waiting ambulance, followed by Isabeau on her stretcher.

"I tried to stop them, boss," she said. "I was in the kitchen and the next thing I knew I was on the floor. I was only out for a second, but I figured out what was going on and pretended to be dead until I could get to my knives." She touched her head. "It looks a lot worse than it is, I think."

"Let's let the doctors decide that," Nessa said. She took hold of Isabeau's hand and walked alongside the rolling stretcher until they got to the doorway.

"I wish I could come to the hospital with you," Nessa said.

"You need to stay here with that boy," Isabeau said.

"Who can I call for you?"

"My phone's in my purse. Just call the one marked Emergency." They wheeled her out to the waiting ambulance.

One of the EMTs examined Daltrey, who woke up during the examination and started to cry.

Amid all the flurry of activity, standing in the front doorway, Nessa saw a pale and shaky Marlon, frantically scanning the crowd until his eyes met hers. He lurched toward her and crushed her to himself.

"I read your suicide blog and I tried to call you," he said, "but it went to voicemail. So I called the cops and then came right over."

"Thank you," she said, and slid her arms around him. He didn't say anything else, just held her tight. He only let go when the EMT handed her Daltrey, who was rubbing his eyes and looking around bewildered at all the people in the house.

Joyce chattered away through all this activity, her wrists in handcuffs behind her back.

"This is a mistake," she said. "Candy's the one who should be arrested. She killed my daughter seven years ago. You should be thanking me. I did your job for you. Found her after all this time. You're welcome."

Everything that came out of her mouth sounded like TV drama dialogue. She couldn't help herself.

Forty minutes later, Treloar and Dirksen appeared, disheveled after being pulled out of bed in the middle of the night.

"That's my troll," Nessa said to Detective Treloar. "She also happens to be my mother. Say hello, Mom."

"I am not her mother," Joyce said.

Treloar and Dirksen glanced at each other.

"And my brother, who also took part, is on his way to the hospital," Nessa said.

"Wait," Treloar said. "Can you start at the beginning?"

"I hope you don't think I'm going to apologize," Dirksen said. " 'Cause it ain't going to happen."

Chapter Twenty-Six

Tuesday, July 5

NESSA WAS FINISHING up an email to her sponsors explaining that she'd be using guest bloggers for the next few weeks due to a family emergency when her phone rang.

"Mrs. Donati, this is Detective Rob Treloar. I wanted to give you an update on a couple of things. Do you have a few minutes?"

"Sure," she said, going to sit on the couch.

"We took Mrs. Gereben's statement and Brandon's statement."

"All right," Nessa said, steeling herself.

"To be honest with you, Mrs. Gereben's story was pretty hard to follow, but what they're both saying is that they found Mr. Donati hanging in the boathouse. The autopsy indicates that he died of asphyxiation, not gunshot wounds. When we were out there, I took samples of the beam in the boathouse and found rope fibers embedded in it, so I'm inclined to believe what they say."

This filled Nessa with nothing but sadness. John had been so tortured by the drugs that he couldn't go on. She knew exactly how he'd felt. Had felt it herself.

"The fact is," Treloar said, "what we have here is not a murder, but a suicide and the criminal desecration of a corpse. And of course, your mom and brother will be charged with kidnapping, attempted murder, criminal trespass, and a few other things. You can call the district attorney to find out the whole list."

"Thank you for everything, Detective," Nessa said. "Would you say 'I told you so' to Detective Dirksen for me?"

"Probably not," he said.

"Just as well," she said.

Wednesday, July 20

NESSA HAD SPENT the last few weeks trying to decide what to do, but her mind kept circling back to "Do the next right thing." She just couldn't seem to escape it.

She sat in the scalding heat of evening and called Marlon. "I've come to a decision," she said.

"And?"

"I'm going to turn myself in. We're going to LA, and I've already got an appointment with the LA County district attorney. I think part of absolute honesty has to include owning up to everything I've done. Wouldn't you agree?"

Marlon said nothing for a moment. He sighed. "I have a grudging admiration for this kind of pointless self-sacrifice."

She smiled.

"When are you leaving?" he said.

"We're flying out day after tomorrow. Once I make up my mind to do something, I want it done right then. You know what I mean?"

"Yes," he said. "But I'm conflicted because though I know it's the right thing to do, on the other hand, doing the right thing is often more appealing in theory than in fact. This is one of those times."

"It is," she said.

"You're prepared to go to prison, if it comes to that?"

"Is anyone ever?"

"I suppose not. Who's going to take care of Daltrey if you have to go away?"

"John's folks will take him." Still, anytime she thought of being away from Daltrey, she cried. She cried now.

"Well, if your mind's made up."

"It is."

"I'll be praying."

"Thank you, Marlon."

"Call me when it's over. Remember to expect the miracle."

"I'll remember."

Friday, July 22

NESSA, ISABEAU, AND Daltrey checked into the Super 8 on Sunset Boulevard, just a mile and a half from the DA's office and three and a half miles from the Seventh Street Bridge.

The three of them spent the day at Disneyland, and it was bittersweet watching Daltrey on the rides and the look of wonder on his face when he came face-to-face with his Disney heroes.

They stayed until closing, full of hot dogs and cotton candy. The next morning she woke up and got ready to go, then she called Isabeau, who was already up and came over to their room.

"Daltrey," Nessa said, "Mommy has an appointment, so you and Isabeau are going to stay here until I get back. Okay? But first Isabeau and I are going outside for a minute to talk about grown-up stuff. Can you stay in here and color?"

He nodded and pulled his coloring book and crayons from his Bing Bong backpack.

Nessa and Isabeau went outside.

Tears stood in Isabeau's eyes. "Are you sure you want to do this?"

"Listen," Nessa said. "Joyce is no doubt at this moment telling her public defender what to say to the *National Enquirer.* One way or another it's going to come out, and it should come from me."

The tears spilled over, and Isabeau cried. She hugged Nessa tight and sobbed. "Love you, Ness."

"Love you too. Now let's get ourselves together. You can drop me at the courthouse."

Nessa carried Daltrey to the rental car, squeezing him until he squirmed, holding on to the feel of him and his scent. She strapped him into his car seat and got in the front passenger seat.

Nessa entered the address into Google Maps, and Isabeau drove them toward Nessa's destiny. When they pulled into the courthouse parking lot, she got out and leaned into the backseat for one last hug from Daltrey.

"I'll call you as soon as I know anything," she said to Isabeau, who stared straight ahead, her chin quivering, tears shimmering in her eyes.

Isabeau drove away. Nessa watched until the car disappeared around a corner.

Nessa couldn't seem to quiet her thumping heart. The seemingly endless supply of sharp adrenaline felt like ocean waves pounding through her system, making her twitch and jerk. Her mind was quiet, but her body was having none of it. She thought about touching up her lipstick but knew her shaking hands would make her look like a slasher victim instead of a contrite offender.

She was walking toward the entrance of the courthouse when "I'm Stuck in a Condo (with Marlon Brando)" began playing on her phone.

"What are you driving?" Marlon said after she said hello.

"Is that like your old-guy equivalent of 'What are you wearing?' "

He ignored this. "Let me guess. White Camry."

"Your mental powers never cease to astonish me," she said, trying to keep the tremor out of her voice, and happy for a distraction before the event that would change her life forever.

"Okay, and what are you wearing? Is it the black suit?"

"Two for two," she said, pausing at the end of the parking lot.

"Look to your left," he said.

She did. There stood Marlon with his phone pressed to his ear, in a coat and tie, hair neatly combed, next to an identical white Toyota.

True astonishment made her mouth drop open and she almost dropped her phone.

He walked toward her, his phone still pressed against his face.

"What are you doing here?" she said.

"I haven't been able to sleep, thinking about you," he said. "Are you absolutely certain you want to do this?"

"Marlon," she said, hanging up. "Why are you here?"

He looked away and pocketed his phone. "I feel responsible."

"You're responsible for the effort, not the outcome," she said, quoting one of his favorite AA aphorisms.

He smirked at her.

"Haven't you suffered enough?" Marlon said. "I feel like you've made amends and then some."

"Since when do you feel anything, Mr. Freeze?"

He just smiled at her and reached for her hand. "I got another call from that reporter at the campus newspaper."

Nessa held her breath. "And what did she say?"

"She said as a professional courtesy she wasn't going to run the story. She said that my friend who works for Altair called and lobbied on my behalf."

"Those tickets to the Adele concert probably didn't hurt," Nessa said.

"Probably not. You are something else."

As she grasped his hand, she felt a thrill go up her spine and spiral into her stomach, but she tried to finesse it. "Aw," she said. "You like me. You really, really like me."

But she heard the trembling in her own voice.

"Don't do that," he said, almost growling. "Don't play it off like it's a joke. It's not a joke. It's a meeting of the minds. We speak the same language, you and I. We're from the same tribe. We fit. If you don't see it that way, I understand. But I came to LA to tell you this. It's that important to me."

She tried to swallow but couldn't, looking up at him. "Marlon, you're just—"

"I'm not *just* anything. You're all I think about, and that's very inconvenient for me. I need to settle this so I can go back to thinking about myself all the time."

She laughed.

"I know I'm ten years older than you, but—"

"Eleven."

He ignored this and went on. "I further know you need time to grieve your husband."

"And I might be going to prison," she said. "You don't have to wait for me."

"I've waited for four years," he said. "A couple more won't matter. You just need to know that I'm coming for you. No matter what happens today, I'm coming for you."

"You don't have to come for me," she said. "I'll meet you in the middle." She stood on tiptoe and kissed him like she'd wanted to since the night she'd told him everything.

He squeezed her one last time, then took her hand and led her toward the building that held her fate.

"You ready for this?"

"I believe I am," she said.

They walked inside.

UNKNOWN LEGENDS

Monday, August 1

For those of you following the saga that was my life over the summer, here is the rest of the story.

D said his first words the other day, and you'll be happy to know they were "More milk, please." You can imagine how relieved I feel, and how surprised Isabeau and I were when he said it.

And not to bury the lead, but the LA County judge gave me three years' probation, which is much less than I deserve. But I'm grateful to my Higher Power, and to the judge, and even, in a bizarre way, to my mom. She's the one who finally forced me to come out of the shadows.

And speaking of my monkey-house-crazy mother. She and my poor brother are awaiting trial on multiple charges, but you can bet her public defender will pull an insanity defense. My brother won't be so lucky, I'm afraid. You may think that crazy runs in the family, but I'm looking into hiring a real lawyer for him. He was her victim as much as her co-conspirator. We were both her victims, nearly from birth. The only difference was that I escaped, and my friend Candy helped me do that.

Unfortunately, my contract with Altair Satellite Radio was not renewed. Instead, dear readers, I'm going to revive the show as a podcast. Stay tuned to the blog for the upcoming schedule. I already have a pretty exciting list of interviewees lined up, many indie artists you simply must get to know, many who are sympathetic to (not to mention outraged at) my unceremonious ousting from Altair. I also have some brand-new sponsors who'd appreciate your patronage.

In the wake of all this media attention, I've decided to use my notoriety for good instead of evil. So if you're out there feeling so lost or alone or confused that you feel like drugs are the only place you can turn, then I want you to turn to me. I'm no longer anonymous, but I'll respect your anonymity. I only want to help you get or stay sober.

Remember, my friends, we're only as sick as our secrets.

Step out of the shadows and into the light with me. I promise you it's a lot warmer out here.

And now comes another new start for me. I'm no longer Rosie, but I'm not Vanessa either. I'm both. So let me introduce myself.

Hi. I'm Nessa. I'm a heroin addict. I've been sober for six years, six months, and twelve days, and I have laid my past to rest where it belongs, under a bridge.

Acknowledgments

As ALWAYS, I am deeply and eternally grateful to the following people:

The world's greatest agent, Michelle Johnson of Inklings Literary Agency, who made all this possible.

Chelsey Emmelhainz, who I hope I'll get to work with again someday. Happy trails, my friend. Until we meet again.

Kacey Pickard, for her invaluable legal expertise.

Bob Byerly, for his guidance in police procedure.

Lori Malone, expert in things that no one should be an expert in, but who lived to tell the tale and help make this story authentic.

99.5 The Mountain Denver radio station peeps: Mike Casey, Mary Farucci, Matt Heager, and Sam Hill, for bringing my radio knowledge into the twenty-first century.

The immensely talented and hilarious critique group, Because Magic, for not throwing me out during this novel's writing: Lynn Bisesi, Deirdre Byerly, Claire Fishback, Marc Graham, Nicole Greene, Michael Haspil (with extra props for coming up with the title—thanks, Mike!), Laura Main, Vicki Pierce, and Chris Scena. Thanks, guys.

Marianne Goulding, who is my own personal Candy, but the good news is that she's alive.

Amanda Deich, my literary agency mate and soul sister, who always speaks truth to me.

Liz Rodgers, whose mischievous smile, generous spirit, and light-filled soul permeates this novel.

My mom, Tanya Stormes, who talked me down off the ledge this time around at just the right moment.

My brother, Rob Stormes, and sister-in-law, Deveney Stormes, for their homegrown PR abilities, and for giving me nieces Sandy and Ailish, and nephew, Ross.

My fabulous daughters: Layla, whose progress this year has been nothing less than miraculous; and Chloe, who, if Harvard Law doesn't work out, will make a stellar editor.

And of course, my amazing husband, my perfect mate and muse, who once again saved the day and this novel in the process.

Want more suspense from LS Hawker?
Keep reading for an excerpt from her debut thriller,
the story of a young woman on the run for her future . . .
from the nightmares of her past:

THE DROWNING GAME

Available now wherever ebooks are sold.

An Excerpt from
THE DROWNING GAME

SIRENS AND THE scent of strange men drove Sarx and Tesla into a frenzy of barking and pacing as they tried to keep the intruders off our property without the aid of a fence. Two police cars, a fire truck, and an ambulance were parked on the other side of the dirt road. The huddled cops and firemen kept looking at the house.

Dad's iPhone rang and went on ringing. I couldn't make myself answer it. I knew it was the cops outside calling to get me to open the front door, but asking me to allow a group of strangers inside seemed like asking a pig to fly a jet. I had no training or experience to guide me. I longed to get the AK-47 out of the basement gun safe, even though it would be me against a half-dozen trained law men.

"Petty Moshen." An electric megaphone amplified the man's voice outside.

The dogs howled at the sound of it, intensifying further the tremor that possessed my entire body. I hadn't shaken like this since the night Dad left me out on the prairie in a whiteout blizzard to hone my sense of direction.

"Petty, call off the dogs."

I couldn't do it.

"I'm going to dial up your father's cell phone again, and I want you to answer it."

Closing my eyes, I concentrated, imagining those words coming out of my dad's mouth, in his voice. The iPhone vibrated. I pretended it was my dad, picked it up, hit the answer button and pressed it to my ear.

"This is Sheriff Bloch," said the man on the other end of the phone. "We have to come in and talk to you about your dad."

I cleared my throat again. "I need to do something first," I said, and thumbed the end button. I headed down to the basement.

Downstairs, I got on the treadmill, cranked up the speed to ten miles an hour, and ran for five minutes, flat out, balls to the wall. This is what Detective Deirdre Walsh, my favorite character on TV's *Offender NYC*, always did when emotions overwhelmed her. No one besides me and my dad had ever come into our house before, so I needed to steady myself.

I jumped off and took the stairs two at a time, breathing hard, sweating, my legs burning, but steadier. I popped a stick of peppermint gum in my mouth. Then I walked straight to the front door the way Detective Walsh would—fearlessly, in charge, all business. I flung the door open and shouted, "Sarx! Tesla! Off! Come!"

They both immediately glanced over their shoulders and came loping toward me. I noticed another vehicle had joined the gauntlet on the other side of the road, a brand-new tricked-out red Dodge Ram 4x4 pickup truck. Randy King, wearing a buff-colored

Stetson, plaid shirt, Lee's, and cowboy boots, leaned against it. All I could see of his face was a black walrus mustache. He was the man my dad had instructed me to call if anything ever happened to him. I'd seen Randy only a couple of times but never actually talked to him until today.

The dogs sat in front of me, panting, worried, whimpering. I reached down and scratched their ears, thankful that Dad had trained them like he had. I straightened and led them to the one-car garage attached to the left side of the house. They sat again as I raised the door and signaled them inside. They did not like this one bit—they whined and jittered—but they obeyed my command to stay. I lowered the door and turned to face the invasion.

As if I'd disabled an invisible force field, all the men came forward at once: the paramedics and firemen carrying their gear boxes, the cops' hands hovering over their sidearms. I couldn't look any of them in the eye, but I felt them staring at me as if I were an exotic zoo animal or a serial killer.

The man who had to be the sheriff walked right up to me, and I stepped back, palming the blade I keep clipped to my bra at all times. I knew it was unwise to reach into my hoodie, even just to touch the Baby Glock in my shoulder holster.

"Petty?" he said.

"Yes sir," I said, keeping my eyes on the clump of yellow, poisonous prairie ragwort at my feet.

"I'm Sheriff Bloch. Would you show us in, please?"

"Yes sir," I said, turning and walking up the front steps. I pushed open the screen and went in, standing aside to let in the phalanx of strange men. My breathing got shallow and the shaking started up. My heart beat so hard I could feel it in my face, and the bump on my left shoulder—scar tissue from a childhood injury—itched like crazy. It always did when I was nervous.

The EMTs came in after the sheriff.

"Where is he?" one of them asked. I pointed behind me to the right, up the stairs. They trooped up there carrying their cases. The house felt too tight, as if there wasn't enough air for all these people.

Sheriff Bloch and a deputy walked into the living room. Both of them turned, looking around the room, empty except for the grandfather clock in the corner. The old thing had quit working many years before, so it was always three-seventeen in this house.

"Are you moving out?" the deputy asked.

"No," I said, and then realized why he'd asked. All of our furniture is crowded in the center of each room, away from the windows.

Deputy and sheriff glanced at each other. The deputy walked to one of the front windows and peered out through the bars.

"Is that bulletproof glass?" he asked me.

"Yes sir."

They glanced at each other again.

"Have anyplace we can sit?" Sheriff Bloch said.

I walked into our TV room, the house's original dining room, and they followed. I sat on the couch, which gave off dust and a minor-chord spring squeak. I pulled my feet up and hugged my knees.

"This is Deputy Hencke."

The deputy held out his hand toward me. I didn't take it, and after a beat he let it drop.

"I'm very sorry for your loss," he said. He had a blond crew cut and the dark blue uniform.

He went to sit on Dad's recliner, and it happened in slow

motion, like watching a knife sink into my stomach with no way to stop it.

"No!" I shouted.

Nobody but Dad had ever sat in that chair. It was one thing to let these people inside the house. It was another to allow them to do whatever they wanted.

He looked around and then at me, his face a mask of confusion. "What? I'm—I was just going to sit—"

"Get a chair out of the kitchen," Sheriff Bloch said.

The deputy pulled one of the aqua vinyl chairs into the TV room. His hands shook as he tried to write on his little report pad. He must have been as rattled by my outburst as I was.

"Spell your last name for me?"

"M-O-S-H-E-N," I said.

"Born here?"

"No," I said. "We're from Detroit originally."

His face scrunched and he glanced up.

"How'd you end up here? You got family in the area?"

I shook my head. I didn't tell him Dad had moved us to Saw Pole, Kansas, because he said he'd always wanted to be a farmer. In Saw Pole, he farmed a sticker patch and raised horse flies but not much else.

"How old are you?"

"Twenty-one."

He lowered his pencil. "Did you go to school in Niobe? I don't ever remember seeing you."

"Dad homeschooled me," I said.

"What time did you discover the—your dad?" The deputy's scalp grew pinker. He needed to grow his hair out some to hide his tell a little better.

"The dogs started barking about two—"

"Two A.M. or P.M.?"

"P.M.," I said. "At approximately two-fifteen P.M. our dogs began barking at the back door. I responded and found no evidence of attempted B and E at either entry point to the domicile. I retrieved my Winchester rifle from the basement gun safe with the intention of walking the perimeter of the property, but the dogs refused to follow. I came to the conclusion that the disturbance was inside the house, and I continued my investigation on the second floor."

Deputy Hencke's pencil was frozen in the air, a frown on his face. "Why are you talking like that?"

"Like what?"

"Usually I ask questions and people answer them."

"I'm telling you what happened."

"Could you do it in regular English?"

I didn't know what to say, so I didn't say anything.

"Look," he said. "Just answer the questions."

"Okay."

"All right. So where was your dad?"

"After breakfast this morning he said he didn't feel good so he went up to his bedroom to lie down," I said.

All day I'd expected Dad to call out for something to eat, but he never did. So I didn't check on him because it was nice not having to cook him lunch or dinner or fetch him beers. I'd kept craning my neck all day to get a view of the stairs, kept waiting for Dad to sneak up on me, catch me watching forbidden TV shows. I turned the volume down so I'd hear if he came down the creaky old stairs.

"So the dogs' barking is what finally made you go up to his bedroom, huh?"

I nodded.

"Those dogs wanted to tear us all to pieces," the deputy said, swiping his hand back and forth across the top of his crew cut.

I'd always wanted a little lapdog, one I could cuddle, but Dad favored the big breeds. Sarx was a German shepherd and Tesla a rottweiler.

The deputy bent his head to his pad. "What do you think they were barking about?"

"They smelled it," I said.

He looked up. "Smelled what?"

"Death. Next I knocked on the decedent's—I mean, Dad's—bedroom door to request permission to enter."

"So you went in his room," the deputy said, his pencil hovering above the paper.

"Once I determined he was unable to answer, I went in his room. He was lying on his stomach, on top of the covers, facing away from me, and—he had shorts on . . . you know how hot it's been, and he doesn't like to turn on the window air conditioner until after Memorial Day—and I looked at his legs and I thought, 'He's got some kind of rash. I better bring him the calamine lotion,' but then I remembered learning about libidity on TV, and—"

"Lividity," he said.

"What?"

"It's lividity, not libidity, when the blood settles to the lowest part of the body."

"Guess I've never seen it written down."

"So what did you do then?"

"It was then that I . . ."

I couldn't finish the sentence. Up until now, the shock of finding Dad's body and the terror of letting people in the house had blotted out everything else. But now, the reality that Dad was dead came crashing down on me, making my eyes sting. I recognized the feeling from a long time ago. I was going to cry, and I couldn't decide whether I was sad that Dad was gone or elated that I was finally going to be free. Free to live the normal life I'd always dreamed of.

But I couldn't cry, not in front of these strangers, couldn't show weakness. Weakness was dangerous. I thought of Deirdre Walsh again and remembered what she always did when she was in danger of crying. I cleared my throat.

"It was then that I determined that he was deceased. I estimated the time of death, based on the stage of rigor, to be around ten A.M. this morning, so I did not attempt to resuscitate him," I said, remembering Dad's cool, waxy dead skin under my hand. "Subsequently I retrieved his cell phone off his nightstand and called Mr. King."

"Randy King?"

I nodded.

"Why didn't you call 911?"

"Because Dad told me to call Mr. King if something ever happened to him."

The deputy stared at me like I'd admitted to murder. Then he looked away and stood.

"I think the coroner is almost done, but he'll want to talk to you."

While I waited, I huddled on the couch, thinking about how my life was going to change. I'd have to buy groceries and pay bills and taxes and do all the things Dad had never taught me how to do.

The coroner appeared in the doorway. "Miss Moshen?" He was a large zero-shaped man in a cardigan.

"Yes?"

He sat on the kitchen chair the deputy had vacated.

"I need to ask you a couple of questions," he said.

"Okay," I said. I was wary. The deputy had been slight and small, and even though he'd had a sidearm, I could have taken him if I'd needed to. I didn't know about the coroner, he was so heavy and large.

"Can you tell me what happened?"

I began to repeat my account, but the coroner interrupted me. "You're not testifying at trial," he said. "Just tell me what happened."

I tried to do as he asked, but I wasn't sure how to say it so he wouldn't be annoyed.

"Did your dad complain of chest pains, jaw pain? Did his left arm hurt?"

I shook my head. "Just said he didn't feel good. Like he had the flu."

"Did your dad have high cholesterol? High blood pressure?"

"I don't know."

"When was the last time he saw a doctor?" the coroner asked.

"He didn't believe in doctors."

"Your dad was only fifty-one, so I'll have to schedule an autopsy, even though it was probably a heart attack. We'll run a toxicology panel, which'll take about four weeks because we have to send it to the lab in Topeka."

The blood drained from my face. "Toxicology?" I said. "Why?"

"It's standard procedure," he said.

"I'm pretty sure my dad wouldn't want an autopsy."

"Don't worry," he said. "You can bury him before the panel comes back."

"No, I mean Dad wouldn't want someone cutting him up like that."

"It's state law."

"Please," I said.

His eyes narrowed as they focused on me. Then he stood.

"After the autopsy, where would you like the remains sent?"

"Holt Mortuary in Niobe," a voice from the living room said.

I rose from the couch to see who'd said it. Randy King stood with his back to the wall, his Stetson low over his eyes.

The coroner glanced at me for confirmation.

"I'm the executor of Mr. Moshen's will," Randy said. He raised his head and I saw his eyes, light blue with tiny pupils that seemed to bore clear through to the back of my head.

I shrugged at the coroner.

"Would you like to say goodbye to your father before we transport him to the morgue?" he said.

I nodded and followed him to the stairs, where he stood aside. "After you," he said.

"No," I said. "You first."

Dad had taught me never to go in a door first and never to let anyone walk behind me. The coroner frowned but mounted the stairs.

Upstairs, Dad's room was the first one on the left. The coroner stood outside the door. He reached out to touch my arm and I took a step backward. He dropped his hand to his side.

"Miss Moshen," he said in a hushed voice. "Your father looks different from when he was alive. It might be a bit of a shock. No one would blame you if you didn't—"

I walked into Dad's room, taking with me everything I knew from all the cop shows I'd watched. But I was not prepared at all for what I saw.

Since he'd died on his stomach, the EMTs had turned Dad onto his back. He was in full rigor mortis, so his upper lip was mashed into his gums and curled into a sneer, exposing his khaki-colored teeth. His hands were spread in front of his face, palms out. Dad's eyes stared up and to the left and his entire face was grape-pop purple.

What struck me when I first saw him—after I inhaled my gum—was that he appeared to be warding off a demon. I should have waited until the mortician was done with him, because I knew I'd never get that image out of my mind.

I walked out of Dad's room on unsteady feet, determined not to cry in front of these strangers. The deputy and the sheriff stood outside my bedroom, examining the door to it. Both of them looked confused.

"Petty," Sheriff Bloch said.

I stopped in the hall, feeling even more violated with them so close to my personal items and underwear.

"Yes?"

"Is this your bedroom?"

I nodded.

Sheriff and deputy made eye contact. The coroner paused at the top of the stairs to listen in. This was what my dad had always talked about—the judgment of busybody outsiders, their belief that somehow they needed to have a say in the lives of people they'd never even met and knew nothing about.

The three men seemed to expect me to say something, but I was tired of talking. Since I'd never done much of it, I'd had no idea how exhausting it was.

The deputy said, "Why are there six dead bolts on the outside of your door?"

It was none of his business, but I had nothing to be ashamed of. "So Dad could lock me in, of course."

About the Author

LS HAWKER grew up in suburban Denver, indulging her worrisome obsession with true-crime books, and writing stories about anthropomorphic fruit and juvenile delinquents. She wrote her first novel at fourteen.

Armed with a BS in journalism from the University of Kansas, she had a radio show called *People Are So Stupid*, edited a trade magazine, and worked as a traveling Kmart portrait photographer, but never lost her passion for fiction writing.

She's got a hilarious, supportive husband, two brilliant daughters, and a massive music collection. She lives in Colorado but considers Kansas her spiritual homeland. Visit her website at LSHawker.com.

Discover great authors, exclusive offers, and more at hc.com.